Polo Fever

ALSO BY KATHERINE REILLY

Match Point
Ride the Wave

Polo Fever

KATHERINE REILLY

An Aria Book

First published in the UK in 2026 by Head of Zeus Ltd,
part of Bloomsbury Publishing Plc

9 7 5 3 1 2 4 6 8

A catalogue record for this book is available from the British Library.

ISBN (PB): 9781035917761
ISBN (ePub): 9781035917778

Cover design: Gemma Gorton

Printed and Bound in Great Britain by Clays Ltd, Elcograf S.p.A.

Bloomsbury Publishing Plc
50 Bedford Square, London, WC1B 3DP, UK
Bloomsbury Publishing Ireland Limited,
29 Earlsfort Terrace, Dublin 2, D02 AY28, Ireland

HEAD OF ZEUS LTD
5–8 Hardwick Street
London, EC1R 4RG

To find out more about our authors and books
visit www.headofzeus.com
For product safety related questions contact productsafety@bloomsbury.com

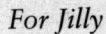

For Jilly

Prologue

Thirteen Years Ago

Mateo can hear the other boys sniggering and jeering as he dismounts. His cheeks flushed with shame and heat, he focuses on patting his pony's neck, refusing to look at them. When he hears footsteps approaching, he glances up and his embarrassment deepens.

'You did well, *mi amorcito*,' his mother says, a reassuring smile on her face.

He shakes his head. 'I fell.'

'You got back on again. That player crossed you. It was dangerous. We all saw it.'

Mateo shrugs. 'It doesn't matter. He won.'

'Winning isn't everything.'

'Yes, it is.' His eyes flash up at his mother, alight with fierce determination.

She sighs. 'You will get there, Mateo. I know it. You mustn't give up.' She places her palm flat against her chest. 'Your heart and your spirit. That is what it takes to win.'

Dejected, Mateo fiddles with the reins. 'I should go cool her down.'

His mother steps aside to let him pass as he begins to lead his pony back to the stables, then calls his name to stop him.

'Rossi believes in you,' she says, his eyes fixed on the dusty ground. 'He can see your natural talent in the saddle. He thinks, with some training, you will make a great polo player.' She takes a few steps towards him and lowers her voice. 'You may not have had the same start in life as these boys, but Rossi still believes you can match them. Sometimes, that's all you need, Mateo. Someone to see your talent and recognise that it's worth their time and effort to believe in you.'

Mateo nods and continues on his way to the stable. Her words reverberate in his head as he begins the process of cooling down his pony. He knows she is right. He has been given a rare opportunity to not just work on the *estancia* of one of the best polo players of all time, but to train with him, too. His mother has sacrificed everything for this chance. And he will not waste it. Mateo lifts his chin defiantly.

Polo is all that matters now.

One

The moment I step through the doors of the club in Soho, I'm surrounded by a flock of frazzled-looking people desperately needing answers to their questions. Shrugging off my trench coat and draping it over one arm, I'm forced to hold a hand up to silence them before calmly requesting that they speak to me one by one, like a teacher handling a bunch of overexcited school children.

'Ash, where do you want the extra chairs set up?' a panic-stricken intern asks me.

'No extra chairs,' I answer simply.

'I thought Ren—'

'He's changed his mind,' I inform her. 'We're now going for a bare and minimalist theme.'

'But... what about the flowers?' checks one of the venue staff, practically buckling beneath the weight of two vases filled with large displays of blooms in his arms.

'No flowers.'

He blinks at me over the giant blue hydrangeas. 'No flowers?'

'No flowers,' I confirm.

'But what do I do with—?'

'Whatever you like. Keep them, give them away.' I shrug. 'But no flowers in here anymore, please. Thanks so much. Next question.'

I begin to walk across the venue to the back, my heels clacking across the shiny floor, my panicked entourage in tow. As I hang up my coat and bag in the cloakroom, I continue to answer questions about the lighting, the music, the caterers, the cocktail menu, the official photographer and last-minute changes to the guest list. On the face of it, I seem cool and collected, perfectly in control despite my boss's sudden U-turn over the theme for tonight's big launch of his latest menswear collection. Under the surface, I'm bricking it.

If I had the liberty to scream, I would.

I never set out to be a fashion assistant. I left university with a degree in history and no set idea of what I wanted to do. I was vaguely thinking something along the lines of a research position or a job in a museum, something to which my skillset would be suited. But after floundering to get a job anywhere, my mum, a TV producer, suggested I apply for the assistant role going with Ren, an up-and-coming designer whose career she'd boosted when one of her breakfast presenters wore a loud shirt of his that got people talking. It was only meant to be temporary while I worked out what I actually wanted to do, but I've worked for Ren for almost four years and am still no clearer on my vocation in life. I should have moved on by now, but the problem is I'm good at this job. It actually helps that I'm not devoted to a career in fashion because I don't feel the need to suck up to anybody or feel intimidated by those in this industry. I'm a good gatekeeper – nobody gets to Ren without going through me first – and, four years in, I know Ren and his dramatics well enough to prioritise what's important and keep him happy.

When I spotted him pacing around his glass-walled office earlier in a flap, I knew instantly something was wrong and I was the only person who could help. I gathered myself. Ren's tantrums can be difficult to manage and no one else who works for him is brave enough to face them. I could see that the office floor had coincidentally emptied and the few left were keeping their heads low and their eyes averted. I marched over to knock on his door.

'Everything all right, Ren?' I asked, peering round it.

'It's no use, Ashley!' he cried, throwing his hands up in the air. 'It's no bloody use! I can't do it. I haven't been true to myself!'

I stepped in and shut the door behind me. 'It's natural to feel nervous in the run-up to the launch of a new collection. Remember what happened last time? And that one ended up being a huge hit.'

I was referring to last season's launch date when Ren didn't show up to work and, after calls and messages went unanswered all morning, I had to use my key to get into his apartment. I discovered him curled up in his wardrobe wearing nothing but a silk dressing robe and sunglasses. He was vaping and eating a bag of peanuts, questioning every step he'd made in his career that had led him to this 'meaningless existence'. After applying some tried and tested persuasion techniques that mostly involved flattery, I managed to get him out of his wardrobe and encourage him to shower and dress while I waited with a car downstairs. He eventually floated down and accepted the flat white I handed him before he reluctantly accompanied me to the office, only to get there and realise his collection was being received well. Then he demanded to know why I'd taken so long to get him.

'This time is different,' he hissed impatiently at me today. 'This is not just any collection. This is... this is—' He stopped pacing, his eyes widening in wonder. 'This is a *cultural moment.*'

While I wasn't sure his menswear had quite the impact on the world he was envisioning, I couldn't deny that this was a big moment in Ren's career. We have secured Australian tennis pro Chris Courtney as the face of this collection, which is a huge deal. He's so famous that the moment we announced the news on social media, we had more engagement than ever before. He's the perfect face for this collection: suave, sophisticated and hot as hell. And when we released a sneak-peek selection of provocative photos from the shoot, there was an online meltdown over his smouldering gaze, carved abs, chiselled jaw and *raw masculine energy*, as one journalist put it. *Real Men Are Back on Top*, the headline of the article claimed, as she went on to applaud Ren's decision to choose someone she described as an 'older' athlete, even though Chris is only in his thirties and reached the Wimbledon final two years ago.

'You're right, this is a big moment and we're prepared for it,' I reminded Ren coolly. 'Chris has already confirmed his timings with me and how excited he is for the launch tonight. It's going to be great.'

But Ren shook his head. 'Nope. No, it won't. I've made a mistake.'

'Ren—'

'I can't do it, Ash, I can't stick with this theme. Every bone in my body is screaming at me to stop it before it's too late,' he declared.

'Stop what? Explain to me what you want to change.'

'The *party*,' he said, bewildered, as though that was obvious. 'I thought I wanted opulence and aspirational luxury. But that clashes with the very heart of the collection!'

Suddenly, I realised where this was going.

'You want to change the theme of the party?' I checked, my voice croaking as panic began to rise in my throat. 'The party that's taking place… tonight?'

He nodded. 'Yes. Destroy the excess. I want *minimalism*.'

I was able to swiftly decipher whether this was a temporary whim I could talk him round from or a serious change of heart. Unfortunately, it was the latter. When he threatened that it would have to all change or he couldn't possibly show his face tonight, I told him I would sort it. Now here I am, hours away from guests arriving, trying my best to persuade everyone else that this is manageable when I'm not entirely convinced of that myself.

I'm talking through Ren's new concept with the lighting designer when my phone rings. I see Chris Courtney's name flashing up on the screen. My heart lurches.

'I have to take this,' I say, excusing myself and going to find a quiet corner where I won't be disturbed before I pick up. 'Hi, Chris.'

'Ash, hey,' he says, his smooth Australian accent making my stomach flutter. 'How are you?'

'Great. You?' I ask brightly.

'I heard there's been a change of plan about tonight?'

'Nothing for you to worry about. A simple switch up, that's all,' I say, jumping as the men carrying the giant gold-painted sculpture of Chris's bare torso clip it on the door frame on their way out. 'Everything is going perfectly to plan and we are on schedule.'

'Are you sure? I heard something about Ren having a meltdown…'

I scan the room of staff scurrying around, wondering who blabbed to Chris's people. If any of this leaks to the press, it wouldn't be a good look for us.

'A major exaggeration,' I assure him. 'He's currently at the spa enjoying a massage, so whoever your source is, they're mistaken.'

Through the window, I spot Sam crossing the road towards the venue carrying a clothes bag and closely dodging the elbow of one of the men lifting the torso sculpture into the back of a van. She stops to ogle it before continuing on her way.

'Okay, I'll choose to believe you,' Chris says, his voice more relaxed now.

'Wise decision. Tonight is going to be perfect, I promise.'

'With you in charge, I have no doubt about that.'

Leaning back against the wall, I smile into the phone. Sam is wandering into the middle of the room now, dodging out the way of everyone and craning her neck to look for me. Her eyes finally land on me and she brightens. I wave her over.

'Uh, Chris, I have to go,' I say a little reluctantly.

'I'll see you tonight,' he says.

'See you tonight. Can't wait.'

As Sam reaches me, I hang up and pull her in for a hug.

'Gosh, it's all going on in here,' she observes, pulling back from me with a wide grin. 'Sorry to disturb your call. Anyone important?'

'Chris Courtney,' I admit, sliding my phone back into my pocket.

She gawps at me. 'Not him *personally*. Oh my God, you talk to the man *himself*?'

'It's been necessary during this campaign,' I reason, a little flustered. 'Much easier to talk direct than keep passing messages through someone.'

'Jesus, no wonder you were smiling so big then. He might just be the sexiest man on the planet. Such a shame he's married.' She hesitates. 'By the way, was that a sculpture of his body I saw out there?'

'One of two sculptures, yes.'

'Why is it being taken away?' she whines, appalled.

'Ren's decided he doesn't want opulence, he wants minimalism. No flowers, no performers, no sculptures.' I gesture at all the staff running around us like sweaty, frenzied ants. 'Tonight is going to look a little different than we've been planning.'

'Shit.' She exhales the air from her cheeks. 'You got this handled?'

'Of course.'

'One day, you'll look back and laugh. When you feel like you want to run away and hide, just remember that. One day, you'll laugh about it all,' she advises.

Sam is no stranger to demanding bosses and intense fashion-industry dramas. The editorial assistant for glossy magazine, *Studio*, she has had her fair share of smoothing dilemmas and soothing divas. We met a while ago when she called in a last-minute favour for a shoot. Ren was so excited to feature in *Studio* that he sent me across London in a heatwave to the warehouse hosting the photoshoot carrying a huge selection of clothes only for the editor to decide on one tie and that was it. Sam brought me a bottle of water while I sat to one side, gearing up to get on the sweaty Tube again, and made me feel better by telling me about the time she was asked by a celebrity they were working with to get a specific salad from a specific shop in North London. She went all the way there to find they were closed on Mondays. When she got back with a different salad, the celebrity in question looked at it and said, 'Where the fuck is the couscous?'

It was the kind of silly story that connects you for life. Bonding over the shitty aspects of our jobs, Sam and I have been best friends ever since and whenever we order food together, we'll look at each other's plates and say in unison, 'Where the *fuck* is the couscous?!'

It's a weird in-joke that is somehow hilarious every time.

'Here,' she says, handing over the clothes bag she's carrying. 'For tonight.'

'Thank you,' I gush, clutching it to my chest. 'You're a lifesaver.'

'Hey, it's no problem. Whenever you need something from the fashion closet, don't hesitate to ask,' she says, putting her hands on her hips. 'I've put a couple of options in there. Both black as you requested but both gorgeous. You're going to look hot.'

'Thank you, thank you. I did have something planned but when Ren changed the vibe to chic and minimalist, I realised that green might not fit so well.'

'Green does look amazing with your red hair,' she says enviously.

Sam has nothing to be envious about, though. She is drop-dead gorgeous with long, blonde hair, tall, slender frame, flawless make-up and an immaculate sense of style which matches with her job description. You can tell Sam works in fashion. I'm constantly having to call in favours with her to dress me from *Studio*'s fashion cupboard for these events. I don't know how much time I'll have to get ready for tonight and whether I'll even be able to get home beforehand. I may have to change in a cubicle here and it's unlikely I'll be able to do much more than attempt to tame my wavy, auburn hair into some kind of loose updo, top up the foundation over my freckles and smudge some eyeliner round my light-brown eyes, disguising tiredness with a smoky effect.

'How are you feeling about tonight?' Sam asks.

'Nervous,' I admit. 'Nothing can go wrong.'

'Nothing will go wrong. And if it does, you'll work out a way to style it out.'

'There will be lots of paparazzi here so styling it out may not be an option.'

'Chris Courtney does attract a crowd,' she muses, before gesturing at the action going on around us. 'But look at all this. *You've* done this, Ash. All that hard work is going to pay off and when tonight goes off without a hitch, you can proudly say it was all because of you.'

'I hope so,' I say on an exhale.

She pulls me into another hug, keeping hold of my shoulders as she pulls away. 'You've got this. I have to go back to work but I'll see you later.'

'Don't be late.'

'Please! The *Studio* crowd are likely to be the first to arrive, we're so excited,' she assures me. 'Oh, quick question, no biggie: are those sculptures I saw for sale?'

I can't stop a smile. 'They will be.'

'Uh-huh. And they're an exact replica of Chris Courtney's body?'

'An enlarged likeness of his bare torso, yes.'

'Uh-huh. And, out of interest, how can one purchase said feats of creation?'

'The artist was planning on auctioning them off from tomorrow. I have to call her to let her know that they'll no longer be on display for the event tonight, though, so I'm not sure how well that's going to go down.'

'Oh, I think she'll have no problem finding them a good home even so.'

I grin at her. 'See you tonight, Sam.'

'Remember,' she says, backing away from me and almost walking straight into someone carrying several LED glitter balloon lamps they've had to remove from the ceiling, 'whatever the stress of today, you'll laugh about it later.'

'That a promise?' I call out after her.

'It's a promise,' she cries back, waving before disappearing through the door.

The moment she's gone, I'm pounced on by someone needing my opinion on whether we still need the menus or if they should be scrapped altogether, whilst someone else asks what I want them to do with the artificial cherry-blossom decor and the gold palm trees.

By the time the event starts, I'm drained, exhausted, and terrified that we won't pull this off. Sam was right: tonight is down to my hard work the past few weeks and if it goes well, everyone will know that I was behind it. They'll also know that if everything goes wrong, too. But I do my best to mask my nerves with a warm smile, on hand to welcome the crowds of VIP guests filtering into his exclusive party. Everyone knows the moment Chris arrives because there's an eruption of noise from the swarm of paparazzi gathered outside, the frenzy of flashing bulbs from their cameras lighting up the windows. I straighten, my mouth dry, heart racing. *Here we go.*

As he breezes through the door, a cheer goes up and Ren glides over to greet him accompanied by a round of applause. The two of them shake hands, smiling at the room, posing for photos and soaking up the attention of their adoring fans.

Chris catches my eye and breaks into a wide, disarming smile.

And just like that, everything feels okay.

Two

The next morning, as I wait for my two soya flat whites in the coffee shop next to the office, I'm in a great mood. Last night could not have gone better. Despite the chaos in the lead-up to it, everything went smoothly. The food and drinks went down a storm, the atmosphere was fun and exciting, the venue was packed, and from the snippets I heard from those that matter who were there last night, Ren's new collection was admired. I had no doubt that this partnership with Chris Courtney was going to do wonders for both their careers.

'He's Wimbledon's answer to David Beckham,' an editor proclaimed to Ren yesterday, and from the way everyone was clambering to speak to him at the party, I'd say she has a point.

Collecting my coffee order when it's called out, I stroll to the office with a spring in my step. I punch the code into the door and push inside, waiting for the lift and smiling as I think about the night before. The first sense I have that something is up is the greeting I receive from the intern as I pass her desk.

'Morning, Natalia,' I say brightly.

She glances up and goes bright red.

'Uh… hi,' she says, looking uncomfortable.

I notice her glance to the person to her left. They share a smirk.

That's weird, I think, but continue to my desk which is by Ren's office at the back.

Things only get stranger on my journey. I notice a ripple of whispers and even some snickering, as though everyone is in on a joke I've missed. Placing the coffees down on my desk, I take off my jacket and hang it over my chair, growing more and more confused at the way people are glancing over at me. I stealthily check the mirror on my desk to make sure I don't have anything on my face, but confirm I'm all good.

'Hey, Raff,' I say, catching our branding manager as he passes my desk, 'what's going on this morning?'

He stops and stares at me, baffled. 'You… you haven't seen it?'

'Seen what?'

His eyes widen with horror and he opens his mouth to say something but is interrupted by Ren, who barks my name from his office, making both of us jump.

'Get in here,' Ren orders, disappearing again.

The blood in my veins goes cold. Ren should be in a good mood after the success of last night. I have to say I was expecting a little more praise from everyone today. Something has definitely happened and now I don't have time to check my phone to find out what it is before facing Ren. I'm unprepared for whatever tantrum is coming my way, so I'm just going to have to wing it. Grabbing his coffee, I step around my desk and shuffle in to his office.

He's waiting for me, perched on the edge of his desk, a cloud of misery descended over his expression. As I come in, he lifts his eyes to look at me in despair.

'Shut the door,' he says through gritted teeth.

I do so before holding out his coffee. He doesn't take it. I slowly lower my hand.

What the fuck is with everyone?

'Is everything all right?' I ask, my brain racing to provide an explanation for this strange atmosphere I've walked blindly into today.

Maybe there's been a bout of food poisoning amongst all the guests this morning that I'm unaware of. Did someone come to the party last night who wasn't supposed to be there? Maybe there's a scathing review of the collection.

'Is everything all right?' Ren repeats in a hoarse voice, looking at me as though I've lost my mind. '*Is everything all right?* Ash, how could you do this to me?'

'Do what?'

Closing his eyes, he sighs. 'You haven't seen it.'

'No. What haven't I seen?' I ask impatiently.

His eyes flashing open, Ren picks up his phone. The page he needs is already up on his screen so he just hands it out to me. Putting his coffee down on the table by the sofa, I step across his office to take his phone from him. It's a picture from last night that's been posted on social media. I gasp, my hand flying to cover my mouth in disbelief.

It's a perfectly clear shot of Chris Courtney kissing me up against the back door in the alleyway behind the venue of last night's event.

'Oh my God,' I whisper, my heart pounding so hard, my ears are ringing and my breath running short and shallow.

This can't be happening. *This can't be happening.*

Numb with shock, I scroll through the comments beginning to spread through social media about it. Reporters are feasting on the scandal of the *sordid affair between the married tennis star and junior fashion assistant*, promising exclusive details if people click on the links provided. Disapproving comments are appearing thick and fast.

Suddenly feeling like I might throw up, I shove Ren's phone back into his grasp and clutch at my stomach, stumbling backwards as though someone had physically punched me in the gut and wishing I had something to balance myself on as my knees feel weak. Ren watches on silently as I fumble back across the room to sink down on the sofa.

'I can explain,' I say weakly, pushing my hair back from my face as my forehead grows moist with sweat. I don't know where to begin.

It's been a whirlwind with Chris. Things have moved quickly but intensely, both of us falling faster and harder than we could have imagined. Contrary to what the headlines are saying, he's not married. Or, rather, he soon won't be. He's getting a divorce, but the problem is, no one knows that yet. He and his almost-ex-wife haven't wanted it to play out publicly, but they've been separated for a while.

He told me everything the first time we went for a drink together; he'd had a meeting with Ren that day in a restaurant in West London and, once Ren had left in the taxi I'd called him, Chris and I were walking in the same direction and got chatting. I've never felt so at ease in someone's company so quickly. He is funny, charming, interesting and captivating. Even though he was separated,

I was wary of getting involved with someone in a complicated situation, but it was hard to keep my distance. I couldn't help falling for him.

We decided it was best to keep things secret because of the delicacy surrounding his divorce proceedings and also the threat the relationship posed to my job. But last night, having spent the entire party acting professionally around each other, our willpower broke and we found a moment to sneak outside the back.

I thought we were alone. But someone saw.

Ren is so incensed, he doesn't seem to want to hear my explanation.

'Do you know how long I have worked on this collection?' he seethes, his knuckles growing white as they grip the edge of his desk. 'Do you know how much blood and sweat and tears has gone into this?'

'Ren—' I begin, but he cuts me off.

'You have put my entire career at risk!' he bellows. 'How could you *do this to me*?'

'It wasn't... we didn't...'

'You have ruined everything. Everything!'

'I'm so sorry, I didn't mean for this to happen. No one was supposed to know.'

'Oh, that makes it okay then!' he cries, pushing himself away from the desk to go stand by the window. 'No one is talking about my clothes. No one,' he says, spinning around to look at me accusingly. 'I finally get someone as big as Chris Courtney to put his name with mine and no one gives a flying fuck! All they care about is that he's screwing my assistant!'

I wince at the blunt language, my hands trembling in my lap.

'What were you thinking?' he hisses. 'Were you drunk last night? Is that it?'

'No, no, I wouldn't… I was working,' I say hurriedly. 'This thing with Chris, it's not… *nothing*. We have something together. Something real.'

He stares at me, looking more perplexed than before. '*What?* Ashley, he's *married*.'

'No, he's not. Er, I can't go into too many details, but he's separated. No one knows; it's still a secret.' I swallow, my heart racing. 'Ren, I'm so sorry about last night. It was unprofessional and… stupid. I promise I'll talk to Chris and we can work out a plan to ensure that this whole thing blows over and the focus is fully back to your clothing line.'

Ren exhales and slumps against his desk.

'Ashley, you know I have to fire you,' he states with a wave of his hand, like he's swatting away a fly that's come too close to his face and is becoming distracting.

'*Fire* me?' I repeat in disbelief. 'I understand you're cross and I'm sorry that I went behind your back, but if—'

'I can't work with you anymore, Ashley; I can't *trust* you,' he emphasises. 'You have humiliated me, you have humiliated my brand, and you have humiliated yourself. Your actions have been deeply unprofessional. You can't possibly carry on here.'

My jaw hanging open, I don't know what to say.

'I recommend you go home and… keep your head down for a while,' he continues wearily. 'I imagine things will get worse for you before they get better.'

I should fight back and remind him how much I've done for him, how heavily he and this entire office relies on me, but I think I'm still in too much shock over the picture. I wasn't prepared for the story to break yet and I'm finding it difficult to process the consequences. Rising slowly and shakily to my feet, I exit his office without saying another word. On autopilot, I pick up my bag and coat from my desk and begin the embarrassing walk back to the lift, trying to ignore the whispers and pointed looks that follow me as I go, my face on fire. In the lift, I muster the courage to check my phone to find hundreds of messages waiting for me across WhatsApp, email, text and my social media platforms. I can't believe how fast this has spun out of control. The photograph wasn't posted that long ago, but in the time it took for me to leave my flat and get to work, my life has blown up. Amongst the growing list of unread WhatsApps from friends and family, there's one name I look for but it's not there. No messages from Chris yet.

When I walk out onto the street, I suddenly feel overwhelmingly vulnerable, terrified that anyone who looks my way has seen the picture and knows who I am. Deciding I can't handle the Tube, I order an Uber and once it arrives, I get in and start scrolling through social media, the horror of it all beginning to sink in. As I read through what people are saying, I sink lower in my seat, wanting to disappear altogether.

Gold-digging slut. Homewrecker. Pathetic social climber. No integrity or morality. Shame on her! Not a girl's girl. She'll get what she deserves.

It's not fair. They don't know the truth. It looks bad, but it's not. I usually consider myself to have quite thick skin, but some of the comments filtering through are personal attacks that no one would be immune to. A tear rolls down my cheek as I exit social media and lower my phone to my lap. I comfort myself by thinking about how remorseful all these people will feel once they know the truth. I feel bad that Chris will have to talk about his divorce publicly before he's ready and I honestly am sorry that he and his ex-wife will have to suffer the attention they were hoping to avoid, but once that's out in the open, at least Chris and I won't have to put up with these unwarranted attacks on our characters.

'We haven't done anything wrong,' I whisper out loud to myself, gazing out the window as my Uber driver battles the city's traffic.

Once everyone knows that, everything will be okay. Ren may regret firing me so quickly. He's definitely going to regret losing me when he realises how much I dealt with every day.

My phone vibrates with a phone call and my heart jumps, but it's not Chris. It's my mum. I can't face her questions, not now, so I let it ring out. I want to turn off my phone completely, but I want to hear from him. He'll have seen this by now, or at least his publicity team will have. I message him, asking him to call me.

When I get back to my flat, he still hasn't replied. He hasn't read it. I send him another. When I check a bit later in the day, the messages remain unread. Looking again late morning, I find his profile picture has disappeared from his WhatsApp. I message him to ask what's going on, but it only shows one grey tick. My messages aren't delivering. I call him but it doesn't connect. I try again. It still won't connect.

He's blocked me.

*

The next day, Chris Courtney uploads a statement to his Instagram:

I have taken the time to reflect on my actions, so I can come to terms with everything that has happened in the last couple of days.

First and foremost, I would like to apologise to my wife, who I love more than anything in the world. I am so sorry for putting her in this situation. One incredibly stupid, spontaneous and drunken moment has caused the person I love to suffer unbearable pain and undeserved embarrassment, and I deeply regret my irresponsible and selfish behaviour. I am so ashamed that I have hurt Rachel and those close to us.

I would like to apologise to her and everyone who feels let down by my drunken, foolish mistake. We will continue to deal with this in our own way and we kindly ask for you to respect our privacy. Thank you to all my fans for the love and support. You have no idea how much it has meant to me during this difficult time for my family.

Chris x

Three

Ash

Have you seen the new photos?

The ones of him and his wife in the park

Sam

Strolling hand in hand?

Putting on a front of being a perfect couple?

Days after he was caught cheating?

Yes, I've seen those

Their fakeness made me want to puke

It's a publicity stunt

Anyone can see through it

Ash

I'm such an idiot

Sam

We've discussed this

You are not the idiot here

HE is the idiot

He is more than an idiot

He's a disgusting cowardly prick

And if I ever see him I'm going to kick him in the balls

If he even has any balls

Which I doubt

Ash

How could I have been so stupid?

I believed every lie he told me

Sam

Anyone would have done the same!

Ash, this isn't your fault

Ash

Actually it is my fault

I got caught up in an idea of him

I didn't know him at all

I'm so embarrassed

Sam

Let me come over tonight and cheer you up?

Or we could go out for dinner? My treat

Ash

In Sainsbury's earlier, a woman tutted at me

I was reaching for some chopped tomatoes

And she TUTTED at me

I'm nationally hated

It will be a while before I can go out for dinner

Sam

It's been a few days now, Ash

It might be good for you to get out the flat for a bit

Ash

You know he hasn't messaged or called

Not once

I lost my job

My reputation is destroyed

And people tut at me in supermarkets

While he strolls happily with his wife through leafy parks

He hasn't even messaged me to break up officially

Sam

He's a coward Ash

The lowest of the low

I'm so sorry he did this to you

I hate him

And I meant what I said when I came over the other day

One day, karma will bite him in the arse

Ash

I can't believe how naïve I was

The biggest fool in the world

And everyone knows it

Sam

You didn't do anything wrong!!

You fell for a guy who told you he was single!!

HE IS THE FOOL

Ash

He is a family man who made a mistake

According to what I've read

I'm the bad guy

Sam

Stop reading all the shit out there

Miserable people comment miserable things

They don't know you

They don't know anything

WE know the truth, that's what matters

Like I said, what goes around comes around

You'll come out of this stronger

Ash

It doesn't feel like it

Sam

I know it doesn't feel like it now

But this could be a good thing

You should have quit that job ages ago

Ren never appreciated you

If it makes you feel any better,

I hear he's falling apart without you

Have you looked at any jobs?

Ash

No

Too busy feeling sorry for myself

Sam

I can ask around if you like?

Ash

Thanks but no one will want me now

Oh

I've got to go, someone's at the door

Sam

Call me whenever you need

I'll come see you soon xxxx

When the doorbell goes, for a fleeting, hopeful moment, I wonder if it might be Chris here to apologise, offer an explanation and beg my forgiveness.

'Ashley, it's me,' comes Mum's crisp voice over the intercom. 'Let me in before I shove this guy's camera lens up his—'

I buzz open the door before she can finish her sentence. The last thing we need on top of the Chris Courtney drama is my mum getting arrested for smashing a reporter's camera. I'm surprised there are any paps still lurking outside my building. The majority of them have given up hope of getting a picture considering I've refused to emerge into daylight since the story broke, except for that one Sainsbury's trip which I instantly regretted. But I suppose now that those photos of Chris and his wife playing happy families have been published today, people are keen to see my reaction so the photographers have returned.

I wait by the door until I hear Mum's footsteps on the stairs getting closer and then open it for her, letting her breeze past me laden with shopping bags, her Jo Malone perfume wafting over me as she goes by. I follow her into the kitchen as she plonks the bags down on the kitchen counter before turning to take me in. She puts her hands on my arms and gives me a good look up and down.

'Uh-oh,' she concludes.

'Thanks, Mum, always a great comfort to have you here,' I grumble, wriggling free of her grasp and going to slump back on the sofa where I've set up camp the last few days.

'Have you been eating?' she demands to know.

'I haven't got much of an appetite.'

'You have to eat otherwise you'll die,' she says bluntly.

'Very profound.'

'I mean it, Ash; it's important. What do you feel like? I got you… well,' she gestures at the shopping bags, 'everything. I wasn't sure what you might want.'

'Nothing.'

'We'll go easy then. I'll make you some toast. Butter and jam?' she suggests, beginning to unload the contents of the bags onto the counter.

I shrug.

'Butter and jam it is. I got you Tiptree,' she says smugly.

Mum grew up in Witham, Essex, which is down the road from Tiptree. She determines the quality of a hotel on whether it serves Tiptree jam with breakfast. If it does, she's happy. If it doesn't, she won't trust it.

I watch as she busies herself, her natural high level of energy making me feel even more exhausted and useless than before. She's wearing an all-black tailored three-piece suit and towering heels.

'Are those Manolos?' I ask, squinting at her footwear.

'Yes, they are,' she replies, opening the fridge. 'Everyone at work has been pissing me off this week so I've been trying to dress with a *come-near-me-and-die* sort of vibe.'

I almost manage a smile at that.

Ever since I can remember, Mum has never taken any crap from anyone. She is the toughest, smartest person I know. Nothing seems to faze or panic her. She has a get-on-with-it attitude and works harder than anyone, which makes her a brilliant TV producer. She's never been a cuddly, emotional sort of mum, and I have to admit that there have been times that I wished she were. But I love that she says it how it is and she's not afraid of anyone, whoever they are. Mum has always worked long hours – she knew no one in the TV business when she started out and was never given any help along the way to get a foot in the door, so she's had to earn every step forward she got. I admire her work ethic and wish I had that kind of drive, although I think it helps if you know what you're driving towards.

When she's done making the toast, she marches over and places the plate down on the coffee table, insisting I take a bite while she sits down on the chair opposite.

'How are you feeling today?' she asks as I chew, flicking her thick mane of impossibly glossy brown hair behind her shoulder.

I get my hair colour from my dad, whose family were all redheads. I don't have much to do with my father.

He and Mum had what she likes to call a 'tumultuous' relationship. They got married quickly after meeting and had my older brother, Jasper. Dad left and they divorced. They were on and off again for a bit, then off for a long time. Then they were back on again briefly which resulted in me.

I remember at one point in my childhood, I got lost in this silly romantic notion that the reason they kept coming back together was because they were meant to be. But I grew up and realised that I wouldn't want that at all. My father is ambitious and selfish, and although I have no ill-will towards him – Jasper and I have never needed anyone but Mum – he's not cut out to be a dad or a life partner. He travels as much as possible, is never in one place for long, and as far as I know, Mum has been the only serious relationship he's ever considered.

He currently works as a reporter in Hong Kong and every now and then will send me messages to check in. It took him over a day to realise I was playing a starring role in the UK media recently, but I did eventually hear from him. He said he hoped I was all right, to keep my chin up and had I seen the latest Crystal Palace football score – the team were doing surprisingly well. I think of all the things he left behind here in England, my dad misses the football more than he misses anything or anyone else.

Under Mum's watchful gaze, I swallow my mouthful of toast.

'I'm okay,' I say in answer to her question. 'The same, really. I haven't heard anything from Chris still.'

'I told you you're not going to,' she says. 'His publicity team will be strongly advising against any contact, and

I imagine his wife may have set down some rules, too. Plus, he's a spineless shithead who doesn't deserve you in his life.' Mum glances around my flat and sighs. 'I don't know why you're not staying with me, Ash. I don't like you being here on your own while this is going on.'

'I like my own space,' I reason, not giving the full details which is: *I like to be on my own so I can rage and cry and drink and check my phone a million times without any judgement.* 'I want to handle this myself.'

'Yes, but there's no harm in leaning on people,' says Mum, who has never leant on anyone her whole life. 'I don't think it's healthy you being cooped up here with nothing to do. You need something to distract yourself from it all.'

I snort. 'I can hardly apply for jobs right now. People hate me.'

'You're not hated; people like to sling mud to feel better about themselves, it's pathetic,' Mum says. 'And I wasn't necessarily talking about getting a job.'

'I'm not really in the mood to take up a new hobby, Mum,' I mutter, attempting another bite of toast.

'This is not going to define you, Ash. This is one guy. You will move on, I promise.'

'Will everyone else, though?' I counter miserably. 'This story is going to haunt me forever. Stuff online doesn't disappear. I will always be the girl who Chris Courtney cheated on his wife with.'

'Sometimes, things that feel like the end can also mark a beginning.'

I narrow my eyes at her. 'Are you repeating stuff that people say on your show?'

'Yes, a life coach said that to one of our viewers last week who called in about her business folding.' Mum tilts her head at me. 'It's a positive way of thinking.'

'Yeah, well, I'm not ready to think positively about any of this.'

She watches me carefully and then straightens, as though she's had an idea. 'You know what I think? I think you need a change of scenery. You need to get away from everything, go somewhere where this doesn't feel like such a big deal, somewhere that doesn't have reporters jumping out at you and lurking around your door, forcing you inside. The city can feel… claustrophobic. This is the perfect time to get away.'

'Yeah, because I'm dumped and unemployed,' I mutter gloomily.

'You're *free*,' Mum counters, 'to do whatever the hell you want.'

'Where am I going to go? I don't want to go on holiday on my own, that will make me feel lonelier,' I reason. 'Although…'

Mum sits up. 'What? What are you thinking?'

'Nothing. Jasper messaged me, that's all, and said I could stay with him for a bit.'

She brightens. 'Of *course*! Why didn't I think of that? It's perfect. He lives in a beautiful part of the country. There's no one better to look after you than your brother.'

Jasper is my older brother by quite a gap – ten years in fact – and runs an idyllic country pub in Sussex that he owns with Mum. We speak a lot, but don't get to see each other as much as we'd like. Managing a successful business takes up most of his time and I was always busy here in the city managing Ren. But since the Chris story exploded, he's been calling often and messaging in the hope of persuading me to come visit. He's a classic country bumpkin in that he thinks the answer to any problem is… the countryside.

'Country air, long walks, nature,' Mum rattles off. 'Very healing.'

'I guess it would be nice to get away and go somewhere a bit more low-key with fewer people around to tut at me in supermarkets,' I admit, rubbing my forehead as the idea grows more tempting the more I think about it.

'Who is tutting at you in supermarkets?' Mum asks before dismissing it with a wave of her hand. 'Never mind. Message Jasper now and ask whether he's happy for you to come tomorrow. I can help you pack.'

'I can pack myself, Mum,' I insist, picking up my phone, typing out a message to him and pressing send. I put my phone down again. 'It's fine. You don't need to—'

I'm interrupted by my phone vibrating with a reply from him already.

'Wow. He says my room is ready and waiting. That was quick.' I glance up to find Mum beaming at me, delighted with the way this has played out. 'Guess I'm off to Sussex.'

'Fantastic.' She inhales deeply. 'I have a very good feeling about this, Ash.'

Four

The train station for Jasper's village is so small that I have to move carriages as we draw into the platform because it's too short to accommodate the entire train. No one else gets off here; it's just me and my case rattling along the empty platform towards the car park as the train departs. As promised, Jasper is there waiting, leaning on the open door of his Land Rover Defender. He brightens as I approach and his warm smile makes my eyes well up. After facing a barrage of hate online, it's nice to have someone look happy to see me.

'Hey, Ash,' he says, striding over, arms outstretched. 'Come here.'

He pulls me in for a hug, holding me so tight, I can't move. Unlike Mum, Jasper *is* a hug kind of person. He's tall and broad, built like a rugby player but with the gentlest soul of anyone I've ever met. He doesn't have the deep-auburn hair I landed with, but his is strawberry blonde, the slightest hint of a redhead.

'How was your journey?' he asks, releasing me and picking up my case.

'Fine, thanks,' I say, trying not to wince as I watch my case of designer clothes and shoes – a perk of being in fashion is, obviously, the freebies that come your way, even if you're a lowly assistant – being tossed haphazardly into the boot of his car, balancing on a pair of mud-caked wellies.

'I'm glad you're here,' he says, shutting the boot and gesturing to the front passenger seat. 'Climb on in and let's go.'

Sliding in next to him, I close the door behind me and put on my seatbelt, exhaling audibly as he turns on the engine. He pulls out of the car park and straight onto a road lined by hedges that separate it from the fields stretching beyond. We get to a crossroads and he indicates, turning his head to look down the road my side and stealing a glance at me.

'You all right?' he asks casually as we turn onto a road that is narrower than the one before and with a few more potholes.

'I'm fine.'

'Really?' he checks.

'Not really. But I am happy to be out of London.'

'Mum told me what happened,' he admits, his brow furrowing with anger as he keeps his eyes on the winding road ahead. 'As in, she told me the truth compared to what the press is saying. It's not fair what he's done to you, Ash.'

'No, it's not,' I mutter.

'Here, you can forget all about that *bastard*,' he says so passionately that I'm forced to look at him in surprise. 'If he dares to contact you, I'll let him know *exactly* what—'

'He hasn't got in touch,' I quickly assure him. 'I doubt he will.'

'Good. He can fuck off,' he spits.

I can't stop a smile spreading across my face. Jasper notices and frowns.

'What?' he says, confused.

'I've never seen you so worked up before. It's weird. Good weird. But weird.'

'Yeah, well, it takes a lot to piss me off,' he admits, 'but Chris Courtney has gone above and beyond to make it happen. The conceit and entitlement. How does he think he can get away with it?'

'Because he can,' I answer simply.

Jasper's jaw clenches and I turn to look out the window as we pass a field of grazing horses. I smile at the sight, watching their long tails flick as they nibble away at the grass, their coats glossy in the sunshine. I have a thing about horses. Mum says I was obsessed with them as a little kid. It was strange, she says, because I didn't grow up around horses. It didn't matter; I loved them anyway.

When I was eight years old, our urban school ran a trial initiative for a year with a south London stables where students were offered group riding lessons. It was a brilliant idea, a programme that was designed to introduce city kids to horses and stable life, building confidence, improving interaction with animals – but I didn't care about any of that. All I cared about was the fact that I was going to get the chance to be around *horses*. At the time, we didn't have much money and I remember going to the fancy stables and enviously watching the girls who rode there often, girls in expensive jodhpurs and tailored jackets with perfect hair and posture and the uncanny ability to let you know exactly what they think about you with a single look. Their superior sneers are burned into my memory.

I was determined to be good at horse riding and I got the hang of it pretty quickly, finding myself naturally confident with a good balance in the saddle. I was the best in the group and I remember the instructor saying that she thought I had real potential if I kept it up. But the programme was cut after two terms. By then, I had a good foundation in riding and was jumping, already envisioning myself as a showjumper for Great Britain. I was devastated. Mum promised me that she was going to get me horse-riding lessons as soon as we could afford them. By the time she could, my obsession with horses had been forgotten. By then, I'd grown up and accepted I was not an equestrian; I'd never be one of those posh pretty girls in the sculpted cream jodhpurs and leather riding boots. I haven't been on a horse since.

Still, I love the sight of them.

'It is beautiful here,' I remark to Jasper.

'I can't believe you've never visited before. Any time I want to see you, I've had to trudge up to London.'

'That's because there's things to actually do there,' I tease.

'Now you sound like Mum.'

'She sends her love, by the way. She's still annoyed about Christmas, though.'

He rolls his eyes. 'She knows it's a busy time at the pub. We're always fully booked around the Christmas period. And as I said last year and the year before, you two could come to me. You'd love it around here during the winter. The pub is very cosy and the village lights are great. A real community atmosphere, you know?'

'Mum couldn't, not with her work. She barely got Christmas Day off. Basically, both of you work too hard and live too far apart.' I rest my elbow on the door and lean my head against my hand. 'Right now, I'm glad you live far away, though. Thanks for letting me stay.'

'Hey, the room is always yours, whenever you want for whatever you need.'

'Thanks. What I need is somewhere to hide.'

Jasper frowns. 'He shouldn't make you feel like you're the one who needs to hide. And anyway, I don't think shutting the world out is an answer.'

'I thought that's why I came to a place I can pretend the world doesn't exist.'

He looks amused. 'It's not *dead* around here, Ash. There's plenty of things going on and people to meet. Speaking of which, I thought you could help me out in the pub while you're here.'

'You're offering me a job?'

'Yeah. Put in a few shifts here and there. Might be better for you to keep busy and keep your mind off things. Work is a good distraction.'

'I'm not sure how long I'm going to be here, though.'

'We'll see how we go.'

He slows and turns off the lane into the uneven, dusty car park of a gorgeous stone-walled pub, its name emblazoned above the symbol of a dog on a green sign hanging above the door: The Old Greyhound. Mum has shown me pictures of it before, emphasising their decision to keep as much of the original character features intact as possible so it retains that quaint country-local feel, like the wooden door with its cast-iron knocker and the wooden hitching posts lined on the grass outside the front that were installed in a time when people would tie up their horses there before nipping inside for a pint. One glance at the pub and I can understand why Jasper fell in love with this place and put his all into saving it – I haven't even gone inside and I already know it's a place worth protecting.

He parks and I climb out the car as he retrieves my bag from the boot, heading up the stone path to the entrance of the building. Admiring the exposed beams and wonky flagstone floors, I follow Jasper through the empty pub to the door hidden behind the bar, up the stairs and into his living quarters. I don't know what I expected but I'm surprised at how neat and clean it is up here.

'It's really nice,' I declare, scanning the vintage patterned rug of the lounge, the prettily displayed cushions on the sofa, the healthy thriving array of plants and the cool arched floor lamp in the far corner. 'Very... stylish.'

'What were you expecting?' Jasper challenges, arching his brow at me. 'A dusty old room filled with cobwebs?'

'No!' I hesitate. 'Maybe a bit of dust.'

He chuckles. 'I'm not completely useless. Here's your room.' He carries my case into the spare room next to the lounge which is small but bright, the sun pouring in through the tall windows. 'I hope it's okay.'

'It's lovely. Thank you,' I say, wandering over to the window to check out the view of the spacious beer garden that looks out over miles and miles of unspoilt countryside. '*Wow.*'

'Not bad, eh? Bathroom is next door and my room is at the far end.'

I sigh, sitting down on the white and blue floral duvet. 'I owe you big time.'

'Don't mention it. This is your home for as long as

you need. Right.' He rubs his hands together. 'I have a few things to do before opening. I'll let you settle in. Shout if you need anything. I'll be downstairs.'

'Thanks.'

Leaving me perching on the bed, he shuts the door behind him and I hear his footsteps disappearing down the stairs. I don't move for a while, listening to the complete silence. No background noise of traffic or trains in the distance or the bustling of people on the streets below hurrying to get wherever they need to be. I fall back to lie down on the squishy duvet and stare up at the ceiling, my hands clasped over my stomach.

As soon as I shut my eyes, images of Chris creep into my head. I think on my stupidity, how much his betrayal stings, how hurtful it is to read comments from strangers all over the world calling me nasty names, wishing me nothing but ill will. My heart starts racing, my breathing quickens with panic and I begin to feel just as suffocated by my foolishness as I did in London.

My eyes flash open and I push myself up, getting to my feet so quick, I get a headrush.

Swinging open my door, I head down the stairs and find Jasper behind the bar studying the menus, twiddling a pen in his fingers.

'I think I'm going to go for a walk,' I announce as he glances up at me.

'Good idea. Clear your head and get some fresh air,' he says with approval. 'Although, I won't be able to go with you right now.'

'That's fine,' I say quickly. 'I want to be on my own. Do some... thinking.'

'You want some recommendations on where to go? The phone signal isn't too good around here.'

'I'll follow a path and see where it takes me.'

'You want to change first?'

I look down at my cropped white sweatshirt, green Lululemon leggings and brand new white and red trainers. 'This isn't okay to walk in?'

'It is if you don't mind it getting dirty,' he says, seeming amused that he needs to explain. 'There's mud around these parts and you're wearing a lot of bright white.'

'It will be fine,' I say dismissively as I head to the door. 'I'll see you in a bit.'

'You sure you're all right going on your own?' he checks, unable to hide the concern laced in his voice.

I shoot him a look. 'Jasper, I'm not a kid anymore, okay? You're right, I don't want him to make me feel like I have to hide away. Besides, I just got here. I want to explore. I won't go too far and I promise I'll be fine.'

'All right, see you in a bit.'

I give him a parting wave before ducking out into the fresh air.

There's a signpost for a public footpath through the woodland straight to my left that seems like a good place to start. I march confidently towards it. Hearing the birdsong in the canopy of trees overhead and sheep bleating in the distance, I take some long, deep breaths as I go, already feeling lighter than I did in the city. At least here I can walk outside without the fear of bumping into anyone.

Jasper was right about the dirt, though. It must have rained here heavily recently as I find myself carefully picking my way around pools of squelchy mud and puddles, trying to keep my new shoes clean. Having successfully made my way around the first few, I'm conned by a patch on the path covered in deeper mud than it looks.

'*Bollocks*,' I huff at the loud squelch beneath my step, lifting my foot and groaning at the mud covering my shoe and splattered all over the other.

From then, I might as well give up on being so careful and by the time the path merges onto an open field, my trainers are no longer bright white and my leggings are covered in mud splatter. Wiping the sides of my trainers on the grass, I continue down the path that's lined by a long wooden fence, looking out across the fields that stretch before me.

I come to a stop. The most beautiful horse is a few metres away. Her chestnut-red coat is impossibly glossy, a white stripe blazing down her nose. Her long, dark tail swishes as she paws the ground with her front right hoof, whinnying and loudly snorting. She notices me, her ears pricking, her bright eyes fixed on me.

'Hello,' I say, moving to lean my arms on the fence so I can study her properly. 'You're a stunner, aren't you?'

Beyond her, at the other end of the field, are a cluster of horses grazing.

'How come you're not with your friends? Have you been ostracized, too? I know something about that,' I tell her.

She dips her head and snorts again. I smile appreciatively at her response. Despite the clicking sound I make out the side of my mouth to tempt her over, she doesn't move closer but she doesn't stalk off either. I stay standing near her for a short while, my chin resting on my hands leaning on the fence, soothed by her company.

Eventually, I concede it's time to get back and climb up onto the bottom rail of the fence so I can reach my arm out towards her. She lifts her head curiously. My fingertips brush against her neck, scratching her there. She allows it before deciding that's enough and lowers her head again to get back to grazing. I like this horse. She's not going to fawn over anyone.

Hopping off the fence, I follow it all the way down along the field until it narrows and comes out onto the road. Checking the Maps app on my phone, I work out I have two options: either go back the way I came, or follow the road to the pub. The latter is the quicker option.

It's a quiet country road and it doesn't have a pavement, but there is a grassy verge, so I stick to that, my spirits lifted by my new equine friend. I'm so lost in my thoughts, I don't hear the car roaring down the road until it's right in front of me. I gasp, stumbling back as the green convertible vintage sports car speeds past me, its top down. The dark-haired, stubbled-jaw driver shows no sign of slowing, even though I know he's seen me, and I can hear the laughter of his passenger, a blonde, angular-faced woman in large, red-framed sunglasses, carry back to me on the wind as they hurtle past.

'Slow down!' I yell after them, adding a mutter of, '*Prick*', for good measure.

I'm still fuming about the driver's idiotic, dangerous arrogance when I get back to the pub, walking in to find Jasper carrying a crate of glasses that he's placing on the bar.

'Good walk?' he asks, brightening at the sight of me.

'I saw some horses and it was all very peaceful until some

dickhead came along, speeding around the narrow lanes in his sports car.'

Jasper doesn't look surprised. 'What was the car?'

'A racing-green sports car. Looked retro.'

'Ah. Sounds like Mateo,' he tells me. 'He's back from the US Open. He may have been driving angrily because his team just lost.'

'He didn't seem angry. He had a beautiful blonde passenger giggling next to him.'

Jasper gives a knowing smile. 'I heard he met a model in Miami who was... uh... a big fan, let's say.'

'A fan?'

'Mateo Pérez is a professional polo player. He's on the Maycourt team. The horses you saw probably belonged to his patron, Lady Maycourt. Her estate is nearby.'

'He plays *polo*?' I say, deeply unimpressed as I pick up the wine menu. 'Figures.'

Five

I don't want to give Jasper the satisfaction of telling him that he's right about the countryside being the answer to my problems, but after a few days, I'm starting to realise that there is something inherently soothing about this setting and way of life. It's easier to be offline here: in the mornings, I go on long walks and in the afternoons, I help out at the pub, during which I can't be on my phone. Keeping busy distracts me from the chaos of the life I left behind in London and I like feeling helpful. I don't feel so lost here, I guess. Or at least, I don't have so much opportunity to think on what's gone wrong – there's always pints to be poured or tables to be cleaned.

I've got to know a couple of the locals too, who couldn't be less interested in my scandalous past. My favourites are Rhys and Noor, both retired, who come in almost daily to have a chat over a pint of local cider or beer and discuss the state of the world or, where Noor is concerned, the polo season ahead. As someone who knows nothing about polo, I don't know what Noor is talking about when I overhear snippets of their conversation but it's obvious he's very knowledgeable on the subject, like a lot of people around here. I'm in the heart of polo country, they've declared, and if I'm going to work here, I'll have to get into it.

'You'll love it,' Noor has told me. 'And considering you're on good terms with the Maycourt ponies, it's only right that you should learn about what they can do.'

He's talking about the relationship I've struck up with 'Chestnut', the horse I met my first day here and the one I've taken to visiting every morning on my walks. As I thought during our first meeting, she's a stubborn and aloof character, preferring to play things on her terms. I like that about her. I haven't been overdoing it and trying to win her over – instead, I've kept my distance, sitting on the fence and chatting to her while she grazes nearby, both of us happy in our own space. After a couple of days of listening to my ramblings about my failed love life and public humiliation, she decided she might come say hello. I didn't act like it was a big deal, even though I was very excited. I patted her neck and stroked her nose, then strolled off. The next morning, she saw me and came plodding over straight away.

Playing it cool doesn't just work on humans. It works on horses, too.

The relationship has become mutually beneficial: she gets nose rubs, I get to talk about what happened with Chris without fear of judgement. It's cheap therapy.

One morning, I'm in my usual spot in the field, having hopped over the fence to be on the same side as Chestnut. I'm leaning back against the fence while I pat her neck and tell her about the latest twist in my sorry saga: Ren has given an interview in which he was asked about his feelings on the launch-party scandal and he flew to the defence of Chris.

'He said he knew Chris well and that he was a dedicated family man who loved his wife dearly,' I reveal to Chestnut as she munches on the grass by my feet. 'Then he said that everyone makes mistakes and he believed people were too quick these days to cancel others. He didn't mention the fact that he'd been very quick to cancel *me*.'

Chestnut lifts her head and whinnies.

Then she shakes her ears and gets back to eating her grass.

'Exactly my thoughts,' I agree, nodding slowly. 'I've had a lucky escape from both of those jerks.' I sigh, adding dismally, 'Still hurts, though. I did a lot for Ren, but he's dropped me without a moment's hesitation. Then there's the injustice of it all. Everyone out there thinks *I'm* the bad guy. I wish I didn't care about that, but... I do.'

As she turns her head away from me, I realise we're not alone.

A man is approaching across the field. I don't notice until he's practically right next to us. Panicking, I straighten, knowing it's too late for me to climb back over the fence to the public path now. His thick, dark hair and square stubbled jaw are familiar. He's the knobhead from the green sports car: Mateo, the polo player.

He comes around Chestnut's front and reaches out to stroke her nose as he passes, but she lifts her head away from his reach, snorting indignantly. In his other hand, he's holding some kind of basket-shaped muzzle, the straps of it hanging loosely down by his side. He stops in front of me. Hands on his hips, mouth set in a serious, straight line, he looks me up and down unashamedly, his forehead creased in puzzlement. He's intimidatingly good-looking, tall and broad-shouldered with dark eyes framed by bold eyebrows and long, full eyelashes. It makes sense that he'd be the type of Argentine polo player to have a legion of 'fans', as Jasper had informed me, whether those fans were into polo or not.

'*Hola*,' he says.

'Uh… hi.'

'What are you doing?' he asks in perfect English with his sexy Argentine accent.

He's not smiling but he's not asking unkindly. He sounds more curious.

'Sorry, I was… um,' I gesture to Chestnut, 'talking.'

The confusion in his expression deepens. 'Talking?' he repeats.

I nod.

'Huh.' He tilts his head at me. 'I've seen you here before.'

'You have?'

'Yes. Were you just… talking to this horse on those occasions also?'

I nod again, feeling nervous under his intense gaze.

'Why?' he asks.

God. This is awkward. Talking to a horse is one thing, but explaining to someone *why* you're talking to a horse is another. It's going to be hard to come out of this sounding sane.

'I like being around horses. I find her presence calming.'

He quirks a brow. 'You find the presence of *this* horse calming?' He points to Chestnut. 'This horse right here?'

'Yes.' I frown. 'Why? What's wrong with her?'

'Nothing. Nothing is wrong with Serafina. She's beautiful. I had hopes she'd make a great polo pony, but she's too wilful and stubborn. She's difficult to ride, near impossible to control. She doesn't listen to anyone.'

'Oh.' I look to her in surprise.

'But *you* find her... calming. Interesting.'

There's a beat of silence as we both study the horse next to us.

'Did you say her name was Serafina?' I check.

'Yes.'

'That's a lovely name,' I muse aloud.

Mateo nods, watching me carefully. 'And yours?'

'Ash,' I tell him, reaching out to pat Serafina's neck.

'I'm Mateo.'

'I know who you are.' I notice a flash of smugness cross his expression, so I feel the need to quash any ego-inflating. 'Not from your polo career. Because you almost ran me off the road the other day. My brother told me who you were from the description of your car.'

He looks thrown and then recognition flickers across his handsome features. 'Ah, yes. I remember now, you were walking near here. I'm sorry about that. I know these roads very well and tend to drive fast around them.'

'You shouldn't. I know you had company, but it's dangerous to show off like that around such tight corners and narrow lanes.'

He doesn't say anything, looking stunned at my directness before his expression softens into amusement. A classic reaction of someone too entitled to ever be put in their place.

I clear my throat.

'I should go. Sorry about trespassing. In the future, I...'

I trail off mid-sentence, distracted as he begins to fiddle with the apparatus in his hand, unbuckling the straps and getting it ready.

'What is that?' I ask, pointing to it.

'A grazing muzzle.' He notices my blank expression. 'It helps to control a horse's natural tendency to overeat. They can still drink and they can eat a little, but they can't eat a lot. It's important to control grazing so they don't get overweight and it can help ponies with stomach problems.' He pauses before adding, 'Don't worry, it doesn't hurt or hinder them. It helps them.'

'Why do you think I'd assume it might hurt them?' I ask defensively.

'City people often have certain misconceptions. I can tell that you have developed an attachment to Serafina through your meetings and I didn't want you to be worried.'

I can't work out if that's nice of him or mildly insulting. It's difficult to tell.

'I'm not worried. And I may be from London, but I'm not completely clueless,' I say.

'I didn't think you were. You obviously have something about you. Serafina usually bolts around anyone who tries to connect with her. Or anyone who tries to make her do something she doesn't want to,' he says. 'Which is why I should take her back to the stable to wrestle her into this muzzle. She eats too much, it's not good for her. But she loves to be out here.'

I glance over at Serafina, who continues to munch the grass. Then without much thought, I say, 'Want me to give it a go?'

He stares at me for a moment. Then, he holds out the grazing muzzle. I take it from him confidently, examining it so I can get a handle on how it works. I can feel his gaze on me the entire time, as though, while I work the muzzle out, he tries to work me out.

This could go very wrong. But the worst that can happen is Serafina bolts when I make my attempt and it sounds like she does that with everyone else. I'm curious to see if the trust I've established with her is mutual or if she's been putting up with me purely because the grass over here is particularly tasty or something.

Mateo steps back as I move calmly towards her with the grazing muzzle in my hand. As I get closer, she lifts her head, her ears turned back and relaxed as I start talking to her.

'Hey, Serafina, nice to have your name right. Sorry I've been calling you Chestnut,' I say. 'On reflection, Chestnut is a bit of a plain name for such a striking horse like yourself. Serafina is more elegant. It suits you.'

I study the grazing muzzle in my hands again and she lowers her head to rub her cheek against my shoulder.

'Mind if I put this on you? Sounds like you might need some help with your eating habits. You can carry on using me as a scratching post while I do it if you like.' I slide the muzzle onto her, reaching up to secure the buckle. She doesn't seem bothered, so I reach up to pat her neck gratefully. 'Thanks for making that so easy.'

She exhales, enjoying the neck rub. With one last stroke of her nose, I turn round to find Mateo still watching me intently, his expression stern and serious. If he's impressed, he doesn't show it.

'There. All done,' I say brightly, walking back towards him. 'Sorry again for being in the field; I know I shouldn't have been. From now on, I'll stay on the right side of the fence.'

He doesn't say anything, looking deep in thought, so I carry on past him and climb back over to the footpath. As I land on the other side and wipe my hands together to dust them off, I notice that someone on the far side of the field is watching us. I can just about make her out: an older woman, sophisticatedly dressed, with cropped, silver-blonde hair. She's surrounded by a pack of dogs of all different shapes and sizes, their tails wagging furiously as they wait at her side. That must be Lady Maycourt, who owns the estate, and she's just fully witnessed me trespassing. I blush furiously and turn to go.

'Nice to meet you, Ash,' Mateo calls out, stopping me in my tracks.

I turn to give him a small nod and then hurry away along the path, too afraid to turn back to check if they're both watching me go.

'So every polo team has a patron?' I check with Noor and Rhys that afternoon, carefully pouring Rhys a pint of Guinness.

The pub is empty apart from the two of them sitting at the bar, so I'm able to quiz them on Maycourt Polo, much more curious about the yard now I've formally met one of the players and seen the team's elegant patron at a distance.

'That's right,' Noor confirms, delighted to talk about his favourite subject. 'Polo is extremely expensive and you don't win any money, so you need someone wealthy to fund the team. The patron pays for everything: the players, the travel, the ponies and their care and stabling. All of it. Usually, the patron also participates in the team of four, but not in this case.'

'Lady Maycourt doesn't play?'

'Her nephew is on the team instead. Fitz. He's the son of her late husband's brother. He's a fairly capable player, but nothing to the three professionals on the Maycourt team,' Rhys tells me as I pass him his pint.

'And Mateo is one of those professionals,' I confirm.

'He's the best of the team and one of the best out there,' Noor says proudly, always talking about the Maycourt team as though he's part of it himself, a feeling shared by a lot of the community here. 'He is a nine-goal handicap.'

'And that means he's good, right?' I check.

'The highest you can get is ten, so yes, that's good,' Rhys says, sharing a smile with Noor. 'In polo, players are rated on a scale from minus two to ten goal. Minus two would be a beginner, and someone with a handicap of ten is the best of the best.'

'Wow. So Mateo is *really* good.'

'His teammates are fantastic, too,' Noor is keen to point out. 'Eric is a seven and Malcolm is a six. And Fitz is nought.'

'Okay,' I say, leaning forward on the bar. 'Polo is complicated.'

'No more than other sports,' Noor contends. 'But to really understand it, you have to watch a match. Come with us to the next one and we can talk you through it.'

'I'd like that, thanks.' I smile as Noor nods, satisfied, before taking a sip of his drink.

As the door to the pub opens, I bend down behind the bar to pick up a dishcloth I dropped earlier, and when I straighten to welcome whoever has just come through it, I start, dropping the dishcloth again.

Lady Maycourt surveys the pub before she sees me and glides over, a corgi on a lead in tow. Jasper, who has been busy in the back, emerges from behind the bar and stops in surprise at our new customer.

'Lady Maycourt,' he says, beaming at her as Noor and Rhys swivel on their stools to greet her with surprised smiles. 'Great to see you! How are you?'

'Hello, Jasper,' she says in a warm, friendly, East Coast American accent that has softened after years in England. 'I'm well, thank you. How have things been here?'

'Business as usual,' he tells her.

'Pleased to hear it.' Her eyes settle on me. 'This must be Ashley. I didn't get the chance to introduce myself earlier when you were with Mateo, so I thought I'd come by the pub to do so. Jasper had mentioned to me his sister was coming to visit and when I saw you this afternoon, I realised that you were she.'

'Yes, hi,' I say, smiling nervously at her. 'I'm so sorry that I was in your field, Lady Maycourt. I know it was trespassing, but I wasn't thinking. I got caught up in admiring your horse and—'

'You don't need to apologise,' she cuts in calmly. 'That's not why I'm here. In fact, I'm delighted to have tracked you down. I'm here to offer you a job.'

I stare at her. Jasper shares a look of bewilderment with the others.

'I'm sorry?' I say, wondering if I'd heard her wrong.

'My daughter, Julia, broke her wrist recently during a showjumping event, which means I could use an extra pair of hands in the stables. I hoped you might consider stepping in,' she explains, as her corgi whines loudly next to her. She gives him a stern look. 'None of that please, Garfunkel.'

Garfunkel stops whining and huffs, plonking himself into a sitting position at her feet.

'I apologise,' she says, addressing us, before gazing fondly down at her dog. 'He had a light lunch today and so I imagine he's peckish. Corgis have bottomless stomachs.'

'Sorry, you want me to come work in your stables?' I check, still trying to get my head round it. 'The Maycourt Polo stables?'

'Yes, as a polo groom. It's extremely hard work but very rewarding,' she states firmly. 'I can see, of course, that you have a job here, but I wasn't sure if it was temporary. I wouldn't want to step on your toes or go behind your back and steal one of your staff, Jasper.'

He shakes his head, baffled. 'Not at all. Whatever Ash would like.'

'I can't be a polo groom,' I blurt out, shocked that Jasper is considering the switch. 'I know nothing about it. I've never worked with horses.'

'You can learn on the job. You seem at ease around them,' Lady Maycourt argues, watching me curiously. 'I've never seen Serafina connect with anyone the way she connected with you.'

'Serafina?' Jasper says, his eyebrows knitted together.

'A very special pony of mine,' Lady Maycourt explains. 'She is the daughter of a pony my late husband was particularly fond of during his own polo career. He made me promise never to sell Serafina and it was a promise I was happy to make; anyone could see her potential. But then we discovered she's rather... difficult. She may be from a brilliant line of polo ponies, but she's developed a personality at odds with her ancestors. She's strong and wilful and won't get on with my grooms or players. Mateo is the only one interested in her.'

'Mateo has an eye for a good pony,' Noor proclaims.

'Yes, he does,' she agrees. 'He's determined to make something of her. He agreed with the Viscount that she had it in her to be an extraordinary polo pony. Nobody loves those ponies like Mateo does, but even his patience is being pushed as far as Serafina is concerned.' She turns to address me again. 'Then you showed up and she took a liking to you.'

Jasper looks at me, his eyebrows flying up.

'Mateo told me he's watched you with her,' she continues steadily. 'He says that around you she's calm, relaxed, *listening*. I witnessed it myself this morning. I saw you slip that grazing muzzle on her. You should have seen one of my grooms attempt to do it yesterday – she was a nightmare. But she trusts you. That's exactly what we need. Mateo is determined to ride her this season and with your help, he might be able to get her into shape.'

My mouth feels unusually dry and I realise it's because I've been gaping at her this whole time. I swallow, licking my lips.

'I... um...'

'Have the weekend to think about it,' she instructs, tapping her hand on the bar as I flounder. 'If you're keen, then you can start Monday morning. Now, I must get Garfunkel home. Lovely to see you, Jasper, and don't let my team make fools of themselves when they next visit your fine establishment.'

'I can't make any promises, Lady Maycourt,' he quips.

'Good luck for tomorrow,' Noor adds. 'We'll be cheering on the team as usual.'

'Thank you,' she says graciously, before swanning out the door, her corgi happily trotting along at her feet.

Six

The pub is packed the following evening. Jasper had put me on the earlier shift, so I've technically finished for the day, but when I hear all the noise of the customers from my room upstairs, I feel the need to go down to offer my services.

'We're fine,' Jasper insists, opening a bottle of champagne to a loud cheer from the crowded bar as it pops. 'You're meant to be having the night off.'

'What's going on? Is it some kind of party?' I ask, marvelling at the number of people in there, whilst dodging out the way of the other bar staff trying to keep up with the orders.

'It's the polo set,' he tells me, placing the bottle in an ice bucket and selecting a number of champagne flutes. 'They won their match today and the team have come to celebrate, along with their supporters. We're in for a big night.'

'Good for business.'

'Very good. Hey, if you want to stick around, I can introduce you,' he offers, reaching for the card machine and punching in an amount. 'If you're going to be working with them, you might want to meet them before you start.'

'You know I haven't made my decision yet, and it's likely a no.'

'I still think you have nothing to lose by giving it a go,' Jasper maintains, holding the machine out to the paying customer who already looks a little worse for wear. 'You always wanted to work with horses when you were a kid, didn't you? And trust me, Lady Maycourt would not offer you the job if she didn't think you could do it.'

'I'll get out of your hair,' I say, acknowledging the jostling crowd waiting for him to take their order. 'Shout for me if you change your mind and need some help.'

'Will do,' he assures me, before turning to greet the next person to grab his attention.

It's a beautiful evening, cold and crisp but sunny, so I make myself a cup of tea and grab my jacket as I head through the back, wandering out into the beer garden. There are only a few people out here, sitting around the picnic tables smoking, so I get a table to myself and take a photo of the view to send to Sam.

Ash
IMAGE
Come visit soon?

Sam
Hell yeah!
Whoa that is STUNNING
Beats my view right now

Ash

What's your view right now?

Sam

I'm in a queue for the bathroom

I'm at a bar in Peckham

There's only one cubicle available

ONE

Ash

Hot date?

Sam

Ha

I wish

Pop-up fashion event

I'm here for work

On Monday, you can cheer me up with pictures of your new
colleagues?

Ash

IF I take the job

I'll inundate you with photos of horses

Sam

I meant the hot polo players

Ash

Oh

Sam
Remind me to take the piss out of you next time we speak
for referring to horses as your new colleagues
Got to go, I'm next up!!
Thank God
I'm about to wet myself
xxxx

Putting my phone down, I sip my tea and look out across the tranquil view, wondering if I'm jealous of Sam at her event in London. It's the sort of thing I spent my weekends doing. Part of me misses the excitement and glamour of it all. But then I inhale a deep breath, gazing out at the fields stretching for miles, and feel a sense of contentment. For now, I'm in the right place. No one here has mentioned Chris Courtney to me.

I'm not alone in having a scandalous past. After Lady Maycourt's spontaneous job offer yesterday, I did some googling on her and discovered that she has had her fair share of the spotlight. She was born into a big polo dynasty in America with generations of her family involved in the sport either as players or patrons, usually both. The daughter of a famous player, she became a popular socialite until she fell for a man her parents disapproved of and eloped with him. By the sounds of it, it was the wrong decision; he spent her money, then left her for a Swiss heiress. Heartbroken and humiliated, she fled to England and later married her perfect match: the Viscount, a passionate polo enthusiast with his own team. From what I've read, Lady Maycourt is very well respected in the sport, known for her extensive knowledge that's been drilled into her since the day she was born.

But that still doesn't mean I trust her judgement when it comes to me.

When I think about her job offer, I get a rush of tingles swirling around my stomach: part excitement, part fear. The idea of working with horses sounds amazing and I never thought I'd have the chance. But the reality is, I know nothing about them or polo.

I'm thinking about it when I hear someone walking towards my table. I swivel on my bench to greet them, assuming it's Jasper. Instead, I find Mateo towering over me.

'Can I join you?' he asks.

'Uh... sure.' Taken aback, I watch as he slides into the bench opposite. 'Congratulations on your win today.'

'Thank you.'

'Was it a good match?'

He considers the question, resting his elbows on the table. 'We could have played better,' he answers eventually.

'But you still won.'

'Yes. There's a lot of work for the team to do, though, before the big tournaments of the British season.'

I nod, not really sure what else to say and wondering why he's come out here. He's not smoking and he doesn't have a drink with him. During the silence that falls between us, I pick up my cup of tea and take a sip. Finally, he speaks.

'Eliza told me that she'd offered you a job.'

'Eliza?' I frown and then say, 'Oh, you mean Lady Maycourt?'

He nods.

'Yeah, she came yesterday. It was a bit out of the blue, to be honest.'

'It surprised me, too,' he says.

'She didn't tell you beforehand?'

He shakes his head. I'd assumed from the way Lady Maycourt had spoken about how Mateo had been the one to notice the bond between Serafina and myself, that he was on board as she was when it came to offering me a groom's position. But from his furrowed brow and hard-set mouth, he doesn't seem thrilled at the prospect.

'Have you ever worked with polo ponies before?' he asks.

'No.'

'But you've worked in a stables?'

'Never.'

A muscle in his jaw twitches. 'Are you a good rider?'

'The last time I rode a horse, I was eight.'

The creases between his eyebrows deepen as he continues to look at me across the table, troubled by this information.

'Hey, I didn't go looking for this job. Lady Maycourt came to me,' I remind him, trying to read his thoughts from his stern expression. 'She told me that she thought I might be able to help you with Serafina.'

He looks thoughtful. 'Yes, I can see why she might think that. You had a way with Serafina and she's given us lots of trouble. I would like to use her this season if at all possible. And maybe she will be easier to control if someone she trusts, someone like you, is around, but...' He trails off.

'But you don't think I should take the job,' I finish for him, affronted even though, as a professional polo player, he has every right to think I'm not right for the part.

I don't think I'm right for the part.

But he doesn't need to know that.

'This is a serious sport,' he says firmly, his dark eyes boring into mine, but I hold his gaze, refusing to be intimidated.

'I want to make sure that my team is the best they can be, rather than thinking of this as an opportunity to play with pretty ponies.'

I snort. 'She didn't invite me to be on the Maycourt polo team, Mateo. She asked me to be a groom.'

'The grooms are as much a part of the team as the players,' he says sternly. 'They do most of the work, they prepare the ponies for the match and the players have to trust their grooms implicitly. Look,' he places his palms down flat on the table to impress his point, 'I want to make sure that if you decide to take this job, you know what you're walking into.'

'Lady Maycourt seemed convinced the most important thing was that I had a connection with Serafina. The rest she said I could learn as I go along.'

'It's hard work and long hours.'

'Nothing I haven't done before.'

'You said you haven't worked in stables.'

'Yes, but I've worked in fashion.'

The corners of his lips twitch. He's fighting a smile.

'Trust me, Mateo,' I say, leaning forward on the table myself, 'if you think that working in a polo stables is hard, you should try working in the fashion industry. I doubt you'd last a day.'

That does it. He can't fight the smile any longer and as it creeps across his lips, I sit back, satisfied.

'Well, I can tell you are Jasper's sister,' he says, amused as he drops his hands from the table. 'There were people who didn't think he had it in him to take over this pub when he first arrived, but he had plenty of fight in him.'

'We're not afraid to rise to a challenge,' I confirm.

'I see. So you *are* taking the job then?'

I hesitate. While I formulate an answer, we're interrupted by someone calling his name across the garden. His eyes flicker over to the girl standing in the back doorway to the pub, beckoning him to come back and join everyone inside. I glance over my shoulder to see who it is. It's a different woman to the one I saw in his car. This girl is blonde too, with charcoal-lined eyes and an unimpressed expression, wearing a butter-yellow maxi dress and cropped white blazer. When I turn back to Mateo, he offers her a polite smile but doesn't seem in any urgency to move.

'I think your girlfriend wants you,' I say when he doesn't budge.

'A friend,' he corrects.

'What are you even doing out here?' she cries. 'Fitz has just bought another bottle of champers. He wants to toast the team. Come *on.*'

'One minute,' he responds, unaffected by her efforts of persuasion.

She huffs and spins round, stomping back inside.

'Can I ask you something?' I say when he shows no intention of following her.

'Please.'

'Did you come out here to persuade me not to take the job? Is that what's happening?'

He raises his eyebrows at the blunt approach, but doesn't flounder at it. 'No. I didn't know enough about you to persuade you one way or the other. And it's not up to me to make that choice for you.'

'But now that you know I have no experience, your worst fears have been confirmed.'

'As I said, I wanted to make sure that if you were to decide to become a Maycourt groom, you understood the weight of the role.'

I wrap my hands around my mug of tea, lifting it to my lips. 'I understand.'

He watches as I take a sip. 'Good. In that case,' he swings his legs out from under the table and stands up, 'I will see you on Monday morning.'

'I haven't said whether I'm taking the job,' I remind him as he walks round the table.

His lips tug into a small, secretive smile as though he knows something I don't. He sticks his hands in his pockets and wanders back into the pub to join his friends.

Seven

I'm still wondering if I'm making the right decision when I shut the door of Jasper's Land Rover on Monday morning and watch as he trundles back down the long drive of Maycourt.

'You can do this,' I whisper to myself, tugging down on the hem of the smart blazer I'm wearing, trying to ignore the butterflies flitting around my stomach as I force my feet to walk in the direction of the stables.

Straight away, I step into a pile of horse muck, grimacing as I shake it off my barely worn Chelsea boots. Taking a deep breath, I regroup, and then continue across the yard. Reaching the stables, I walk in and look down at the rows of ponies, their heads hanging over their half-doors staring at me. The smell in here, an earthy mix of hay, dust, leather and horse hair, is at once nerve-racking and comforting, haling me right back to the time I spent in stables as a kid when I didn't want to be anywhere else, yet still felt like I didn't quite belong. The latter part still rings true. A horse whinnies down the way, the sound echoing around the stables.

'Can I help you?' a clipped, formal voice says behind me.

I jump, spinning round to see a girl standing behind me carrying some kind of rope. Her light-blue eyes peer out from beneath a fringe, her brown hair tied back into a ponytail. She's about my age or a bit younger and wearing a t-shirt and faded blue jeans.

Her wrist is in a sling.

'Are you Julia?' I ask, brightening at finding the person I'm supposed to.

'Jules,' she corrects.

'Jules, sorry. I'm Ash. Lady Maycourt said she'd tell you to expect me.'

'Oh right,' she says slowly, her eyes roaming down me and back up again, deeply unimpressed. 'The new groom who isn't a groom.'

'That's me,' I confirm, my heart sinking at the lack of a warm welcome.

'I didn't think you were coming,' she says, turning to go put the rope away in a small room to the side.

I follow her, peering in at all the saddles, bridles and equipment hanging in there. This must be the tack room.

'Well, I am here and ready to start,' I say chirpily.

'You should have been ready to start about four hours ago.'

'Four...' I trail off, pulling my phone out my pocket to check the time. 'It's nine o'clock.'

'Exactly. You're very late.'

'You start work at *five* in the morning?' I say in disbelief.

'You've missed most of the day,' she claims, turning to face me. 'Grooms start at five when we give the ponies their breakfast, clean out the stalls and exercise them. If you want to help with working sets, you have to be here bright and early.'

'Working what?'

'Riding a set.' She stares me down. 'You do know what that is, don't you?'

'Afraid not,' I say, trying hard to stay polite and cheerful in the face of weary hostility.

'It's when you ride one horse while you pony three others.'

I blink at her. 'How do you pony... ponies?'

'It means you lead the others off the side of the horse that you're riding,' she says impatiently, looking at me as though I'm an alien. 'So you really know nothing about being a polo groom?'

'I thought your mum would have told you that.'

'She did, I just didn't expect...' She exhales. 'I'm not sure this is going to work out.'

I frown at her quick dismissal. 'We haven't even started.'

'Yeah, but we're starting from scratch with you. I mean, you don't even know the language and you're dressed for a *Country Life* magazine fashion shoot, not a day's work in the stables,' she points out, exasperated.

I glance down at my blazer, crisp white shirt, designer blue jeans and boots.

'I doubt you can help with one pony, let alone seventy,' she concludes.

My jaw drops. 'You have *seventy* ponies here? Fucking hell. That's... a lot.'

'Uh, yeah?' She wrinkles her nose at my alarmed reaction. 'It's a polo yard. See? This is what I mean. You don't know anything about anything. I don't think this is worth my time.'

She marches past me and I stand still for a moment, astounded, until a bubble of rage swells inside my chest and I spin round to go after her, refusing to scuttle away from this job with my tail between my legs before it's even started.

'You won't give me a chance?' I call out, my voice echoing through the stables.

She stops and sighs heavily, turning to face me. 'It's not personal, okay? But this is a busy place and I don't have—'

'So let me help you,' I interrupt, taking a few more steps towards her and gesturing to her broken wrist. 'You're slowed down so take advantage of someone offering to do the jobs you can't do right now. I know I've got a lot to learn, but I'm here, aren't I? Surely having *someone* to help you is better than having no one.'

She doesn't look convinced.

'Oh come on,' I say, lifting my eyes to the ceiling. 'You can't think I'm *that* useless. You haven't let me try yet. As I told Mateo yesterday, I didn't come looking for this job. Lady Maycourt came to me. She thinks I might be good at it and I don't know,' I shrug, throwing my hands up in exasperation, 'I want to see if she's right.'

Jules is watching me quizzically. 'You spoke to Mateo yesterday?'

'Yeah. He was as doubtful about me as you are.'

'And you persuaded him you were right for this.'

'Not exactly. He just didn't persuade *me* I was *wrong* for it.'

She nods, looking a little more swayed. I seize on the opportunity.

'Let's at least give it a try and if it's a complete disaster, I promise I'll bow out,' I assure her. 'I have the job back at the pub ready and waiting for me.'

She lifts her chin in the air. 'All right, Ash. We'll give it a try.'

'Great.' I shrug off my blazer and go to toss it on the floor of the tack room. 'Where do we start?'

'We need to do some cleaning and then we'll prep the ponies that the players want to use for stick and ball this morning,' she says.

'Okay, I know I'm a beginner, but you don't need to dumb the sport down quite so much to "stick and ball". You can call it polo.'

She purses her lips. 'Stick and ball is what you call the practice of hitting the ball with the mallet. It's training exercises for the players.'

Whoops. 'Oh. Got it. Makes sense. Stick and ball.'

I force a laugh. She doesn't laugh with me. But at least she doesn't tell me to go home. Instead, she rolls her eyes and jerks her head to the other end of the stables before heading that way. I follow, my cheeks blushing at my ignorance.

'In polo, there's a lot of tack,' she tells me briskly. 'You've got bridles, saddles, standing martingales, running reins, bandages, breastplates, bits. After tack is used, the grooms give it a wipe down, but once a week, we give everything a thorough clean.' She stops in front of a large box that contains a variety of buckets, sponges, cloths, disinfectants, oils and, somewhat strangely, toothbrushes. 'It's difficult for me to do that with one hand but, lucky for me, you're here to help now.'

I start unbuttoning the cuffs on my shirt so I can roll up my sleeves.

'Tell me where to start,' I say.

It was a blink and you'll miss it kind of moment, but I swear Jules looked almost impressed.

By the time I'm done washing and scrubbing the tack, I feel like I've done a solid workout at the gym. My clothes are damp and dirty from the splatter of the wash buckets, a thin layer of sweat has formed on my forehead and back of my neck, and my hands are covered in gunk, grime and grease. I've learnt that there's such a thing as leather conditioner, which smells like lavender and eucalyptus, and that a toothbrush is a really good way to get to the nooks and crannies that can be hard to clean: for example, buckles. It's not just about brushing and scrubbing when cleaning tack either; you have to take it all apart and put it back together again. It turns out there are a lot of pieces when it comes to bridles and I was not quick to get which bit goes where.

'That's the throat latch,' Jules told me wearily when she asked me to grab the cheek pieces. I put that down and tried again. 'That's the noseband. Nope, that's the browband.'

'Okay, why are there so many *bands*?' I muttered under my breath.

I picked up another one and held it up for her.

'That's the throat latch again,' she said.

Honestly, I felt just about ready to strangle myself with whichever band of the bridle was closest, but I didn't crack under the pressure of Jules watching me like a hawk. Instead, I practised lots of deep breathing, listened carefully, and finally, by the time I'm done, I feel like I have a much better handle of all the tack and what goes where.

Relieved to have finished, I'm wiping my brow with the back of my hand when another of the grooms comes in carrying more tack after exercising one of the ponies. An Argentine man in roughly his forties with kind dark eyes and a bashful smile, he speaks to Jules in Spanish. She responds to him in Spanish before gesturing to me. He nods and then walks towards me, holding out the tack expectantly. I assume he wants me to take it from him, so I do, my tired arms almost buckling from the weight of the saddle.

'*Gracias*,' he says, before leaving.

I look to Jules. She shrugs and says, 'You'd better go refill the bucket.'

Fighting the urge to collapse, I casually put the tack and saddles down and pick up the bucket as though it's not a bother, even though my limbs feel like they're about to fall off.

'Wait, Ash,' Jules says, stopping me before I exit the tack room. 'You have to change.'

She points at a navy polo shirt folded on one of the shelves. Lowering the bucket, I go to pick up the shirt and see that it's a Maycourt branded one. I spin round to beam at her.

'Is this your way of saying I'm officially one of the team?' I ask eagerly.

'Oh. Uh, no. Your white shirt has gone see-through from all the water. You can see your bra,' she explains, nodding to my chest.

I glance down to see that she's correct, my neon-orange bra on display through my sopping wet shirt. *Great.* My patience is really being tried today, huh.

'Thanks,' I mumble, feeling like an idiot for my assumption.

'Sorry,' she says, at least sounding genuinely apologetic. 'You can change quickly in here. I'll go see to a couple of the ponies.'

I wait for her to leave the room before slumping back against the wall and closing my eyes, gathering myself. The first day was always going to be a bit shit. Surely things can only go up from here. After some whispered affirmations that *I can do this*, I open my eyes and balance the polo shirt on one of the saddles. Unbuttoning my shirt and taking it off, I let it drop to the floor.

'Hey, Jules, I—'

I yelp as Mateo appears in the doorway of the tack room, startled by my appearance.

'Ash!' he says, as I grab the polo shirt and wrap it across my chest to cover my bra, while he purposefully looks away, lifting his hand over his eyes. 'I… what are you *doing*?'

'I'm changing!'

'Sorry. I didn't… I didn't realise. I was looking for Jules.'

'She's… somewhere,' I say, fumbling with my shirt before I hurriedly yank it on over my head. When it's on properly, I put my hands on my hips and sigh. 'You can look now.'

He turns to me apologetically. 'I'm sorry about that. A lot of people walk through here. Maybe next time, close the door.'

'Yes. Good advice.'

We fall into awkward silence as he hovers in the doorway. I push the loose strands of hair back from my forehead, starkly aware of how bedraggled and flustered I must look. He, on the other hand, looks as though he's just strolled off a Ralph Lauren runway, his toned arm muscles straining against his polo shirt, a glimpse of dark chest hair on his tanned skin at the bottom of the neckline, his hair falling in that sexily tousled way that makes you want to run your fingers through it. I can smell his cologne, a delicious musky scent which is in stark contrast to what I imagine mine to be right now: sweat mixed with disinfectant.

'How is your first day?' he asks eventually.

'Everything is going very smoothly.'

'Good. Good.' He stands awkwardly, his eyes shifting as though he's not sure where to look or what to say. 'Anyway, I wanted to tell Jules that I'd like to take Byron out. So if you wouldn't mind getting him ready…'

'Of course,' I say with no idea who Byron is. 'Leave it with me.'

'Thank you.'

He lingers for a moment longer and I wait for him to say something else, but he doesn't. Eventually, he gives a sharp nod and turns to leave. My heart racing and cheeks burning at his unfortunate timing, I bend down to pick up my wet shirt from the floor, folding it up and tossing it next to my blazer. A minute later, Jules returns and I give her Mateo's message as I grab the bucket.

'Leave the cleaning for now; we'll come back to it,' she instructs, gesturing for me to follow her as she strides out the stables. 'Byron is one of Mateo's favourite polo ponies. He wants him prepared for training.'

'Okay. How do we do that?'

'For now, *we* won't do anything. Eduardo and Federico will prepare him, but I want you to watch, so you can see how it works.' She stops in the middle of a yard and nods at the beautiful black horse being led out by a groom. 'Ash, meet Byron.'

I stare at him in wonder. 'He's stunning.'

'Isn't he?' she says, her voice softening as she gazes adoringly at the striking horse. 'He's a big softie. Mateo loves him because he's a good listener and does what you say.'

She goes to grab a tough-bristled brush and hands it to me, instructing me to get to work brushing off any dirt or loose hairs on Byron's sides. As I do so, I notice one of the grooms picking his hooves, while the other waits until I'm done before he puts on the saddle pad, placing it high and sliding it back before lifting the saddle on top of it.

Taking a step back, I observe the slick operation while Byron stands still and calm the entire time. Jules talks me through each action: the breastplate going on, the martingale that stops the horse throwing its head in the air and smacking the player in the face, the two sets of reins so the player has extra control for manoeuvres and turns, the bandages going around Byron's legs to support the tendons and protect them from mallets, and how tight the braid of the pony's tail is plaited to keep it out the way of the tack.

As I watch Federico and Eduardo fastening the many buckles and straps, completing each stage in incredible speed with perfect precision, I swallow nervously, wondering whether I'll ever be able to get to grips with it. To them, it seems second nature. They're relaxed and efficient, chatting to each other and patting Byron as they go.

When Mateo appears, he launches into a conversation of rapid Spanish with Eduardo, and Jules tells me they're discussing tactics for the next match. Mateo wants Eduardo's opinion on which ponies to use for which chukka – a match is divided into six chukkas and the players will use at least one pony per chukka.

'I thought Mateo was the pro. Doesn't he make those decisions for himself?' I ask.

'Mateo knows the ponies well, but Eduardo knows them better. The grooms are the *true* experts. They work, exercise and care for the ponies every single day, so they know their fitness, their temperament, any issues they've been having. Polo players rely heavily on the advice of the grooms.'

'Right. Okay, so for professional players, the sport is the passion. But for the grooms, it's the ponies.'

'Now you're getting it.'

'And you'd rather be a groom than a player?' I ask curiously. 'How come Fitz is in the team and you're not? I'm guessing you could easily have his spot when your mum is patron.'

'I like polo, but I prefer eventing,' she explains, glancing regrettably down at her wrist. 'As soon as this thing heals, I'll be back jumping again.'

Mateo mounts Byron in a swift, rapid motion and guides him out of the yard, while Jules and I walk along behind. She takes the opportunity to point out some important areas of the estate as Mateo takes Byron to warm up in the vast green field that Jules tells me is the 'stick and ball field'. Other areas she points out are the sandy corrals, the turnout paddocks, exercise tracks and the polo field.

We come to a stop at the side of the stick and ball field. The sky has clouded over and I fold my arms across my chest for warmth, while Mateo canters down one side of the field before turning sharply, bringing Byron back the other way.

After warming up, he begins some drills. Gripping the reins in his left hand, the mallet in his right, Mateo gallops towards one of the many balls lying in wait for him, swinging the mallet back and hitting it hard with a loud *thwack*, sending it flying out in front of him. He races after it and hits again with unbelievable accuracy despite the speed at which he's going, before charging after it again and changing direction.

It's mesmerising.

'It's going to rain,' Jules announces as the clouds above get darker. 'He'll be coming in soon. I'm going to go back to the yard, but you can stay a bit longer if you want and help Eduardo when Mateo brings him in.'

I nod, unable to tear my gaze away from Byron majestically galloping across the field, Mateo manoeuvring him calmly and effortlessly. He looks as though he's barely moving up there in the saddle, completely in control. He seems completely fearless. Dangerously so.

Jules's prediction is correct; just a few moments after she's left, I feel the first droplets of rain on my forehead and nose. It begins to get heavier, but I don't care. A flicker of something has sparked once again in my belly, a passion I'd suppressed a long time ago. Watching Mateo, I remember how it felt to be up in a saddle, galloping down a field, the thrill and exhilaration of the speed of the horse, the power of its long, rhythmic strides beneath you, the wind beating against your cheeks. I feel an overwhelming urge to ride again, desperate to feel that rush of adrenaline.

Alone at the side of the field, I stay watching Mateo until the end of his session, completely entranced. He dismounts, his sopping-wet shirt plastered to his muscular torso, his face glistening with raindrops and sweat. He takes off his helmet and runs a hand through his hair, dishevelling it. He leads Byron over and stops in front of me, holding my gaze as the rain trails down my face and flattens my hair, his chest heaving from the exercise. Mateo's eyes flicker down to my lips, his forehead creasing.

'You… you should get Byron out of the rain,' he says, holding out the reins.

I nod, taking them from him.

Mateo starts striding back towards the stable and I traipse through the rain behind, my mind set on one day getting back up in the saddle.

Eight

Two days later, I witness my first polo match. I feel like a spare part in the lead-up to it, constantly dodging out of everyone's way behind the scenes as they prepare. I wish I could be of more help. I've learnt a lot the last couple of days though, spending long hours cleaning tack, brushing down and feeding the ponies, and shovelling a lot of horse muck. I'm fast becoming an expert at manoeuvring a heavy wheelbarrow. The work is exhausting and I can barely function when I get home in the late evenings, flopping flat onto my bed, hardly able to budge, but I've liked working around the ponies and feeling like I'm part of something important, even if I'm at the bottom of the food chain.

I've not spent as much time with Serafina as I would have liked, but I've visited her in her stables when I've been able. She wasn't all that welcoming to begin with. I was disappointed the first time I swung by and she didn't even bother lifting her head over the stable door to see me. She just stared at me, as if to say, *What are you doing here?*

But yesterday, she did let me stroke her nose and pat her neck and I stayed long enough for her to scratch her cheek against me, which felt like a win. Eduardo looks after her but he agreed to let me help. When I asked Jules if I could have a go riding Serafina, she laughed as though I'd said something funny and then noticed my expression and went, 'Oh, you're being serious?' It was a flat-out no. I asked if I could ride *any* of the ponies and she pointed out that as a beginner, I couldn't take one out alone, and none of the grooms had the time to break from work or hang around in the evenings to teach me.

I tried not to let the disappointment get me down, but it does feel useless being a groom that can't ride. The main perk of this job is riding the ponies to exercise them. At least Jules is a little more welcoming. I think she's secretly enjoying teaching me the ropes – when you're passionate about something, it can be fun to talk about it. So maybe soon, once she and the other grooms have got used to me and I've earned my dues, someone will take the time to give me a lesson.

'Hey, Ash, can you take these to Eduardo?' Jules asks the day of the polo match, passing over the saddle mats she's awkwardly carrying in one hand.

I jump to attention, happy to get involved and taking the mats with gusto. Knowing that Eduardo will be in the pony lines near the polo field, I set off in that direction. As I watch the other grooms busying themselves around the estate, I'm reminded of the lead-up to a fashion event. The stress levels are high, but you get a thrill from the buzz of the anticipation.

Hurrying along the long rows of ponies tied together near the polo field – each player uses six to eight ponies per match and the team needs reserves, too – I look for Eduardo somewhere amongst them and almost walk straight into Mateo as he emerges from behind Byron. We both come to a sudden halt.

'Shit, sorry!' I say, juggling the mats as they almost slip from my grasp.

'It's okay.' He steps back and gestures for me to go ahead.

I scurry past him. 'Thanks.'

'Ash,' he says, stopping me so I turn round to face him, 'have you ever seen a polo match before?'

'No. This is my first time.'

He nods. 'I hope we put a good show on for you then,' he says, before patting Byron's hind leg and continuing on his way.

Slightly dazzled by his attention, I stare at his back until Eduardo comes up behind me to ask for the mats and makes me jump. Handing them to him, I glance back at Mateo as he goes to talk to his teammates, wishing I'd had the sense to say good luck.

A polo match starts in what looks like absolute chaos. The players line up on their ponies, facing each other – in this case, Maycourt in their purple shirts and their competition, Orchid Park, in lime green – and an umpire throws the ball along the ground between them and the battle commences to get the ball out. I stand at our end of the pitch, watching the ponies jostle for position, mallets knocking and players shouting, with no fucking clue what is going on. Suddenly, the little white ball appears from the fray, rolling out from beneath the flurry of trampling hooves, and there is Mateo chasing after it before anyone else knows where it is. He fires it upfield, hurtling after it with green players, his teammates and the two umpires tearing after him.

The play is so far away, it's hard to see, but I can make out Mateo, with the number one in black emblazoned on the back of his shirt, glance up for his teammates and spot Fitz in position. He taps it his way, offering a beautifully set-up pass right in front of the goal posts. Fitz wallops it between them, the person behind the goal waves a white flag, and a cheer comes up from the Maycourt side. A group of girls, including the blonde from the pub, shriek with delight, clapping eagerly and gazing out at the field as though a bunch of rock stars were out there. Lady Maycourt, standing next to a man in a mustard-yellow blazer and red trousers by his parked Range Rover over by the sidelines, looks on, pleased. Even when entertaining his conversation, she doesn't take her eyes off the match for a moment.

'What do you think you're doing?' Jules says, walking by with a pony and jerking her head towards the others. 'All hands on deck.'

I hurry over to the pony lines where Eduardo hands me a hose, ready to wash the ponies down with cool water as they come off the pitch. Every groom is working at a hundred miles per hour, whether it's prepping a pony for a chukka – wrapping bandages, plaiting tails, warming them up at the end of the field – or cooling a pony down when it comes off the match covered in sweat, untacking it and walking it up and down and round in circles, steam rising off its body as its hosed down with cool water. They monitor the ponies closely and constantly, checking them over to make sure they're okay; they're standing ready with mallets should the players need to change theirs; and they're on hand for any calm, concise advice about which pony to use for the next chukka and why.

As the match nears the end, Maycourt is leading but Orchid Park is catching up thanks to a few mistakes on Fitz's part. I've been entrusted by Eduardo to walk one of the most docile ponies, Lyra, near the pony lines for her cool down, and I watch as Fitz charges towards the ball, swings heavily and loses his balance a little, causing him to mishit the ball. One of the Orchid players scoops it up, takes it back upfield and whacks it neatly between the posts of their goal.

'Fuck! Fuck! *Fuuuuck!*' Fitz howls, while Mateo mutters something under his breath, his expression twisting with anger.

I've never known so many expletives to be thrown around in a professional sport, but Fitz has been cursing at the top of his lungs throughout the match and he's not the only one. Whenever they mishit or helplessly watch a goal scored by the other team, the players have no qualms in roaring and yelling swear words either to themselves or each other. Mateo doesn't swear like the others, but there's no doubting his flares of temper, revealing themselves through his hostile and stony expression and tightened jaw.

As the ball comes back into play and he bolts past with one of the Orchid players racing alongside him, I gasp at their proximity and the roaring thunder of the hooves, my heart leaping into my throat at the idea of one of them falling in a ride-off.

'It looks so dangerous,' I say to Jules. 'Aren't they scared? The ponies are going so fast!'

'It's like any sport; they're addicted to the rush – a bit like Formula One, but on horseback,' she explains. 'For most of these guys, this sport is in their blood. It's part of their heritage. They eat, sleep, breathe polo. It's hard work and dangerous, but it's who they are. They can't not play. It's an addiction.'

I turn Lyra round and walk back again, looking over just in time to see Mateo fire the ball between the goal posts, securing the win just before the final chukka finishes, prompting an eruption of cheers from the Maycourt pony lines.

As the players dismount, greeted with high fives and claps on their backs, I continue leading Lyra back and forth. Jules congratulates each player, doing a good job of telling her cousin Fitz how brilliant he was. While the other players greet their adoring fans now spilling onto the pitch from the sidelines, I notice Mateo have a quiet moment with the pony he's ridden for the final chukka, a strikingly beautiful and fast black horse called Violet.

He glances up and catches me staring.

Blushing, I offer him a congratulatory smile. Our eyes locked, he smiles back and a flutter ripples through my chest. A beaming Eduardo approaches him to lead Violet away and I turn Lyra round again, relieved that the moment between us has been broken. *Shit. What is wrong with me?* I can't develop a crush on someone like him. I've learnt my lesson about falling for an athlete. I won't let myself become so vulnerable again.

That night, the Maycourt team celebrate with some drinks at the clubhouse. I'm on the fence about going, but Jasper persuades me otherwise.

'You're a part of the team now,' he reminds me, dropping me off after I've been home to shower and dress once I'd helped the other grooms to sort the ponies after the match and put them to bed. 'You deserve to celebrate this win as much as they do.'

I'm not sure that's completely fair since I'm not even trusted to plait a pony's tail for a match yet, but I am hopeful that tonight, I might get to know some of the grooms better.

The moment I walk into the clubhouse, I realise I haven't got the dress code right. I've rocked up in a mini dress, leather jacket, ankle boots and gold hoop earrings. After a couple of days of smelling like horse hair and hay, and having suffered a knock to my confidence thanks to Chris, I was excited to smell and look good, taking my time earlier with choosing my outfit and applying smoky eye make-up, styling my hair in soft waves around my shoulders. But scanning the room on entering, I realise my mistake. All the other girls are dressed in long, floral dresses and tailored, cropped, preppy blazers, some wearing panamas and straw hats. They look like they've stepped out of a Tommy Hilfiger photoshoot, while I wouldn't be out of place in the smoking area of a Camden nightclub.

As I take in everyone sipping champagne, laughing loudly together, chatting and embracing, I recognise this churning feeling in my stomach from when I first started attending fashion events with Ren: the uneasiness of knowing I don't belong here amongst these people. Not yet anyway. I spot Jules talking to her mum in the corner and make my way over, keen to talk to Lady Maycourt or 'Lady M' as the other grooms call her. I haven't spoken to her since I started and I want to thank her, but by the time I've weaved my way through the crowd, she's slipped away, leaving Jules on her own.

'Hi,' I say, pleased that at least she doesn't look irritated by me joining her.

'Veuve?' She jerks her head towards the bottle of champagne in the ice bucket surrounded by spare glasses on the table near her. 'Courtesy of my mother.'

'Thanks.' I help myself, standing awkwardly next to her and taking a glug before I notice her intently watching the group of girls who were on the sideline earlier. 'Are they your friends?'

She raises her eyebrows at me. 'The High Fives? No.'

'The High what?'

'High Fives,' she repeats drily. 'It's what we call Clara Fennel and her friends. They're essentially polo groupies and won't shag anyone with a handicap below five.'

'Oh. Right. Who's Clara Fennel?'

'The Honourable Clara Fennel is the blonde in the middle of them and the leader of the pack,' she tells me in a strained voice, nodding to the girl who'd brazenly beckoned Mateo to her in the pub when he'd been sitting with me. 'And the brunette next to her is Paige Potter, my ex-girlfriend.'

I stealthily check out Paige, who is very pretty with tight, brown curls, big, dark eyes and wearing a red, floral dress that shows off her curves and matches her bold-red lipstick.

'Clara and I didn't get on at school and since the break-up with Paige, she dislikes me even more, which means her entire entourage aren't allowed to like me, either.' Jules heaves a weary sigh. 'It's all very stupid.'

'Sounds it.' I notice Clara look over at me, her friends following suit, before a sneer appears on her face and she whispers something to the other girls, who snigger. 'For some reason, I don't think she's a fan of mine, either, even though we haven't met yet.'

'You're new and you're pretty. That's enough to get on her bad side,' Jules mutters.

'You must be Ash!' a voice says behind me and I spin round to see one of the polo players, Malcolm, giving me the once-over. 'Word on the grapevine is that you're fairly new to all this. How come you're Lady M's latest hire, then?'

'Probably something to do with Fitz,' chips in Eric, another one of the team, his voice slightly slurred as he joins our group.

'That right, Fitzy-boy?' Malcolm says, ushering Fitz to come join us, too. 'You were the one to bring this new groom to Maycourt, were you?'

'Nothing to do with me, but can't say I'm complaining,' Fitz declares as Clara and her friends watch on, wearing similar distinct scowls.

'Don't be a slimeball, Fitz,' Jules snaps at her cousin, but he shrugs it off with a laugh.

'It was Mateo who spotted her... *talents*,' Fitz says, his eyes scanning down my body as I wrinkle my nose in disgust. 'He has an eye for these things.'

'I can't take any credit for Ash being here,' Mateo says calmly.

I hadn't noticed he was even in the room, but as he speaks, people surrounding us part slightly to turn to look at him. At odds with the other players in their pastel designer shirts and chinos, Mateo is in a t-shirt and jeans, leaning on the bar on his own.

'Lady M saw that she was good with Serafina and brought

her on to help us work with her,' he continues, before taking a sip of his drink.

Eric sighs, shaking his head. 'That pony is *never* coming round. She's reactive and doesn't suit the pressure of polo. She should be sold.'

'Mum will never do that,' Jules says, frowning at him.

'She shouldn't. Serafina is the quickest pony in the yard,' Mateo adds.

'She cannot be controlled,' Fitz proclaims. 'She bit me, you know. She's a feisty bitch and makes it damn clear she doesn't want anyone riding her.'

'Maybe it's just *you* she doesn't want riding her,' Eric suggests.

'She wouldn't be the first, eh, Fitzy-boy?' Malcolm jeers, sending a ripple of laughter through the room.

'Oh ha bloody *ha*,' Fitz mutters into his drink.

'It will be impressive if you can get Serafina into shape for the season, Ash,' Malcolm says, stroking his chin. 'Have you worked with ponies before?'

I shake my head.

'I've heard you don't even ride,' Clara jumps in, her plummy voice booming around the room and holding its attention. 'Is that true? It *can't* be.'

'No, it's true,' I say.

The players share looks of surprise, while a smirk creeps across Clara's lips.

'How *fascinating*,' she emphasises, her eyes flashing at me as she begins her fun. 'And what about polo? You must be very knowledgeable in the sport at least?'

I hold her steely gaze without flinching. 'I've never seen a match before today.'

'*What?*' Fitz balks. 'And my aunt still hired you?'

'That seems odd,' Clara says, tilting her head at me. 'Do you have any expertise whatsoever to offer Lady Maycourt's stables? Or are you just another stray she's picked up, like one of her little dogs?'

Her friends laugh. Jules looks down at the floor uncomfortably.

'Personally, I find it bizarre the way people who have no idea about polo suddenly try to get involved with it,' Clara continues, bemused. 'Every year, it's the same at the start of the season. All these,' her eyes land on me pointedly as she relishes the attention of the room, '*wannabees* come along and get excited by the prestige and then think that after watching one polo match, they're suddenly an expert. I mean, it's laughable. Quite entertaining, really.'

I watch her with interest as she takes a glug of her drink.

'How lucky we are to have a polo expert such as yourself then,' I remark coolly.

My comment takes her by surprise. She lowers her glass slowly.

'I wouldn't be so crass as to refer to myself as an expert,' Clara replies, 'but I do tend to know a lot about the game, having been brought up in the polo world.'

'Ah, so that's your accepted criteria? That you have to be born into the polo world to come to understand it,' I surmise.

She lifts her chin, her eyes not budging from mine. 'I think you need to at least have a basic grasp of such a world and respect every aspect of it to deserve to be a part of it. And some people,' her eyes drift down my outfit to my boots and back up again, her lips curling into a sickly sweet smile, 'clearly don't fit the bill, despite how hard they try. That's what I find particularly pathetic.'

'You don't think it's more pathetic to close ranks on those who want to learn about it and contribute to it, just because they're, what, not like you?' I point out, unimpressed.

A pink tinge appears on her cheeks.

'I merely mean that the polo world needs to be protected, in the same way that any tradition with foundations rich in heritage, skill and knowledge must be,' she claims, momentarily flustered before relaxing, a triumphant smile returning to her lips. 'My point is that *class* isn't something that can be acquired. It's something one is born with.'

'I see, we're talking about *class* now, rather than the sport of polo,' I say, watching her with interest as she takes a sip of her drink. 'Oh, well, that's funny, because I was thinking that those with titles might have a bit of that, but you've proven me wrong.'

She splutters on her drink. Paige pats her on the back as Clara hastily wipes her chin with her hand. Jules disguises a snort of laughter with a cough.

'I think it's great to have new blood,' Malcolm interjects, raising his glass.

'Me too, me too,' Fitz slurs, leaning in towards me. 'And what an honour to have taken your polo virginity today, Ash. I hope you were impressed with my *stick*.'

He guffaws at his lewd joke, prompting several eye-rolls from our audience and a weary sigh from his teammates.

'Not really,' I say, bored. 'I've seen much bigger ones.'

There's a ripple of laughs through the room and I hear Malcolm turn to Eric and go, 'Oh, I like her.' Fitz looks put out, and Clara mutters something to her friends, who nod in agreement, shooting disapproving looks my way.

Knocking back the rest of my drink, I place the empty glass down on the table and excuse myself, the crowd parting as I head to the door. I might have been making it up but I could have sworn I heard Mateo chuckling quietly at the bar as I left.

Nine

As my confidence in the stables grows, so does my determination to ride. I'm getting into my new routine now and Jules has to monitor my tasks less and less, which is useful for both of us, although since the party, she's definitely warmed to me more. But despite my improved abilities for tacking up a pony and caring for them, not to mention how at ease I am around them, Jules still hasn't set time aside to give me my first lesson. Every morning, I give the ponies their breakfast and prepare them for their sets and then have to stand aside and enviously watch on as one of the other grooms pulls themselves up onto one and leads a group of them out to exercise. Meanwhile, I'm stuck stuffing washing machines with saddle mats.

Clara didn't get under my skin – I've faced a hundred Claras in the fashion world and, frankly, her jabs were mild in comparison – but she had a point that a groom who can't ride is strange. It was embarrassing that my lack of skillset was highlighted in front of everyone that night. I came home after the party with a fire in my belly, determined to ride better than someone as pompously entitled as The Hon. Clara Fennel by the end of the summer. As the week has gone on, I've been getting more and more impatient to start. When it becomes clear that no one's going to help me, I realise there's only one thing for it.

'I'm going to have to take matters into my own hands,' I say to myself out loud one morning as I park up the old Volkswagen Polo I'm renting from a friend of Jasper's.

That evening, I wait until Jules and most of the other grooms have gone home, finding things to busy myself with, and then I go to Serafina's stables and start tacking her up. I've chosen her because she's the horse I've forged the best connection with. I've purposefully put aside time to spend with her each day and Eduardo has let me take over most of her care now. Mateo took her out this week and she was still stubborn as hell, but even he made a comment at how much calmer she was when I was around her in the stable. I felt so elated and proud when he said that, my affection for Serafina swelling in my chest. There wasn't anything else around here I could claim to be the best at, but at least I had my bond with her. It was like the two of us understood each other, accepting that neither of us quite fit in. I think that's why she's taken to me – I'm learning how horses tune in with our energy.

'Okay, my girl,' I say to her, tightening my helmet and then reaching up to grip the saddle, one foot up in the stirrup. 'Don't let me down, yeah? Let's do this together.'

Hoisting myself up onto her, I hold onto her reins and focus on nice steady breaths as she shifts beneath my weight, getting used to me. Muscle memory kicks in as I get comfortable in the saddle and I sit up tall and straight, urging her to walk on to the indoor arena by applying pressure to her sides with my legs. When we get into the arena, I start slow and easy, just walking around in a loop until I'm confident enough to shorten my reins and encourage her into a trot. I break into a wide grin as my body seems to remember what to do, my core muscles engaged as I lift myself up from the saddle and back down again in a controlled and rhythmic manner.

'We've got this,' I say to her, tingling with excitement.

My courage is growing and I want to go faster. I can't wait for that feeling of cantering again. I didn't realise how much I've missed it. Serafina is working well with me and when she pulls her head down sharply, likely bored with trotting round and round in circles and as eager as I am to make things a bit more exciting, I regain my balance in the saddle and say, 'No, you don't. I'm the one in control here.'

I'm trying to think back on what I learnt about cantering all those years ago when Serafina loses her patience and picks up speed before I'm ready.

I gasp. 'Hang on,' I say, my voice wobbling with nerves.

My instruction has the opposite effect. She launches into a canter and, not just any canter, but a Serafina-speed canter, which is *fast*. The sudden acceleration throws me into a panic as I grip onto the reins. I remember that my heels are supposed to be down, but jerk my foot too quickly and my boot slips out from the stirrup, which is left knocking against her as she hurtles around the arena. I'm too frightened to think about body position or taking back control, instead desperately trying to apply the brakes and slow her down, jerking back sharply on the reins.

'Wait!' Mateo's voice echoes around the arena. 'It's all right, don't—'

Serafina whinnies and slows, bucking and rearing until I feel myself slip, the reins tugged from my grasp as I fall from the saddle, landing on the ground with a solid thud.

'*Ash!*'

I hear his footsteps thundering towards me as I grimace in pain and embarrassment.

'Are you okay?' Mateo asks urgently, looming over me as he kneels at my side, his eyes wide with panic.

'Yes,' I croak, though it doesn't feel like it.

As I begin to push myself up, he places his warm hands on my arms to urge me back down again. 'Don't move. I need to check you over. You can't rush this.'

'I'm fine,' I assure him, slowly bringing myself up to sit and unclipping my helmet, letting it drop to the ground before I look up to find Mateo's face etched with concern just inches from mine as he continues to scrutinise me.

My mouth feels impossibly dry, mostly from the shock of the fall but a little from our proximity. He really is breathtakingly handsome. I must be a bit dazed from the fall because as he asks me questions on where the pain is, I'm unable to answer coherently, too distracted by the intensity of those dark eyes and long eyelashes, the sharpness of his jawline under the stubble, and the fullness of his lips up close.

He must notice me studying him, because something changes in the way he's looking at me. At first, he's all serious and concerned, his forehead creased, his brow furrowed, his eyes darting this way and that as he tries to work out if I'm okay. But now, as I repeat that I really am fine, just a bit bruised, the expression in his eyes softens. His hand lifts to cup my jaw and my breath hitches.

'Are you sure?' he asks, his throat bobbing as his eyes search my face. 'Your head feels okay? Your neck? Do you have a headache? Do you feel sick at all?' His hand drops to run down my arm as I shake my head in answer to his question. 'Your arms? How do they feel? Any tingling anywhere?'

'Fine, everything's fine,' I assure him. 'Serafina slowed to a stop before she reared. I basically fell off a stationary horse.'

'She wasn't stationary; as you say, she reared.' He draws back to look around the arena for her, finding her standing in the far corner, looking bored. He shakes his head, glowering at her. 'She is such a little—'

'Don't insult her,' I say, rubbing the back of my neck with my hand. 'This is my fault.'

He stands up and holds out his hand for me, using the other to support my back as I get to my feet. I brush the dirt off my jeans and move all my limbs a little to make sure I am genuinely okay and Mateo's beauty hasn't distracted me from serious injury.

'That I won't argue with,' he says disapprovingly. 'Ash, what were you thinking taking her out on your own? She's the most difficult pony in the yard. You're a beginner!'

'I'm not a complete beginner. I've ridden before. It's been a while, that's all.' I look over at her, my shoulders slumping in disappointment. 'I thought I could handle her. It was stupid of me.'

'You were giving her conflicting commands, jerking those reins back suddenly when you were cantering. And your positioning wasn't great. I could see how tense you were. She would have sensed that, too. She likely panicked. Both of you could have been seriously hurt.'

I hang my head and nod.

He seems to take pity on me, adding, 'Although, you did well at first. She was responding to you nicely when you were trotting.'

I glance up at him in surprise. 'You saw that?'

'I happened to be passing. I didn't realise anyone else was still here,' he admits, which is no surprise. The most dedicated player on the team, Mateo is always the first to arrive at the stables along with the grooms and usually the last to leave. 'It was lucky someone was around. Please don't do this again.'

'I won't,' I say, my hands still trembling a little from the fall. 'I know now, I'm not meant to ride, after all.'

He looks puzzled. 'I meant don't go out here on your own, not that you shouldn't ride again. At your level, you need an instructor.'

'No one round here has the time, and anyway, I think I've had my fill for a while,' I say glumly. 'I should get Serafina to bed.'

'I'll do that. Go and sit down for a bit while I get one of the grooms to look over you and then you can get home. I'll ring your brother and talk to him about the signs of concussion so he can keep an eye on you,' he mumbles, seeming troubled by something.

'Honestly, I'm fine.'

'Symptoms can be delayed.'

Relenting, I thank him again and pick up my helmet from where I dropped it on the floor before I make my way to the exit, my body bruised, my ego shattered.

In bed that night, I wince at every movement, my limbs aching and my heart sinking at how I'd made such a fool of myself.

I go into work the next day, hoping to bump into Mateo at some point to apologise again for my stupidity, but I don't see him until two days after when he comes to seek me out as I'm finishing my jobs for the night.

'Ash, there you are. How are you feeling?' he asks, his brow furrowed.

'Better, thanks,' I say, pushing my hair out my eyes as I shut and lock a stable door. 'I'm so sorry for taking Serafina out. I feel like such a—'

He waves his hand dismissively to cut me off. 'It's fine. What are you doing now?'

'I... uh... I'm about to go home. Why? Is there something you need?'

'I need you to tack up Elinor,' he says.

'Elinor,' I repeat in confusion, knowing her to be the most docile pony in the yard.

'Yes, I'm going to give you a lesson,' he states.

'What?'

'You want instruction. I'm going to teach you how to ride. I can't promise it will be every day, but when we have the time, we can do it. I have the time now.'

'But...' I stare at him, stunned. '*Why?*'

'Because it's important that you don't let the fall put you off riding completely, and you should keep riding. You don't have any experience, but you're good at it. I think you could be very good.'

'You... you do?'

'Yes, Ash, I do.' He turns on his heel to stride out of the stables, calling, 'I'll meet you in the indoor arena,' back over his shoulder while I stand frozen to the spot, speechless.

Ten

It's difficult to tell if I'm making good progress with an instructor like Mateo who isn't naturally talkative and seems guarded in his expressions. He doesn't give much encouragement, focusing on pointing out the things I'm doing wrong, but at the end of my third lesson, he nods and says, 'Better,' with the hint of a smile. I grow about two inches taller.

I was shaken after my fall, so he took it slow the first lesson and went through all the basics. The second lesson, I felt less nervous and he told me that my pony, Elinor, was naturally responding to that lift in confidence, making both of us look more comfortable. And by the third, I've been too focused on his stern voice nitpicking every detail as I went from trotting to cantering to feel afraid of falling: *don't rush the transition, engage your core, upright posture, legs relaxed, heels down, don't tense your shoulders...*

His instructions were drowned out by the whooshing of the wind in my ears and my heart rate accelerating with the rush of thundering on a horse down a field, before

I executed a smooth, sharp turn, and pelted the other way again. It was euphoric and I'm on such a high afterwards, it's hard to fall asleep that night. I only wish Mateo had more time for lessons, but I'm lucky he's given me any time at all, especially with his training in the run-up to the Prince of Wales Trophy tournament, the high-goal tournament held at The Royal County of Berkshire Polo Club that essentially kicks off the official British season of polo.

When we arrive in Berkshire with lorries of ponies in tow, the estate is calm and serene, grey skies over stretches of beautifully maintained green polo grounds lined with pristine white fences. All the grooms are in a good mood. Match days are exciting, but this is the first high-goal tournament and there's a crackle of excitement in the air as I help tie up the ponies to the iron rails before embarking on the first of many coffee runs of the day. A steady stream of cars begin to trickle into the grounds later in the morning, either flashy sports cars or mucky old Defenders, fans arriving early to get a good parking spot at the side of the pitch so they can picnic by their car whilst watching the matches.

The sun eventually breaks through the clouds and, as the grooms warm up the ponies for the first chukka, spectators mill around the edge of the ground in their sunglasses, wide-brim straw hats, linen shirts, colourful trousers and floaty dresses. Champagne bottles are popping, jugs of Pimm's are filling, and the stand is swarming with people taking their seats.

All four of the Maycourt players are with their patron, her dogs pestering Mateo for a fuss while he sits to zip up his boots. As I hold some spare mallets on Eduardo's instruction, I spot Mateo crouch down to give Lady Maycourt's two lurchers a neck scratch and a kiss on the head, before Garfunkel the corgi succeeds in getting a belly rub from him.

I'm smiling dreamily at the adorable exchange when someone knocks into my shoulder from behind as they pass by, causing me to stumble forwards.

'*Perdón*,' a voice says hastily, and I turn round to find it's a polo player.

With light-brown hair, sharp cheekbones, a clean-shaven jaw and the way his lips naturally form a resting pout, he looks like a model. I know he's a player on an opposing team thanks to the branded polo shirt clinging to his muscular and sculpted torso.

Jesus, I think, drinking him in.

It's like an unwritten rule that you're only allowed to play polo if you're handsome.

His eyes widening at me, a warm smile begins to creep across his lips.

'I'm so sorry,' he emphasises, in English this time. 'Are you all right?'

'Fine, thanks. Don't worry about it.'

His smile grows wider. 'I'm Basilio. I play for Dominance Quarter.'

'Oh right, DQ,' I say, nodding in recognition. 'You won the US Open this year.'

'Yes,' he says, looking at the ground with suitable modesty before lifting his eyes to meet mine again. 'And you are?'

'Ash. I'm a groom for Maycourt.'

'Ash,' he repeats. 'I haven't seen you before. I would remember.'

My cheeks flush with heat. 'I only started the job recently.'

'That so? Lucky Maycourt.'

I can't fight a smile in the dazzling glare of his charm. His grin falters as his eyes drift over my shoulder. I turn my head to follow his eyeline and find Mateo has come over to join us, standing tensely behind me wearing a grim expression.

'Mateo,' Basilio says with forced cheer. '*Cómo estàs?*'

'Basilio,' Mateo responds through gritted teeth.

'Uh-oh.' Basilio laughs, raising his hands as though in surrender. 'Sounds like you're still sore from Palm Beach. Surely you're used to me beating you by now? It's been, what, thirteen, fourteen years?' He addresses me with a twinkle in his eye. 'Mateo and I grew up together near Buenos Aires.'

'You should get back to your team,' Mateo advises gruffly.

'I was just meeting the latest member of yours,' Basilio responds, gesturing to me. 'Ash, I hope Maycourt is treating you well. If not, then you should consider DQ. We have the best of the best working for us and I can tell you'd fit in perfectly. You might find being a part of a polo yard that wins once in a while a lot more rewarding.'

I glance at Mateo as a muscle in his jaw flickers and his fists clench. He looks like he's fighting the urge to punch this guy in the face. Basilio, on the other hand, is completely relaxed in his company.

'I'm happy at Maycourt, thanks,' I tell him.

'Okay.' He shrugs. 'Things can change.' His attention returns to Mateo. 'You had better start preparing for your match, Mateo. I hope you win this one. That way, we'll have the chance to meet later on in the tournament. It's always a lot of fun. *Chau*. A pleasure to meet you, Ash. I look forward to seeing you again.'

He turns to saunter back to join the rest of his team, all of whom listen to something he says before looking our way. Basilio glances back at me and one of his teammates grins, slapping him playfully on the arm. As well as being handsome, it seems that every polo player also needs an inflated ego, a dash of charm and a pinch of fuckboy energy. I check in on Mateo, who hasn't moved, his features scrunched with anger as he glares at them.

'You okay?'

The question forces him to look at me and I catch something there in his eyes that wasn't there before. A flare of hurt or sadness. It's gone too fast for me to work it out.

'I'm fine,' he says in a low, terse voice that tells me he clearly isn't. Shaking out his hands, he clears his throat. 'When you're ready, Lady M wants a word.'

His expression still thunderous, he marches off in the direction of the pony lines before I can thank him for delivering the message. Wondering what the deal is between Basilio and Mateo, I pick my way over the grass to our patron, waiting to the side while she finishes her conversation with Fitz.

'Ah, Ash,' she says once her nephew has left. 'Everything set for today?'

'We're raring to go,' I confirm, still holding the spare mallets Eduardo gave me earlier. 'Is there something you need? Mateo mentioned you wanted to talk to me.'

'Yes.' She comes closer to me and lowers her voice. 'I thought you should know that one of the official photographers for the event here today recognised you. He asked me earlier if I could confirm that you were working for me. He knew your name.'

'Oh. *Ooh*,' I say, my heart sinking as it dawns on me why a photographer would be interested in me. My eyes fall to the grass. 'I should have… talked to you about this before, about why I came here from London in the first place. You've probably read a few things about me and I—'

'Ash,' she says gently, 'I hope you don't think I need you to justify anything. None of that interests me. All I care about is your passion and care for my ponies, and your work and dedication in the yard and, so far, I've heard good things. That's all I need to know about your character.'

I force myself to look up at her, smiling gratefully.

'I wanted to warn you in case he approaches you today. I didn't want him to catch you off guard,' she emphasises, before she waves at a fellow spectator making a beeline for her. 'All right, I imagine Eduardo and Jules are looking for you. Back to your duties.'

'Thanks, Lady M.'

I rush back to the pony lines as the players mount for the first chukka, pretending as though my heart isn't pounding with dread against my chest. I knew I wouldn't be able to escape this story, but it's been nice not to have been living in its shadow the last few weeks. Surrounded by new people, distracted by my busy daily routine and with the online onslaught lessening over time, I could almost pretend it hadn't happened at all. But as I glance nervously around at the photographers setting up in their positions at either end of the field, I start to feel the overbearing weight of it descending upon me once again.

The match against Momentum, a team in neon-pink shirts, starts off by heavily leaning in favour of Maycourt.

Mateo scoops up the ball from the throw-in and speeds off with it, knocking it through the goal posts with a smooth offside strike and putting us in the lead in the first minute. Momentum seem stunned by the early goal and it takes them a while to shake off the pressure it creates. Whenever I look up, it seems that it's a pink shirt chasing down a purple, with Maycourt dominating the first half mostly thanks to Mateo's ability to break away with ease. At one point, it feels like Momentum player Delfina Moreno has managed to get her team back into the match, charging towards their goal confidently, but she mishits with the pressure of Malcolm alongside her and Eric is there, ready and waiting. He taps the ball to Mateo, who takes it back the length of the ground before slotting it in between the posts, bringing the score to five-one by the end of the second chukka.

During the third, I notice the lens of the photographer set up at our end of the pitch directed at me as I hold a spare mallet should one of the players lose theirs during a particularly enthusiastic hit or if an opponent hooks their stick in defence. I immediately tense, glancing back at him to make sure I'm not mistaken, but I know I'm not being paranoid when the action of the match comes our end and he ignores it. The ball sails through the posts and I fix a smile, clapping the players as they canter past.

'Hey, Geoff,' Mateo calls out to the photographer, circling his horse back our way, 'in case you didn't notice, the polo field is over here.'

Geoff lifts his head and winks at him. 'Not all the action is, though.'

Mateo's expression hardens. 'You're paid to capture the sport on film, not our grooms.'

'Come on, Mateo, we're all freelancers in this line of work and we need to get paid. I get the shots that are going to pay the highest; that's how it goes.'

I swallow the lump in my throat. Mateo's jaw sets.

'Mateo, get over here!' Malcolm yells urgently.

Turning his pony round, Mateo gallops off to rejoin the match.

Moments later, as the ponies charge up this way again, Mateo steals the ball, lofting it up through the air directly at Geoff. He yelps, jumping out the way as it sails at him, crashing into his tripod and toppling it over. His hands on his head, Geoff straightens shakily, looking at Mateo, aghast. Mateo shrugs.

'Mishit,' he says simply, tearing away back up the field.

Grumbling expletives, Geoff gets to work checking his camera and setting it up again. He doesn't point it my way the rest of the match.

In the final chukka, Momentum are down ten-three and desperately trying to step up their game, but the player marking Mateo, clearly exhausted and frustrated, fouls him, handing Mateo a forty-yard penalty to the goal near our pony lines. Steering Violet into position, Mateo sends it through the posts and canters past me as I lead a pony nearby. He pulls up Violet a little so that we have time to smile at each other before he goes galloping off, leaving behind a flutter in my stomach.

The final score is twelve-three to Maycourt.

That afternoon, while the players celebrate their win in the VIP area of the clubhouse, I join the Maycourt grooms at the sidelines of another pitch to watch DQ play their first match of the tournament. The DQ team is strong and

Basilio is particularly good. He produces two goals in the first chukka, beautifully balanced, charging courageously down the field and whacking them between the posts with ease. When he scores his third goal, he rides towards the DQ lines to change ponies, effortlessly jumping from one saddle to another without touching the ground. Trotting back into the field on his new pony, he glances my way, lifting his fingers to his helmet as though tipping his cap at me, before cantering off.

'Ash, you know Basilio?' Jules asks, her eyebrows lifting in surprise.

'Not really. We met before the Maycourt match.'

'You've caught his eye.' She glances over at Clara Fennel, who looks appalled, before muttering with a notable hint of pleasure, 'The High Fives will be furious. Basilio is a nine.'

At half-time, the spectators are invited to honour the tradition of treading in divots, everyone pouring onto the field with their glasses of champagne in hand to repair the uneven turf. I haven't actually had a chance to take part in this age-old polo tradition before. I throw myself into it eagerly, scanning the ground for opportunities and flattening the loose wads of grass beneath my shoe. The stomping and squishing of turf is amazingly therapeutic, a great stress outlet.

When I'm content there's no divots left in my vicinity, I lift my head and put my hands on my hips, blowing a loose tendril away from my face with a satisfied exhale at a job well done. I notice Mateo, now changed into a smart shirt, pale trousers and sunglasses, standing in the exclusive part of the outside area of the clubhouse with a beautiful and recognisable blonde actress and Lady M. While they talk, he seems distracted, looking out in my direction. He pointedly lifts his glass to my divot-stomping efforts, a playful smile on his lips. I give a bow in response and his smile widens, before the blonde actress brushes his arm with her hand and he's pulled back into her orbit.

Eleven

Later in the week, Maycourt have a good start in their semi-finals match against The Buzzards, a team in orange and yellow, with a two-one lead in the first chukka.

Malcolm does a spectacular ride-off, galloping down the field and pushing an opponent off course before stealing the ball and passing it to Mateo, who takes it upfield and knocks it between the goal posts to make it three-one. Eric cheers along with the Maycourt grooms and fans in the stands while Fitz circles his pony, slumped in the saddle, his head wobbling like those bobblehead toys you sometimes see on dashboards.

'What's wrong with Fitz?' I ask Jules after the second chukka which has seen The Buzzards close the gap to four-three. 'He's playing badly.'

'Because he went out last night, like a fucking idiot,' Jules seethes, handing me two of the ponies who need cooling down, their coats drenched with sweat, their nostrils flaring with fast, heavy breaths, eyes alert and bright with exercise. 'Mum told him not to, but he got goaded by the High Fives who were on the prowl. Did he score then? No, course not. Is he going to help us score today? No, doesn't look like it. So it's a lose-lose situation.'

In the third chukka, The Buzzards slip into the lead and in the fourth, Eric manages to get the ball out in the throw-in, hitting it on and watching in horror as Fitz attempts to make up for his performance so far by tearing after it. An opposing player seizes the opportunity, chasing after him and swiftly hooking his stick. Without much encouragement, Fitz's stick falls from his grip and he's left floundering on the field as the ball is blasted the other way by his opponent. I hold up the spare mallet, wielding it like a sword, as Fitz comes over.

'Here,' I say, passing it to him. 'Come on, you can do this!'

'No, I fucking can't,' he mutters glumly. 'This bar better have Bloody Marys.'

Maycourt crash out of the tournament, losing the semi-finals thirteen-ten.

Mateo dismounts and storms over to the Maycourt-branded tent, unclipping his helmet and chucking it to the ground, releasing a cry of frustration. Running his hands through his damp, sweaty hair, he looks up to find Basilio strolling past, showered and dressed smartly after DQ's win this morning. Peering at Mateo over the top of his sunglasses, he stops.

'Bad luck, Mateo,' he says.

Glowering at him, Mateo turns and storms away, kicking the leg of one of the fold-up chairs in the tent as he goes so it tips before rocking back into a stable position. Basilio notices me hovering nearby.

'I hope you'll still come to watch the final, Ash? It's

always a great party afterwards and I'd like you there to celebrate our win.'

'How can you be so sure you're going to win?' I challenge.

He shrugs. 'You get used to it.'

Rolling my eyes, I turn to go back to the ponies, as Basilio calls out after me, 'I'll see you there then, yes?'

Pretending not to hear him, I search for Jules in the pony lines to help start loading the ponies back into the lorries, only to find Mateo having a quiet moment with Byron. I stop abruptly. Mateo has his forehead resting on Byron's nose, his eyes closed, listening to Byron's steady breathing. When Byron dips his head to snort, Mateo lifts his, opening his eyes and realising the interruption.

'Sorry, I didn't mean to disturb you.'

He rests his palm gently on Byron's nose. 'I find him calming.'

'I know what you mean,' I say, gazing admirably at the pony nuzzling into Mateo, his favourite person in the yard by far. 'Byron's like the BFG. Big Friendly Giant. Majestic and gentle all in one.' I hesitate, adding quietly, 'Sorry you lost.'

'It happens. We learn from our mistakes and go again.'

'I don't know whether this will help, but I thought you played brilliantly.' I shrug. 'Probably not much of a comfort, but you should know that anyway.'

He turns his head to look at me. 'Thank you, Ash. That does help.'

Aware that he came here for some time alone, I turn to go. And as I walk away, he mutters something almost inaudible, but it sounds like, 'More than you know.'

My stomach erupts with naïve butterflies at the thought

of being the one to lift him up in a moment of disappointment and hopelessness. The sensible, despairing part of my brain reminds me that I've felt that before, when Chris Courtney acted as though I was the one getting him through his divorce. The butterflies evaporate on cue. Nothing good can come of a silly schoolgirl crush on an aloof polo player with models and actresses falling at his feet.

The end of the tournament is celebrated with a glamorous bash at Fairfax Manor, the Berkshire country estate owned by Lord Vane, an oil tycoon and polo fanatic who travels too much to own a team but is determined to get involved as soon as he retires. He keeps a hand in by throwing an annual polo party.

I'm wearing a satin, emerald-green dress that an up-and-coming designer who worked on a collaboration with Ren sent me as a thank you after her intern left behind a suitcase of designs on the train on the way to the photoshoot. He'd been distracted by filming a 'Come With Me' video for TikTok and completely forgot he had a case at all. A few frantic phone calls later and a helpful National Rail staff member tracked it down for me – the photoshoot was so delayed, it ran into the night, but we were all so relieved, none of us cared, and the designer gifted me this dress afterwards.

On entering the country mansion and taking a pink cocktail handed to me on arrival, I find Jules with Malcolm and Fitz in the corner of the ballroom surrounded by a huddle of elegantly-dressed women, clinking their shot glasses and downing them.

'Welcome to your first proper polo after-party,' Jules says to me as Fitz catches the attention of a staff member to order another round of shots. 'This is where you'll witness everyone let loose.'

She's right about that. The booze is free and flowing, the music is thumping through the house, making the chandeliers shake, and the competitive spirit from the tournament has lifted. You can see how the polo community works on nights like this as players of opposing teams greet and tease each other with friendly banter. They may be enemies on the pitch, but they're only signed up to a team for a few months, the players changing around all the time depending on assigned handicaps and international tournaments. Which is why patrons are treated like royalty, revered and adored by their players, even if they played like shit in the tournament – those patrons are the players' meal ticket and if you want to be signed next season, you don't want to piss them off or burn any bridges for the future.

At one point in the evening, I leave the others to go to the bathroom and on the way back, unfortunately bump into Clara and Paige, who are here with the rest of the High Fives.

'Interesting tactic, Ashley, flirting with the enemy,' Clara says. 'We all saw your little exchange with Basilio. Can't say much for your loyalty. I'm curious, though, should you be entertaining other men when you're already in a relationship with Chris Courtney?'

I instinctively tense.

'Oh no, wait, you must have an open arrangement with him, on account of his *wife* and everything,' she says, her innocent smile making my stomach churn. 'You obviously have a thing for sportsmen.' She reaches out to pat me on the arm as my jaw clenches at her ice-cold touch, leaning in to whisper loudly, 'Leave some for the rest of us, won't you?'

Drawing back, she winks at me before gliding away, her cackling entourage following. I try to shake off her comments, weaving my way through the crowded rooms back to where I left the rest of my team, but they've dispersed by now. Floating around aimlessly, I feel someone tap my shoulder and spin round to see Basilio next to an older man in a mauve velvet smoking jacket with thick, grey hair and light-blue eyes.

Greeting me warmly with a kiss on each cheek, Basilio introduces me to the DQ patron, Ambrose Moore, an American technology and software billionaire.

'Congratulations on your win,' I say as he gives me a firm handshake, while Basilio snaffles a flute of champagne for me from a passing tray.

'Thank you. We had fun out there.' He claps Basilio on the shoulder. 'Best team going. US Open in the bag, now the Prince's trophy – it's going to be one hell of a summer.'

They clink glasses and I take a large glug from mine, still smarting from Clara's comments. If she sees me talking to Basilio now, it won't help my case, but I'm not doing anything wrong. I take another gulp of champagne.

'Ash is a groom for Maycourt,' Basilio informs his patron.

'I'm so sorry,' Ambrose jokes, stroking his chin. 'I haven't seen Eliza yet, but I assume she's around here somewhere. Hiding from me, probably. She's had a bit of a losing streak. Then again, she's used to that.'

'The season has only just started,' I say, bristling.

'True, true. It's all to play for. I hope Maycourt can give us a bit of a challenge. It does get boring after a while if you make it too easy,' he teases. 'Don't mind me, you can ask Basilio here – it's all harmless; I like to poke the bear. I'm afraid your boss is one of my favourite targets, but believe me, she gives as good as she gets.'

'I hope so.'

He cackles with laughter. 'What about you, Ash? You a horsewoman?'

'I'm trying to be. But I haven't played any polo yet.'

'Why not?' Ambrose demands to know.

'I should probably master a few more technical details in my riding first.'

'You're confident up on a horse?' he checks, waiting for my nod. 'Then to hell with technical details. This is the problem with Maycourt: they never take any risks. Here you are, a confident, keen rider, and they stick you in the back with the hose pipe.'

'If you want to learn to play polo, you should come to a real polo yard,' Basilio says. 'What do you think, Ambrose? Space for another groom in the stables?'

'There might be space for another polo player if Basilio doesn't fetch me another drink,' he jokes, shaking his empty tumbler. 'What do I pay you for?'

Basilio forces a laugh and then catches the attention of a waiter, putting in an order for another round of drinks. It's then that I feel a presence at my side, someone else who has joined our circle with a gentle waft of cologne. Mateo looks devastatingly good wearing a suit jacket over an open collared shirt, and my eyes linger a little too long on the slope of his tanned neck and his Adam's apple as he reaches out to shake Ambrose's hand, his arm brushing against mine.

'Congratulations, Ambrose,' he says in a way that seems passably sincere.

'Mateo!' Ambrose greets him with delight. 'Shame about your own tournament. Next time, eh?'

'Next time,' Mateo echoes.

'We've been trying to poach your groom,' Basilio reveals, grinning at me.

'Sly and conniving. Why am I not surprised, Basilio?' Mateo glances down at me, his hand pressing lightly and momentarily on the small of my back, my skin beneath the thin satin there tingling long after his hand has dropped. 'Hey.'

'Hey,' I reply, before finishing off my glass, happy to see the next round has arrived.

'Another of these for my friend here,' Basilio says to the waiter, pointing to his own drink, before he tilts his head at Mateo apologetically. 'You'll need something to drown your sorrows.' He turns to his patron. 'What do you think, Ambrose? Is it the Maycourt players or the ponies that's the problem this year?'

'A bit of both, I'd say. Eliza thinks she knows ponies, but she doesn't have the eye of her father,' Ambrose claims jovially. 'As for the team, you know my thoughts, Mateo. You're a top-class player. Your man Malcolm isn't bad, either.'

'Good of you to say,' Mateo notes gratefully, before Ambrose is distracted by a friend, deserting our conversation for another huddle of people nearby.

'Don't get too excited, Mateo,' Basilio sneers. 'Ambrose was being polite.'

'Threatened?' Mateo counters. 'I hear he's interested in shaking things up for Argentina.'

Basilio snorts. 'Be serious. If he thought you were good enough for Argentina, he'd have tried to sign you for the English season. He didn't consider you. And after your performance in the US this year? I'm surprised the Maycourt team still wanted anything to do with you.' He sighs. 'Plus, we all know how you fare under the pressure of Argentina.'

Mateo tenses next to me, his eyes cold and angry beneath a furrowed forehead.

Someone bumps his shoulder and he staggers forward, muttering, 'Excuse me,' and sliding through the gap of a group of guests sashaying past, disappearing into the crowd.

Shooting Basilio a look of disapproval, which he misses since he's busy greeting another player, I grab Mateo's drink from the waiter who's reappeared with it and slip out of the room. I check the various areas in the downstairs of the house that are being used for the party before I finally spot him through a window sitting alone outside at a garden table on the patio. I step out to join him.

Twelve

'Here,' I begin.

He snaps his head up at my voice.

'I brought you your drink.'

He takes it, resting it on the table. 'Thank you.'

Carefully gathering the fabric of my dress in my hand, I sit in the spare seat next to him under his watchful gaze, setting my glass down next to his.

'I've been meaning to properly thank you for having my back with that photographer the other day,' I say, wiping away a speck of dirt that's fallen onto my satin lap. 'You didn't have to do that, especially in the middle of a chukka.'

He looks at me innocently. 'Do what?'

'Try to take him out with the ball.'

'Mishits happen all the time.'

'Sure, okay. Thank you, anyway.'

We fall into silence for a bit, the muffled sound of the raucous party inside providing entertaining background noise.

'Why do you and Basilio seem to hate each other so much?' I blurt out, my directness encouraged by the champagne. 'I know it's a competitive sport, but most players are enemies on the field but then all jokey with each other off of it. With you two it seems... personal.'

He exhales a deep breath, leaning back in his chair as though relenting. 'That's because it is. Like he said, we grew up together. We trained together, came up on the polo circuit together. I've known him longer than anyone else here.'

'The way he talks to you and the way you act when he gets to you,' I frown at him, trying to work it out, 'it's pure dislike.'

'Mm.'

He takes a moment, pressing his lips together and inhaling through his nose before speaking again in a soft, low voice, his fingers tapping on his lap every now and then. This is not a comfortable conversation for him.

'When you're somewhere like this and at the clubs, it's easy to think that polo is only for the privileged. I was not born into this. I fell in love with polo late, but enough that I was able to hold my own on an estate near Buenos Aires. That is where I met Basilio, who learned polo there. He's from a polo dynasty. A long line of excellent polo players in his family. He and I are from different backgrounds. We couldn't stand each other, right from the start. When he mocks me, I remember how it felt back then, to be a little boy so different to everyone else. Different in every way, except our love for polo.'

He pauses, reading my expression and giving me a knowing smile.

'When you saw me driving too fast in my car, I bet you thought I was one of them,' he muses, jerking his head back at the roaring party inside the mansion. 'Privileged and pompous, yes?'

'And arrogant and entitled, yes.'

He gives a light laugh. 'Polo is a sport of billionaires and royals, a world of money and power. But it's also a sport of ponies,' he breaks into a smile so big and sincere, it takes me by surprise, a smile so beautiful, it knocks the breath right out of my lungs, 'and it was ponies that brought me to polo. I did everything I could to be around them when I was growing up. I was lucky that Rossi gave me a chance. Polo saved me.'

I nod, still a little dazed by that smile. It was like the little boy in him had reappeared for a moment to express the pure joy of being around horses, all the layers of seriousness, restraint and sadness that life piles on temporarily stripped away.

Realising I'm staring at him dopily, my brain kicks back into gear.

'Who's Rossi?' I ask.

'A professional player my mum worked for. He let me train and play on the estate. In return, I helped out in the stables. Something Basilio will never let me forget.' He reaches for his drink, taking a swig before continuing. 'I owe Rossi everything. He looked after us.'

'Does your mum still live in Buenos Aires?'

A crease appears between his eyebrows. 'She died when I was a teenager.'

'I'm so sorry.'

'It was a long time ago and...' He trails off, clearing his throat before reaching for his drink again. 'Anyway, she was dedicated to my career. Thanks to Rossi, I became a pro when I was nineteen. I joined the Maycourt team, then.'

'Whoa. You were so *young*!'

'A lot of players start young, especially the ones who grow up in a polo family like Basilio. He turned pro even earlier.'

'So you've been at Maycourt a long time. No wonder you and Lady M are close.'

'Actually, we weren't that close then. I was scared of her,' he admits. 'But Eliza was the one who believed in me right from the start. I played for Maycourt for two seasons, then I joined an American team for a while.' His smile fades at the memory. 'It did not work out.'

'Was it Ambrose's team?'

He shakes his head. 'No, but Basilio was on it, too. We clashed. I played very badly and was substituted, then rightly dropped during the Argentine Open. It was... humiliating.'

'Oh.' I shift in my seat. 'Shit. Sorry.'

'I think it was a good thing in the end. It made me work harder, fight harder. I became a better player. A pro's career is filled with ups and downs; you're always on the hunt for the next season, never allowed to get complacent. Your handicap changes after a bad patch and then that's it, you can find yourself without a team.'

'Ruthless.'

'That's part of the rush. When things are going well, you're in a world of luxury and high-adrenaline,' he pauses as a huge cheer comes up from inside the house, perfectly timed, 'but it can all suddenly slip away. I don't want to lose it quite yet.'

'You're talking like you're at the end of your career, but you're, what, mid-twenties? I know you became a pro a while ago, but that's still so young. This is just the start. I don't think Lady M would ever want to lose you. You're the best player on her team and you work harder than anyone else. You're the first pro at the stables and the last to leave.'

He studies me for a moment, as though he didn't know any of that. 'I don't want to let anyone down. This is all I've ever wanted.'

A player stumbles out onto the patio, chugging from a champagne bottle with a woman draped round him and pressing him up against the wall. She's frantically kissing his neck and opening his shirt to nip at his collarbones.

'I can see why,' I mutter, before the player sees us and holds his hand up apologetically, leading his companion back indoors, both of them giggling.

Mateo grins down at his lap. 'There is a lot of fun attached to the job. But none of it is important. All that matters is the ponies and the sport. Everything else is just...' He trails off, searching for the right word.

'Distraction?' I offer.

'Yes, distraction.' He brings his eyes up to meet mine. 'Although some things are more distracting than others.'

My heartbeat quickens, thudding hard against my chest.

We're interrupted by Malcolm, who bursts outside and throws his hands up in the air.

'There you bloody well are!' he cries at Mateo. 'You'd better come in.'

'Why?' Mateo asks, finally tearing his eyes from mine so I can gather my thoughts.

'Ambrose and Lady M got into a bit of a spat. All jokey at first but then he said something below the belt, the tosser. Now both teams have got involved and you know what Fitzy is like after a couple of drinks. Things are getting heated.'

His chair legs scrape across the stone as he rises to his feet. 'Where are they?'

'The drawing room. The music was too loud in the ballroom, but now I'm thinking it would have been better to stay in a room where they couldn't actually hear what the other was saying. Let the beat drown out the banter.' Malcolm guffaws. 'Anyway, I've been looking for you everywhere so you can come help me hold Fitzy back before he does something he regrets. He's a liability, that idiot.'

'I'll come with you,' I tell Mateo, standing up.

'I would save yourself and enjoy the party,' Mateo advises.

'If DQ and Basilio are involved then you might need someone to hold *you* back.'

His mouth tilts. 'You think you could hold me back?'

'I can try.'

There's a beat of silence as he looks down on me with amusement until Malcolm clears his throat pointedly and says, 'Sort of a time-sensitive issue here. Shall we?'

Thirteen

Mateo heads back inside, Malcolm wiggling his eyebrows at me suggestively behind Mateo's back before gesturing for me to go ahead of him. I bashfully follow Mateo through the door, parting the crowd of guests partying in the hallway until we step into the drawing room. It's a vast space with tall windows and patterned floral wallpaper, gold chandeliers hanging from the high ceiling, and a statement fireplace at one end with mismatched furniture including a soft pastel-green sofa, two red velvet armchairs and a pink chaise longue.

In the middle of the room stand Ambrose, now holding a cigar in one hand, and Lady Maycourt, also holding a cigar, both flanked by their teams and their teams' entourages. Clara is perched on the arm of the sofa, the other High Fives gathered behind her like they're posing for a portrait with their matriarch, and the DQ team have brought along their groupies, too: a mixture of men and women in designer suits and dresses, Cartier watches on their wrists, the diamonds embedded in their jewellery glinting in the dimmed light of the chandeliers.

The scene looks at once surreal and spectacular.

'This is like a posh English version of *West Side Story*,' I whisper to no one.

'I say we settle this outside right now!' Fitz is saying, getting in Basilio's face, who smirks with his teammates while Eric grabs a fistful of Fitz's shirt and yanks him back.

'Your team is as big an embarrassment off the field as it is on it,' Ambrose says drily to Lady Maycourt. 'Why don't you control your nephew before he hurts himself?'

'Fitz, calm down,' she snaps, turning back to her fellow patron. 'It was you and your team who insulted me first, Ambrose, and the boy is fiercely loyal. Can't fault him for that. You wouldn't know much about loyalty, though, would you?'

Ambrose looks bored. 'If you're referring to Claire, I can assure you that she was perfectly aware of what was going on, no matter what she might say for the courts.'

'I was talking about your business and polo endeavours, not your third wife, Ambrose,' Lady Maycourt mutters, scowling at him. 'For goodness sake, I wouldn't stoop so low as to make this personal.'

'Oh please,' he spits. 'You can act all high and mighty, above it all with your British title, but I know the real you, and I know there's nothing you wouldn't do when it comes to winning. Shame it's all for nothing. Maycourt is a joke this season.'

'Oi!' Fitz roars, before Eric tells him to pipe down.

'It's not worth it,' Eric adds. 'We'll beat them at Cowdray.'

Lady Maycourt smiles fondly at Eric, pointing her cigar

in his direction as she says to Ambrose, 'Now *that's* what I call class.'

'Class? You lot?' One of the DQ players with bloodshot eyes and a red wine stain on his shirt snorts with laughter. 'Maycourt is scraping the barrel so low, you guys hired a fashion model with no idea about ponies to work for you.'

'Hey,' I say, putting my hands on my hips and causing all eyes in the room to turn towards us, having been oblivious to our presence before. 'I wasn't a model.'

Two of the women on the DQ side of the invisible line through the room snicker behind their hands. I realise it would have been better if I hadn't bothered correcting him.

'Ash is testament to my yard's brilliance,' Lady Maycourt declares, saving me as she regains the room. 'Thanks to my team's tutelage, she is becoming as good a groom as anyone working in the stables, and, according to reports, a bloody good rider, too.'

I glance at Mateo, but he's too busy glowering at Basilio to notice.

'Safe to say she'll be one of the best grooms in the business when the season's over,' Lady Maycourt continues loftily.

'Oh yes,' the wine-stained DQ teammate says, his eyes trailing down my dress and back up again, 'we all know from her previous job how good she is at making her way to the top.'

Mateo, who has remained silent and still up until now, bursts into life, striding up to him so fast, it causes him to stumble backwards, growling, '*What did you say?*' in his face.

'I... um,' the wine-stained man stammers, leaning on an antique writing desk for balance.

Basilio steps in front of his teammate, blocking Mateo.

'You'd better step back,' Mateo warns in a low, venomous tone.

'Or what?' Basilio challenges. 'What will you do, Mateo?'

'Calm down, boys,' Lady Maycourt orders in a weary manner. 'You're meant to be gentlemen, so start behaving like it. Save the fury for the polo field. *Mateo. Para!*'

His eyes blazing and fists clenched, Mateo reluctantly draws back from Basilio and I feel like the whole room breathes a sigh of relief. I'm staring at Mateo in awe, my heart hammering as he moves to stand to the side of the room on his own, folding his arms across his chest. He refuses to look at me and I don't know if that's a good or bad thing.

'How gallant,' Ambrose remarks.

'We look after our own,' Lady Maycourt states simply.

'You have to, considering what you go through. My God, I'd need a dedicated support group if I suffered the amount of losses on the pitch that you do, Eliza!' Ambrose hoots with laughter, his team laughing behind him while the Maycourt team glare at them. 'You can never quite find the right combination. Something just won't click for you, will it?'

I don't know why I suddenly feel the urge to defend this team. Maybe it's because Lady Maycourt looks stung by that last comment, as though Ambrose has touched a nerve, and she's been so good to me. Maybe it's because I've genuinely grown to love the Maycourt yard and the ponies and the way of life there. Maybe it's because I've been bullied and harassed online by cowards on keyboards and I won't let it happen in person. Maybe it's because, moments ago, Mateo was willing to punch that DQ guy to a pulp in the name of defending my honour. Or maybe it's the champagne.

Either way, I'm jumping in.

'The only reason you're talking like this is because you're scared,' I accuse loudly, inviting everyone's eyes back on me.

This time, I'm prepared to be in the spotlight, though.

Ambrose balks at the idea. 'I beg your pardon?'

'If you weren't threatened by Maycourt, you wouldn't bother to engage in whatever this is,' I explain, gesturing to the two teams. 'The reason you're giving it any time at all must be that deep down, you're scared that our team is a serious threat this year. I can understand why. Maycourt has better ponies, better players, and,' I shoot him a smile, 'better grooms.'

My little speech causes a stir. I hear Jules tittering behind the others somewhere. Lady Maycourt lifts her chin with pride. Even Basilio can't stop a smile, despite which side he's on. I'm too nervous to look at Mateo, so I don't know how he's reacting.

Ambrose is too stunned to speak at first but then he forces a laugh, pointing his cigar in my direction. 'I like her,' he tells Lady Maycourt. 'Look, Ashley, I applaud your attempt at insight, but you're hardly a polo expert. If I want to know which team is or isn't a threat to mine, I'll ask a DQ groom, thank you. They tend to know what they're talking about, having played polo *themselves*.'

'That means nothing,' Fitz cries, leaning on the mantelpiece. 'With my help, I bet Ash would be twice as good at polo as any of your lot.'

I wince at his slurred sentences and casual arrogance, but I'm grateful for his confidence in me, even if he's too drunk to know what he's talking about.

'That so?' Ambrose brightens. 'Why don't we put that to the test?'

Lady Maycourt narrows her eyes at him. 'What do you mean?'

'We can have some fun here! How about a charity match? The DQ grooms versus the Maycourt grooms.' Ambrose claps his hands, making me jump. 'What a brilliant idea! We can raise some money for a good cause I'll let you pick, Eliza, as a courtesy, on the grounds that it has an equestrian theme – and put on a match that will prove DQ is not only superior on the main stage but behind the scenes too. Superior in every way: players, ponies, stables, grooms... and patrons.'

A chorus of gasps ripples through the audience.

'A grooms' polo match,' Lady Maycourt says slowly. 'The DQ grooms versus the Maycourt grooms.'

'That's right.' He points his cigar at me again. '*She* has to be on the team, since this all stemmed from her claim to be as good at polo as any of my grooms—'

'*I* didn't actually claim that,' I cut in as this spirals out of control.

'And, to make things fair, you have my word that the least experienced DQ groom will be selected for our team,' he continues brazenly, ignoring me. He pauses to sneer at her. 'What do you say, Eliza? Just a bit of fun between two friendly rivals.'

The room descends into a tense silence, everyone watching the two patrons as they stare each other down. Lady Maycourt breaks into a smile, her eyes flashing with mischief.

'You're on.'

My mouth drops open while everyone erupts into cheers.

I watch in horror as Lady Maycourt places the cigar between her lips to extend her right hand to Ambrose, who mirrors her action, clenching the cigar with his teeth before shaking her hand vigorously to whoops and applause.

Oh God. What have I done?

The tension between the two teams now dispersed as the party atmosphere returns, Lady Maycourt picks her way through the drawing room and exits, sauntering down the hall with me in hot pursuit.

'Lady Maycourt, wait. Lady M!' I call out.

'Yes?' she answers without looking back, stepping out through the front door and down the steps to the gravel of the drive.

'We can't do this,' I say, lifting my dress to descend the steps.

She turns to face me. 'Why not?'

'Because!' I throw up my hands. 'It's ridiculous! I can't play in a polo match. I can't play polo! And if I do, I'm only going to embarrass you and Maycourt. It's going to make everything worse. We can't beat the DQ grooms.'

'I don't see why not,' she says calmly. 'I meant what I said in there. Mateo has every faith in your riding ability, so I do, too. You dedicate yourself to polo the way you have to the stables and you'll be a pro in no time.'

'Lady M, if you go ahead with this, *we are going to lose*!'

'No, you won't,' Mateo says, coming down the steps behind us.

'Mateo,' I groan, looking at him in wide-eyed panic, 'I've only just started *riding* again. How am I going to learn how to play polo in one summer? There's no way I'm going to be good enough for us to win!'

'Yes, you will. I'll teach you.'

'But... this is serious,' I say, pleading for him to see sense. 'I'm going to need a *lot* of training to get anywhere near their level, and you don't have time for that. This isn't only my reputation on the line, it's Maycourt's, too. Please, we can't do this.'

'You have my word that I will be dedicated to your training.'

'Mateo—'

'With your natural talent and me teaching you, I think you can be better than anyone DQ have got,' he says in a manner that won't be argued with. 'I can tell that it's worth my time and effort to believe in you.'

Fourteen

Mateo makes it clear early on in our polo lessons that he's not going to take it easy on me. We start by covering all the basics – the rules, equipment etc. – and then he teaches me to master the different strokes with the mallet while I'm still on the ground. I practise forehands and backhands and learn the nearside shots, before I'm declared ready for the wooden horse. I hit the ball nicely on that, practising my swing and being rewarded with satisfied nods and even a few comments of, 'Good,' from my instructor.

Since the party, I've been trying to manage feelings I've developed for Mateo. I think they've been simmering under the surface for a while, but they violently flared when he practically slammed that DQ jerk against the writing table without even touching him, backing him into a corner with pure protective rage.

On top of that, there's the sweet, vulnerable side to him that he's revealed glimpses of to me: when he was talking about his childhood and when I fell off Serafina and he knelt down beside me with an expression so adorably worried and terrified, it's burned into my memory. Then there's the matter of how sexy he is, with that thick, dark hair I want to thread my fingers through, broad, muscled shoulders, and dangerously beautiful, intense dark eyes. And the way he effortlessly and fearlessly commands a horse going at breathtaking speed, yet how gentle and playful he is with them. Of all the players, the ponies love him the most, whinnying and kicking their stalls whenever they spot him as if to say, *Pick me! Pick me!*

I'm starting to think he may be the sexiest man I've ever seen.

But when my stomach flutters at the mere sight of him, it's not difficult to remind myself of the recent pain I've suffered after making the mistake of falling for someone I work for. I'm starting to rebuild my life and reputation. Mateo admitted to me openly that nothing else matters but polo to him. If anything were to happen, I'd be a temporary distraction to him. He implied as much. Allowing my heart to run away with itself has already cost me everything. I won't let myself make such a silly and reckless mistake again.

When it comes to Mateo, I have to keep things strictly professional.

Anyway, it doesn't take long before he takes the shine off those feelings himself. When I mount one of the smaller Maycourt ponies, Lyra, after a positive stint on the wooden horse, I'm distracted by the fantasy of what it would be like to throw my arms around Mateo and kiss him – but by the time I dismount Lyra, I'm ready to throw this stupid mallet at his stupid head. His stern instructions and criticisms are relentless, a few levels up from when he was teaching me to ride for fun. The stakes are higher now and we're both feeling it.

'Stop going so fast! You're getting overexcited!'

'Don't yank the reins so much! Polo ponies are incredibly responsive.'

'You're leaning too far back! You're not at a bloody rodeo.'

'Your weight is too far forward. Why are you acting like a jockey?'

'Up out of the saddle!'

'Stop worrying so much about hitting the ball and focus on the positioning of the pony as you approach it.'

'You didn't hit the ball because you're not watching it.'

'You're too tense up there. Try to relax into it. She's reading you.'

'Don't slump your shoulders!'

That is a small selection of the orders he barks at me throughout the first lesson, and when he comes to grab Lyra's bridle as I slip off her, exhausted, frustrated and irritable, there's no, *Well done*, or, *Good job for your first proper lesson*.

Instead, he says, 'Now you know how heavy the mallet feels when you're riding with it in one hand, and the importance of using your core, you should focus on strength training outside of our lessons. Yoga or Pilates, as well as cardio and weights.'

I glare at him, but he's too busy fussing Lyra to notice.

The second lesson is even worse. Whatever gentleness I thought was lurking beneath his serious, muscled exterior is either gone completely or only reserved for ponies, because he seems to be incapable of giving me any compliments, even when I think I've done okay. The ponies respond well to me, I feel comfortable up in the saddle so am going quick and turning nicely. I admit that my success with hitting the ball at speed has been less than good, but from his teaching methods, you'd think I was utterly hopeless.

During our third lesson, I'm starting to wonder if I can take any more of this. I'm tired and fed up. Managing these lessons around the day job is becoming impossible, not just physically but mentally. My patience is wearing thin. I'm not getting it like I hoped I would.

'You're overswinging,' he grumbles, seeming irked when I miss the second ball in a row. 'Don't take the mallet so far back; you lose control. Watch your grip. And your posture was all wrong; you're sitting too far forward. Do you want to come flying off the horse?'

'No! I want you to *fuck off*!' I rage, the frustration and tiredness that's built over the last few days exploding out of me. My face hot and flushed and beading with sweat, I pull up the pony and kick my feet out the stirrups. 'You know what? Fuck this!'

'What are you doing?' he asks, looking genuinely confused as I swing my leg over to dismount.

'Quitting,' I snap, landing on the ground and tossing my mallet on the grass.

'*What?* You can't quit!'

I pull off my helmet, shaking out my hair. 'Yes, I can.'

He dismounts his pony too, leading her over to me. 'You're giving up?'

'Yes, I'm giving up!' I say, spinning to face him. 'There's no point. I can't do it!'

'That's it, you're going to give up and walk away,' he says, taking a step closer.

'*Yes.*'

'Then you're not who I thought you were,' he says, frowning at me.

'Clearly I'm not, since all you can do is sit there and shout at me!'

'I'm not shouting,' he protests, taking another step forward to close the gap between us. 'If I raised my voice, it's only because you weren't listening.'

'I am listening, but it's hard when you're being told a million new things at once. Would it kill you to tell me I'm doing something *right* every once in a while?'

'This is polo, Ashley,' he says sharply, using my formal name for effect. 'It's fast and it's dangerous, and I'm trying to make sure that as well as hitting the ball, you don't hurt the pony or, worse, yourself. It's important you don't make mistakes!'

'You're making me feel as though that's all I do!'

'You want me to fan your ego, is that it?' he huffs, peering down at me.

'No, I want you to... I want...'

I trail off as I suddenly realise how close we're standing. I have to tip my head back to look up at him now as he looms over me. His dark, expressive eyes, flaring with anger, are boring into mine, his chest heaving heavily, while my shaky breath is coming thick and fast. It's incredible how good he smells. Seriously, even after a day of riding, I can still inhale the woody scent of his cologne and it's making my thoughts muddle and flutters erupt in my chest – or maybe my body is reacting to the fact that he's pissing me off so much. My eyes track the little creases between his eyebrows, the fullness of long eyelashes that I would kill for, the gentle slope of his nose, the shape of his lips.

Nope, it's not the frustration that's sending my pulse into overdrive anymore; it's him.

I part my lips, my breath hitching at his prettiness. His eyes flicker down to them, his irritated frown softening. Suddenly, the air between us feels charged with something other than anger.

A voice of reason at the back of my head trying desperately to be heard above the racket of every other part of me screaming, *Kiss him*, knocks something he said at the party back to the forefront: *There is a lot of fun attached to the job. But none of it is important. All that matters is the ponies and the sport. Everything else is just... distraction.*

You hear that? 'None of it is important.'

Remember how good Chris made you feel?

Remember how important you turned out to be to him?

Using all the willpower I have left, I drop my gaze to the ground and step away from him, breaking the spell. I breathe in deeply, glugging in air like I've come up from deep water and broken through the surface. For a moment, he looks startled, like a deer in headlights, before resuming motion, turning towards the pony waiting patiently at his side.

'I... I'm sorry,' he stammers sincerely.

I roll back my shoulders, already feeling ashamed of how I flew off the handle.

'Me too,' I admit quietly.

'No, you're right. I should be more encouraging. I'm learning here, too – I've not done much teaching before.'

'It's not...' I dig my teeth into my bottom lip. 'Mateo, this grooms' match idea was a big, drunken mistake. We need to cancel it. I'm setting myself up to be the fool again and there's only so much I can take.' I read the confusion in his expression and feel the need to explain further: 'The whole Chris Courtney thing.' I wearily rub the back of my neck. 'I'm already the wannabe homewrecker who lost her job because I was naïve enough to believe a famous athlete who told me he was getting a divorce. Things have been better here. I don't want to lose my job by being naïve again and thinking I can do this when all I'm on course to do is humiliate myself, the team, and Lady M in front of her greatest rival.'

'Chris Courtney told you he was getting a divorce?' he checks, the pony nibbling at his shoulder impatiently now, wanting to play again. Mateo swats him away, his eyes fixed on me, his attention solely mine.

'Yeah. He said they were separated and divorcing. But my point is—'

'So he tricked you into kissing him and then let you take the fall?'

I sigh, running a hand down my face. 'He tricked me into more than that.'

'You... you were dating?' he asks tentatively.

I nod shamefully. 'Like I said, he told me he was separated.'

'You are not the fool, Ash. He is. He is a *coward*,' he spits with such venom, it's like he suffered the experience personally himself. 'A true villain. A weasel in tennis whites.'

The insult is so ridiculous, a bubble of laughter rises up my throat and escapes.

Mateo looks surprised but pleased that I'm laughing at least. 'That's an insult to weasels,' he adds.

'You have no idea.'

Lyra snorts impatiently behind us and Mateo's pony has another nibble at his arm.

'So.' Mateo tilts his head at me. 'Want to try again? You can pretend Chris Courtney's head is the ball. Then you might hit it.'

'Is that a formal tip?' I question, amused.

'Polo doesn't work without passion. You have to put your heart into it. Don't hide away from everything you're feeling – use it. When you're up on the pony, you are powerful and imposing. No one can stop you.'

'That does sound like a good feeling.' I heave a sigh. 'All right. I'll try again.'

Moving to Lyra's side, I pull myself up and, when I'm ready, Mateo picks up my mallet from the grass and holds it up for me to take.

'Half the battle is confidence and trusting yourself and your pony,' he says, checking my heel position. 'I know you've got lots to think about, but all those things will become second nature with practice. You and your horse are partners. For the rest of this lesson, just focus on enjoying playing with her – she'll relax and respond when you do.'

Walking her on, I start circling the field, bringing her into a canter before turning her to come down in a straight line towards the ball. Before my head can get overwhelmed with instructions – *eye on the ball, check grip on the mallet, stand in the stirrups, up from the saddle, swing the stick smoothly, watch the ball* – I try to focus on enjoying the ride, this feeling of going so fast, my breath catches and my heart soars. I set my sights on the ball, a determined smile spreading across my lips as we thunder down the field towards it.

'Come on,' I whisper to both my pony and myself, the two of us soaring together.

I rise up from the saddle. *Fuck being the worst groom in the yard.* I lean forward. *I'm going to be the groom who took on DQ and won.* I begin my swing. *Let's do this.*

The loud *thwack* of my mallet striking the ball with perfect timing echoes across the field. I gasp and then cheer with excitement, going into a celebratory lap while Mateo punches the air and cheers from his pony. When I make my way over to him, he's laughing.

'Did you see that?' I ask breathlessly, bouncing as my pony trots towards him.

'It was brilliant. A perfect shot. You should have kept going!'

'I was too excited!'

'I could tell.'

'I can't believe I did it,' I gush. 'That was incredible!'

'Now you know the feeling, you will keep chasing it. Like the rest of us.'

I nod, my whole body tingling with adrenaline. 'Thank you, Mateo.'

'It was all you.' He smiles, his eyes glistening at me. 'Brilliant you.'

Something tugs in my heart as we grin stupidly at each other.

He notices something over my shoulder and his smile falters. Shifting in my saddle, I look behind me to see someone waiting at the edge of the field: a gorgeous woman in a mini dress with long, blonde hair and huge sunglasses. She wiggles her fingers in our direction.

'Isn't that…?' I peer at her and then turn to face Mateo again, recognising her while my stomach twists itself into jealous knots. 'It's the actress you met at the Berkshire.'

He looks sheepish. 'She joked about surprising me one night, I didn't think—'

'I won't keep you. Our lesson is finished anyway. End on a high, right?' I babble, patting my pony before I dismount. 'I can take the ponies back and sort them, and come back to pick up the balls and mallets and stuff. You head out. Don't want to be late for your date.'

God, why am I talking like this? It's so weird and forced. He'll see through it. But I can't seem to stop. I'm on a frantic mission to prove I'm at ease.

'Thanks so much for the lesson. I'll see you tomorrow. Have a good time!' I call out, leading my pony away.

'Ash, wait,' he says, and I spin round, turning the horse with me.

'Yes?' I say, my breath catching in my throat.

'I... I haven't got off my horse yet,' he says, brow furrowed.

I slap my forehead with my palm as he hops down onto the grass and leads him over to me. 'Almost forgot a pony. It's the high of hitting the ball. It's made me dizzy.'

'Ash—' he begins, pained.

'I'll see you in the morning,' I say, cutting him off and leading the ponies away before he can say anything else and refusing to look back over my shoulder at them as I go. Soothed by the rhythmic clopping of the two ponies walking with me across the yard, I remind myself in a quiet voice out loud why this is a good thing: 'He only wants flings and you're better than that. Forget him before it's too late.'

Fifteen

When you're around someone a lot, it's hard not to constantly think about them. I see Mateo almost every day and we're spending a lot more time together thanks to my polo lessons and his training with Serafina. I've had to stop myself from asking him outright about his date with the actress, desperately wanting to know what happened and at the same time dreading it, uncontrollable envy swirling in my stomach at the thought of them together.

'Serafina is doing brilliantly,' Jules gushes a few days later as she helps me untack her now that her wrist is healed and her cast is off. 'She's calmer, she's controlled, she's listening to Mateo. And she's quick. She's becoming a fantastic little polo pony! If she keeps this up, Mateo might even consider bringing her to Guards. Good work, Ash.'

'I haven't done much. Mateo is the one riding her.'

'Yeah, but he wouldn't have won her trust if it weren't for you. Take the compliment.'

'Okay.' I laugh. 'Thanks.' I pause, fiddling with the buckles before asking innocently, 'Will Mateo's date be coming to watch him play at Guards?'

'What date?'

'You know,' I say casually, 'that beautiful actress he met at the Berkshire. They're seeing each other aren't they?'

'Oh, her. No, that didn't go well,' Jules shrugs. 'I heard Malcolm ask him about her and he said he wasn't interested. Apparently, he cut the date short. Strange, right? She's hot.'

I silently continue with my task while my heart swells.

That evening, after a late lesson with Mateo, he helps me lead the ponies back to their stalls, untack and sort them before bed, which has become a bit of a routine of ours. We usually talk about tactics or upcoming matches or ponies – I do my best to keep it professional so my growing feelings for him are, at least, a little restrained. Tonight, though, I'm gabbling on about my love for the sport, the adrenaline still pumping through my veins after a brilliant lesson.

'It's impossible to describe that thrill,' I gush, exiting Lyra's box.

'I know what you mean.' He laughs, leaning on the door of the stall belonging to the handsome grey horse he was riding today, Wickham, who nudges Mateo in the hope of a treat – Wickham is *always* hungry. 'When you hit the ball right, it's an amazing rush.'

'Actually, I was thinking more about the moment just before you hit it.'

He raises his eyebrows. 'Before?'

'Yeah.' I grin, enjoying his surprise. 'When you're going at it full speed, I mean. Obviously, if you're fighting for the ball or if it's a penalty, it's different. But when you're charging full pelt down the field and you can feel the power of your horse and your heart jumps into your throat as you begin your swing, not knowing how it's going to go.' I blow out the air in my cheeks. 'That's the moment I'm addicted to.'

He laughs, his eyes gleaming at me.

'What? Why are you laughing? Have I embarrassed myself by talking shit?'

'No, no,' he insists, grinning from ear to ear. 'It's... you're adorable.'

I grimace with mortification. 'Adorable. *Christ.*'

'I mean, it's nice to hear you talk about it that way, with that level of passion. You're a true player now. Completely hooked.'

'I think so.'

We smile at each other and I notice his eyes flicker to my cheek.

'What?' I ask.

'You... you have some mud on your face from the training.'

My hand flies to my cheek. 'Oh God, where?'

'Just,' he steps towards me, brushing my hand away with his own as he runs his thumb along my cheekbone, 'here.'

I stop breathing at his closeness, my face on fire beneath his touch. He drops his hand but he doesn't step back, remaining so close to me that if I raised my chin, if he dipped his head, our lips would brush together. The thought of it sends a shiver down my spine and I have to pull myself away before I lose control and throw myself at him.

Stepping backwards, I knock my arm against the stable door, the bang echoing through the stables and causing Lyra to peer out curiously.

What the fuck are you doing? she seems to be saying, munching her hay lazily.

I don't fucking know! I tell her telepathically, pretending to check the lock on her door.

Mateo looks down at the ground with a grim expression.

'Right, everything's sorted here,' I announce, as though I've fixed the lock that wasn't broken in the first place. 'Home time.'

'A few of us are going to the pub tonight,' he says, still looking rattled. 'You should join us. It is at your house, after all.'

I consider it. 'Who's "us"?'

'The team and a few friends.'

I quirk a brow at him. 'Friends as in the High Fives?'

He grimaces. 'They're all right when you get to know them.'

'Yeah, if you're a sexy polo player with a high handicap. Not if you're me.'

The words are out before I can realise what I've said. He stares at me while heat flushes up my neck. I called him 'sexy'. *To his face.* It hangs in the air and my brain flounders with ways to take it back but I come up short. The only thing I can do is pretend I didn't say it and act normal for his sake. He'll be feeling just as awkward.

'Thanks for the invitation, but I'll skip it,' I say adamantly.

'Another time?'

'Another time.'

'I'll hold you to that,' he says, before leaving.

Watching him go, Lyra nudges me crossly, shaking me out of my dreamy daze.

'*What?*' I say defensively to her, but I get the message, blushing as I gather my stuff.

Later that night, I can hear the muffled voices of the team and High Fives downstairs and I try to convince myself that I'm listening because I'm nosy and not because it makes me smile every now and then when I hear the faint sound of his voice amongst them.

A couple of days later, I'm saying goodnight to Serafina – a long, drawn-out process because I find it hard to leave her – when Mateo comes strolling in carrying two mugs and a bottle of wine. I look at him quizzically and he holds a mug out for me to take.

'If you won't come for a drink with me at the pub, I'll bring one to you,' he says by way of explanation, pouring wine into my mug before filling his. 'Sorry about the presentation. Mugs are all we have around here and I hoped you wouldn't mind too much.'

'I… I'm meant to be driving home,' I stammer.

'We can just have one if you want.' He grabs a couple of fold-out chairs that have been stuffed away in the corner by the door for someone to move but never have been. 'Or you can leave your car here and we'll call you a taxi later.' He hesitates. 'Unless you have other plans tonight?'

'No plans,' I admit.

'Then, if you'd like to,' he gestures to one of the chairs, 'please join me for a drink.'

I stare at him.

'If you'd like,' he repeats, his confidence starting to wobble at my reaction. 'No pressure. If you want to go home, then of course, you don't have to hang around here with me. It's been a long day, you've worked hard, I thought…'

He trails off as I smile, finding his panic endearing.

'No, I want to,' I assure him as his shoulders relax. 'I wasn't expecting this, but thank you. It's very sweet and thoughtful of you.'

'Sometimes, I can be both those things.'

He waits until I sit down before he does, and we knock our mugs together before having a drink. It's expensive wine, chilled and crisp, and goes down nicely. Suddenly feeling nervous, I self-consciously brush my hand over my top and jodhpurs.

'Are you okay?' he asks.

'I wish I wasn't wearing clothes covered in horse hair, but yeah, I'm fine.'

He pinches a horse hair from his own top between his thumb and forefinger and lets it drop to the ground with a shrug. 'We match.'

I grin, taking another sip of wine. He takes a gulp of his, before looking around the stables silently, the heel of his right boot tapping from the way his leg is shaking.

Is he nervous, too?

'How are you feeling about the Queen's Cup at Guards?' I ask.

His leg stops. 'Good. Ready. I want to face DQ and beat them.'

I tilt my head at him. 'DQ or Basilio?'

'Both. Mostly Basilio. If he wins the Queen's Cup, he'll be unbearable. He won last year, too.'

'Was he playing on the DQ team then?'

Mateo nods. 'Like everyone, he's switched teams a lot over the years, but he did well with DQ last season and it looks like they're on another winning streak.'

'It won't last,' I tell him, sounding more confident than I feel. 'It never does.'

'Hopefully, our luck will kick in soon.'

'It's nothing to do with luck. You and the boys are playing much better together now *and* you have your secret weapon.' I gesture at the stall behind me. 'Serafina.'

'If she does what I tell her.'

'And if you trust her instincts in return,' I add, shooting him a look.

He smiles into his mug. 'Right.'

I lean back in my chair. 'Would you ever play on the same team as Basilio?'

He almost chokes on his wine, spluttering and wiping his mouth with the back of his hand. 'What? Why would I do that? I told you it didn't work out so well.'

'What if your dream team asked you to join them for a season? Would you turn it down just because he was on it, too? Surely, you could put your past rivalry aside to form an unbeatable allegiance.'

He laughs at my wording. 'You make us sound like knights going to battle.'

'Polo isn't so far off that. Horses, long sticks, adoring waiting partners, and way too much testosterone – there's definitely a whiff of ancient cavalry there.'

'The sport of kings, they say.' He sighs. 'I respect Basilio as a player. We'd need to have some serious talks before I joined a team with him. We'd have to make sure we got it all out of our system. Why do you ask? Are you forming a fantasy polo league?'

I pick at the handle of my mug. 'No. I was just curious since we were talking about how players switch teams so much. I can see why most of you are friends off the field. It's a small community and you don't know who you'll be playing with next.'

'Mm.' He nods. 'If you're a lead player, you can encourage your patron to sign someone you think is good. Lady M has always valued my input. You know I was in talks with Ambrose to join DQ last year?'

'Seriously?'

'But I feel a strong loyalty to this yard,' he admits. 'Eliza saw something in me long before anyone else did. The first time she ever saw me play, I was playing against Basilio and he was fire that day. He scored more goals than anyone. That's what it was like playing with him when we were young – he was so brilliant, most people only saw him and no one else. That's what makes him so cocky.'

'How strange for a polo player,' I remark sarcastically.

'Don't think too badly of us. You *have* to believe you can win if you play professional sport,' he points out. 'Otherwise you never will.'

Serafina whinnies, kicking at her stall and making me jump. Mateo knocks back the contents of his mug before placing it on the ground and standing up to go over to her.

'It makes me happy she's doing so well,' he comments, one hand gently scratching her cheek, the other rubbing the end of her nose. 'William loved her so much.'

'The Viscount? Lady M was saying how he made her promise never to sell her.'

'Thank goodness.'

'Otherwise you wouldn't have the fastest pony in the yard.'

'And you and I might not have met.'

I freeze, my mug halfway to my lips. Serafina snorts, pulling away from him, done with the cuddles for now. He leans on her stall door. I bring the mug to my lips and take a big gulp of wine, finishing it. I can feel his eyes on me and my heart is thudding loud and fast, my whole body tingling with anticipation and hope and fear. I place the empty mug down on the floor.

'Top-up?' I offer, unable to look at him.

'Sure.'

Rising to my feet, I take a step over towards the wine bottle that's next to his chair before I feel his fingers brush down my arm, landing at my wrist and staying there, my breath catching at his touch.

'Ash.'

I turn to face him, hardly trusting myself to speak. Lifting my chin, I gaze up into his eyes as they desperately search mine.

'Yes,' I whisper, everything around us fading into a blur. It's just me and him.

He takes my face in his hands and swallows.

'I can't… I can't do this anymore,' he says in a strained, hoarse voice.

'Do what?'

'Be around you all the time and pretend like I don't want to kiss you.'

I swallow audibly, any crumb of willpower in my body vanishing without a trace.

'Then kiss me,' I say, like I'm challenging him.

He doesn't need telling twice.

Dipping his head, he presses his mouth to mine and kisses me urgently, like he might burst if he doesn't. A small moan of relief and pleasure emits from my throat, my hands finding his waist and sliding up the ridges of his abs I can feel through his shirt as he drops his hands to my hips and pulls me into him, pressing his body against mine.

I loop my arms around his neck, wanting to lock him in forever if it means this kiss, this amazing, spectacular, earth-shattering kiss, doesn't have to end. My breath hitches as his tongue parts my lips and glides against mine, his stubble rough against my skin. I feel instantly intoxicated by this man, the way he smells of freshly-sprayed deodorant and cologne, how warm and hard his body feels up against mine, how good he tastes, as though I've been craving him my whole life and I've finally got my hit of him.

The kiss is so frenzied and urgent, I stumble backwards dizzily but he styles it out for me, taking control and moving me backwards until my back hits the wall. *Fuck me*, this is hot. This is the hottest fucking kiss *I've ever had*. Nothing has ever been like this, so passionate and desperate and demanding: a kiss that sends shivers down my spine and leaves me begging for more with my lips and hands, a warm ache gathering between my legs. My nails dig into the firm muscles of his shoulders. He's so strong and toned and powerful. I feel tiny, enveloped by his huge frame. I gasp for breath as he trails kisses down my jawline and my neck, his warm, large hands slipping under the fabric of my shirt and roaming over my waist. I can feel his hard erection pressing against my hip and it's driving me wild.

When he tries to take a moment to look at me, his breath ragged, his eyes dark and piercing, I pull his lips back to mine so quickly, he smiles against my mouth. He frees a hand from under my shirt and, insisting on breaking the kiss, his gaze drops to my lips as he brushes his thumb along my lower lip before giving it the gentlest of tugs, teasing me. He rests his forehead against mine and sighs, closing his eyes.

'Fuck, I want you,' he says in a low, raspy growl. 'What do you do to me, Ash?'

Raking my fingers through his hair, I arch into him needily and he brushes his lips against mine, slowing down the pace. Suddenly, it feels different. My heart is pounding as his nose nudges mine, his lips soft, gentle, almost tentative. Before, I was spellbound by his desire, a willing captive to a kiss that sent feverish pulses of heat through my body, but now, the way he's kissing me, it feels... intimate and meaningful. Which I know it can't be.

Whoa. *What am I doing?*

My sensible brain kicks in to gear. This is too dangerous. In a flash, I see how this plays out from here. I see how devasting it could be. I know him and what he can do. I know if I let this go on, I would not walk away unscathed. Not from him.

He can sense my hesitation. 'What's wrong?' he asks, drawing away, his eyes nervously darting around my face as he tries to read my expression.

'We can't do this,' I say quietly, my voice cracking. 'I can't do this again.'

'What? Do what again?' he asks in confusion, stepping back from me instantly. 'Ash, tell me what's wrong? Did I do something?'

'No, no, you were perfect. Too perfect. I... I'm sorry. Thank you for the wine.'

'It's okay, you can talk to me. Wait,' he calls out after me as I hurry out of there as fast as I can. 'Ash!'

Convinced I'm doing the right thing and desperate to run back to his arms, I don't allow myself to look back at him. I know what will happen if I do.

Sixteen

Sam

I need to ask you something important

Ash

Yes, of course!

What is it?

Sam

When the polo hottie kissed you in the stables, were you on hay bales?

Ash

SAM!

You said it was important

Sam

It IS important!

I need to know!

Ash

Aren't you supposed to be at work?

Sam
I'm on lunch break

                                        Ash
                                        It's 11.30am

Sam
Early lunch
Stop deflecting
Answer the question

                                        Ash
                              No it wasn't on hay bales!

Sam
That's disappointing

                                        Ash
                       It was up against the stable wall

Sam
OH MY

                                        Ash
                                        I know

Sam
I googled him
He's an underwear model

                                        Ash
                 I think you googled the wrong person

Sam

Nope

It's him

Seriously

I had to take a cold shower after I saw it

I'm sending you a picture

IMAGE

Ash

WHOA

What the fuck?!?!

How did I not know this?!?!

Sam

Because you've been avoiding the internet

Tell me again why you turned him down?

Ash

He doesn't do anything serious

Polo is his life

Sam

So?

This could be exactly what you need

Just a bit of fun, a nice summer fling, no strings attached

Ash

My last fling didn't work out so well

Sam

This is different

We know he's not married

This could be a simple sexy stable boy romance

Wait

YOU ARE ACTUALLY A STABLE GIRL

You've switched the fantasy on its head and brought it to life

Disney will want to buy the rights to this heartfelt true story

                                                            Ash

                                    Are you having wine with lunch?

Sam

You're definitely not going to go there, then?

IMAGE

                                                            Ash

                            Why have you sent me the same picture twice?

Sam

You might need some encouragement

His muscles are very defined and oily

Those boxers are tight

And filled

                                                            Ash

                                    It's probably socks

Sam

You're over that tennis scumbag, right?

Ash

Ugh YES

I actually am

He's made it quite easy

Lying to me, ghosting me, blaming me

Disappearing from my life

Sam

So why not enjoy yourself?

Don't put any pressure on things with polo hottie

If you both know it's just a bit of fun, then what's the harm?

Unless...

Ash

Unless?

Sam

Unless you like him

If you liked him, then I can see why you'd be nervous to go
there

It would be understandable

Especially after everything that's happened

You're protecting your little heart, I get it

...

Ash? Ashley Slater?

You LIKE him, don't you?

Ash

I don't know

I don't want to

Sam

I mean, I did have my suspicions

You talk about him a lot

Almost as much as the horses

Ash

Shit, I've got to go

It's chaos here in the lead-up to Queen's Cup

Sam

I don't know what that is but GO MAYCOURT

Also call me tonight

We can talk about him

Ash

Xxx

Sam

Quickly before you go...

He might like you, too, Ash

Don't let what Chris did get in the way

of giving a good thing a chance

You deserve to be happy

Ash

You're the best xxx

Sam

Also...

IMAGE

Ash

Really?
A third time?!

Sam

As your friend, I support your choices
But I think you should consider doing some important
research that will benefit us both

Ash

What research?

Sam

Find out if that is a pair of socks down there

'What have you done to Mateo?' Jules asks bluntly a few days later as we shuffle forwards in the queue at Clara's Cocina Café in Guards Polo Club.

'Nothing! What do you mean?'

'The whole week, he's been so tense and brooding, and he can't keep his eyes off you. Everyone's talking about it. Did you guys shag and then you binned him or something?'

'*No!* God,' I hiss, checking around us to make sure no one's listening.

At this time in the morning at Guards, the queue is mostly made up of grooms from other teams and the security stewards who are pulling up in their golf carts to get their coffee before they zip off again, inaudible information blasting from their walkie talkies every now and then. I made friends with one of them, Alvin, the morning of the first round because he has his gorgeous German Shepherd who drives round with him in the front passenger seat of the golf buggy. It was too cute for me not to go over and ask if I could take a picture.

'Maybe Mateo is annoyed because he knows DQ made it through to the Queen's Cup semi-finals, too, so Basilio will be around here somewhere,' I continue, flustered.

'No, that's not it. They see each other all the time and openly hate on each other. No, there's something bothering Mateo.' She sighs impatiently. 'Whatever's going on with him, it's made him play like a fiend this tournament. I've never seen him so fired up.'

We reach the front of the queue and order the coffees before sitting down on the bench at the nearest table while we wait for them. Jules replies to a message on her phone while I try not to think about Mateo and that world-altering kiss. Things between us have been tense and confusing ever since. Neither of us said anything the next morning, acting on edge around each other in front of the other grooms, and then when we found ourselves alone in the yard, he'd asked if we could talk about it.

'I want to make sure you're okay,' he said in a low, urgent voice, his eyes filled with concern. 'Ash, if I did something wrong, if I crossed a line, I'm so sorry. I don't want you to be uncomfortable or unhappy.'

'You did nothing wrong. It was... it was wonderful.'

His brow furrowed as he stepped closer to me. 'Then why can't we—'

'Mateo, please,' I said, moving away from him, knowing I wouldn't be able to stop myself from giving into temptation and melting into him if we stayed too close.

'I don't understand,' he'd mumbled.

Glancing around the yard to make sure no one else could overhear, I said, 'Polo is a small community. As soon as you got this out your system, I'd be left as the idiot again. I'm sorry Mateo, but I won't take that risk.'

He flinched. 'Is that what you think this is? Me getting something out my system?'

'Isn't it?' I challenged. 'Nothing matters but polo. Everything else is distraction.'

Mateo stared at me, anguished but unable to deny it.

We hadn't spoken since then about anything but the job, and as much as I ache to be near him all the time, I know it's best this way. It will be awkward for a little bit, but then with time, we'll both move on and we can be colleagues and friends.

Not that he's listened to me regarding work, though – during the first match of the tournament, I reminded him that Serafina was here in his selection of ponies, but he told me he'd be sticking with Violet for the final chukka. I tried not to let his dismissal of both me and her put me in a bad mood, which is actually easy to avoid when you're experiencing the Cartier Queen's Cup at Guards Polo Club.

Not to be dramatic, but it's magical here. The grounds are vast and immaculate, the sun has been shining all week, and the atmosphere is electric. I like the bit in the mornings, though before the spectators arrive – the calm before the storm – when there are pockets of activity around the tranquil grounds. Grooms are busy preparing the ponies and stewards are being briefed, making their way to their checkpoints and chatting with each other about the teams and their chances. Dog walkers strolling through Windsor Great Park will stop at the side of the field and watch the warm-ups before the first match of the day, some of them polo fans who strike up conversation with any grooms and trainers lurking around, others simply entranced by the ponies. The waiters in the clubhouse are double-checking the place settings and the shine of the glasses; the staff at the main bar and the pop-up bars behind the grandstand are stocking up the fridges with bottles; and a bright-red tractor with a roller mower attached behind it is methodically trundling up and down the Queen's Ground.

The café is busy first thing, providing coffee and traditional Argentine breakfasts to fuel the hard-working grooms keeping everything together and aid the patrons' hangovers.

'We really might win this tournament, you know,' Jules declares, putting away her phone and tapping her fingers on the wooden table whilst watching someone's scruffy terrier yap at a striking-looking and startled rough-coated vizsla on his lead.

'Don't jinx it.'

'If we win the Queen's Cup, we'll be going to Paris on such a high.'

I smile as the barista calls out our order and we get up to retrieve it. 'I'm so excited about Paris.'

'Surely you travelled to Paris when you worked in fashion.'

'It was always flying visits. I never saw any of the city. Apparently, we get time off when we're there, right?'

'Yeah, a little,' she confirms. 'Paris is amazing; you'll love it. I'll make sure you get enough time to do some exploring.'

'Thanks,' I say warmly as she shrugs like it's no big deal.

She may not be the most open of people, but I've learnt that beneath the guarded exterior, Jules is thoughtful and kind.

I like working with her and we've grown closer over the past few weeks, especially now I don't hinder her work so much.

'Do you get to travel a lot with polo?' I ask as we both carry a tray of coffees each past The Prince's Ground on the way back to the pony lines.

'Paris, Florida, Dubai, Sotogrande, Aspen, Argentina,' she lists. 'You go all over the world. It's pretty exciting.'

I sigh, getting my sunglasses out my back pocket and sliding them on. 'One day, you're shovelling horse shit; the next, you're flying private jet to Paris. Fucking hell. The polo world is straight up bonkers.'

'I know, right?' she says as Alvin rattles by on his golf buggy, giving us a salute, his dog up front next to him wearing goggles and a neckerchief. 'You can't beat it.'

In the final chukka of the semi-finals, the entire Maycourt team is on edge. In a spectacular shake up, DQ crashed out of the tournament earlier in the midday match, losing thirteen-twelve to the Breakwater team. I couldn't hear Ambrose from where I was standing but from his thunderous expression and his wild gesticulation, it was safe to say he wasn't happy about the result. Basilio dismounted, snapped at the groom ready to take his pony, and stormed off the pitch, punching the side of the DQ tent as he passed. I glanced over at the spectator stand of The Prince's Ground and Lady M happened to catch my eye.

She smiled serenely.

The result gave our team a boost of confidence, but has also served as a stark reminder ahead of the late-afternoon match that, in polo, no matter how well you've been playing up until go-time, nothing is guaranteed. Anything can happen.

We're leading the match against Ember Crest eleven-eight, largely thanks to Mateo, who is playing so aggressively that I'm worried it's going to lead him to foul at any moment. He's dominated the match start to finish and the Embers have picked up on it, leaving other Maycourt players open to mark him together, but despite their harassment, he's managing to slip through any gaps they leave him. When he whips the ball away from a scuffle and sweeps upfield with it, Fitz gallops to the goal posts waiting for the pass that soon comes his way only to hit it at the post, swearing loudly as it bounces back into play. But Mateo is somehow there, like he predicted it all, like it's played out exactly as he meant it to, and as he sails past the posts, he knocks the ball in between them with an unhurried nearside backhand.

He doesn't need to look over his shoulder to see if it's a goal.

He notes the reaction of the spectators, satisfied.

'Mateo is unbeatable this week!' Jules exclaims, as we pass each other on different ponies, cooling them down.

The whistle blows for the end of the match and the Maycourt team erupts into cheers, the players holding up their mallets in victory as they canter back towards us, grooms running to each other to high-five and embrace, jumping round and round in celebration, and Lady Maycourt behind the white picket fence raises her glass of bubbles to the players and takes a long, triumphant sip. Elated, I reach to pat the warm, sweaty neck of Wickham who I'm cooling down. *We're through to the final!*

Seventeen

It's a beautiful day for the finals match between Maycourt Polo and The Redwoods for the Cartier Queen's Cup. Clear blue skies, bright sunshine, and a crowd dressed to the nines, jittery with excitement and anticipation. The grandstand is packed with spectators, and the garden of the bar that lines the Queen's Ground is bustling with people, an ice bucket of champagne or pale rosé on every table.

It's much busier today than it has been earlier in the week, but this is a weekend match and the grand final of one of the most prestigious tournaments in the polo circuit. Not to mention, royalty is here: HRH The Prince and Princess of Wales are watching and will be presenting the trophy to the winner.

I feel sick with nerves. There's as much pressure on the grooms as there is on the players. The operation behind the scenes has to be slick and rapid with no room for error. My hands are trembling as I plait tails and wrap bandages, asking Eduardo and Federico to check everything I do, refusing to leave anything to chance.

Just before the match begins, the atmosphere in the pony lines is tense and serious. I'm so nervous, I actively seek out Mateo, finding him on his own behind the tent, drinking from a bottle of water. He lowers it slowly on seeing me approach.

'Hi,' I begin.

'Hi.'

'I haven't seen you properly all day – I mean, obviously I've seen you, but we haven't had the chance to…' I frown, my heart hammering as he watches me. Just being in his vicinity is scrambling my thoughts and words. 'I wanted to say good luck.'

He gives a small nod. 'Thank you.'

Not knowing what else to say, I turn to leave, shaking out my hands to try to get rid of the tingles. And then it's time to go, the clock ticking nearer and nearer to the first throw-in.

The Redwoods control the first two chukkas, scoring early on and infuriating Fitz with their smug celebrations that cause him to lash out irresponsibly, handing them an easy penalty when their number three has line of the ball and he crosses over to steal it. Mateo snaps at him to calm down when Fitz complains about the umpire, but Eric does a better job of mellowing things by speaking to Fitz in between chukkas and talking to him calmly. After that, Maycourt mount a good comeback, channelling their anger into fiery play and narrowing the gap in goals that leaves the stands cheering with enthusiasm.

At half-time, The Redwoods are leading seven-five. I can feel the sweat across my forehead, my shirt is damp from hosing down hot ponies and there hasn't been one moment of rest, but I don't care. It's been exhilarating and brilliant. Mateo is with the other players discussing tactics and I can see Fitz nodding along vigorously to whatever he and Malcolm are saying. Even Fitz has been motivated enough that he didn't go out last night.

The team go into the fourth chukka, reinvigorated and ready, and at the end of the fifth, the score is tied. The tension is high and the poor umpires have had their work cut out for them with the number of fouls from both teams as players begin to feel the pressure. Plied with champagne, Pimm's and beers, the spectators are getting louder and rowdier, and the two teams couldn't have given them a better match. The play today has been extraordinary.

In the short few minutes before the final chukka, I'm walking Wickham up and down the end of the pitch to cool him down, proud of his excellent performance, and praying that Violet doesn't let Mateo down in the next. I still think he should be giving Serafina a try, but he thinks it's too important to risk her stubbornness, while I argued that it's *so* important, it's the perfect time to finally take that risk. She can outrun any of the Redwoods ponies, of that I'm certain. I was overruled.

'Ashley!'

Glancing over my shoulder, I find Basilio sauntering towards me in aviators, navy chinos, a white shirt and a cream linen blazer with two glasses of Pimm's in his hand. Smiling broadly, he offers me one of the drinks, which I politely decline.

'I'll drink yours and then buy you another after the match. How does that sound?' he says, taking a sip of one of the drinks and mercifully not waiting for me to answer his question. 'I have a confession for you.'

'Really?' I say, distracted, glancing nervously over at the Maycourt team in their huddle discussing the forthcoming final chukka.

'I've been watching you ride. In the mornings when you've been helping warm up the ponies. You're brilliant. You ride as though you've been doing it all your life,' he says.

'Thank you. I love it.'

I turn Wickham to circle back again and Basilio turns with us.

'It's made us all nervous about the grooms' match, I have to admit. I think Ambrose may have been over-confident. Clearly, you are an excellent addition to the Maycourt yard. I have no doubt that you will be the best on the field when it comes to the polo.'

'Mateo is a great teacher.'

His easy-going smile falters. 'Is that right? I find that surprising. Mateo isn't the sort of person who puts time aside for someone else, especially to teach them. I would have thought he'd think that beneath him. Even as kids, he never had time for anyone else. He wasn't a team player. He always put himself first.'

I don't say anything.

'I only hope he's giving you his time for the right reasons,' Basilio adds.

I shoot him a look. 'What does that mean?'

'You know what he's like, surely,' he says, looking surprised I'd even have to ask. 'He has a reputation for... using people. Every woman he dates knows not to get attached. I think dating is his way of blowing off steam. I, of course, am a little biased.'

'Because you don't like him.'

'It's more complicated than that. He hasn't told you about Emma?'

I shake my head.

'Emma was my girlfriend a long time ago. A sweet, lovely girl. Then she met Mateo and, after he pursued her, she left me for him. A week later, he dumped her. That's the truth.'

I chew the inside of my cheek.

'She thought she was special to him, but in the end, he broke her heart just like everyone else's,' Basilio continues, 'and he broke mine too. For what? To prove he was better? That he could have whoever he wanted? It was all for nothing. Mateo is like… a hunter. He sets his sights on his quarry and he won't be satisfied until he's got it. Then he disregards it once it's served its purpose.'

'Why are you telling me this?' I mutter, turning Wickham around again.

'Because… I like you,' he says with a shrug. 'I don't want to see you get hurt. You don't know him like we do.'

'I can look after myself, thanks.'

He laughs. 'Yes, I could tell that the moment we met. In fact,' he strides a few paces ahead and then spins around, facing me and walking backwards, 'I knew that you were quite unlike anyone else I'd ever met.'

I bring Wickham to a halt. 'I have to go. The final chukka is about to start.'

'Nice talking to you,' he says, leaning in to give me a kiss on the cheek.

Glancing instinctively towards Mateo as Basilio draws back, I find him up on Violet watching us, his eyes blazing, his jaw set. Oh *fuck*.

Basilio starts waltzing away from me before spinning

round to shoot me a dazzling smile and call out loudly, 'I'll see you after the match, Ash. I'll make sure of it.'

Head down, I lead Wickham back to the pony lines while Mateo turns Violet sharply and canters away.

From then, Mateo takes no prisoners. In the first minute of the final chukka, Fitz is dribbling the ball along the centre of the field and, in a momentary lapse of concentration, misses it as it slows from bouncing along the divots, him and his opponent having to pull up their ponies when they realise the ball's left behind them. Mateo, who was following, positions Violet perfectly and from there, thwacks the ball with an exquisite nearside forehand that sends it soaring up into the air past all the players and sailing through the goal posts up ahead. It's such an incredible, risky goal, I gasp in amazement and the people in the stands are up on their feet applauding as Maycourt slip into the lead. As Mateo circles on Violet, he looks my way as I stare at him in awe.

His next goal comes soon after when a Redwoods player offers a clumsy pass to a teammate who isn't there. Mateo scoops it up and you can see his opponents panic as he thunders back the other way with it, taking Violet full-throttle. The Redwoods number four hunts him down for a ride-off but is left behind as Mateo picks up the pace to knock the ball between the posts, the flag going up and waving once more. Malcolm is laughing atop his pony, he's finding Mateo's fresh determination so incredible.

'What did you take before this chukka, mate?' he asks. 'Share it out, would you?'

The final is nearing the end and work in the pony lines has slowed because we're all distracted by the match, so close to the win but knowing that it's not secure until it's over. The ball is at the end of the pitch we want it to be, but so are all the players, the Redwoods doing all they can to get it out of there while Maycourt won't let up. After a frantic minute where it's hard to tell what's going on between all the pony legs and mallets, we see Mateo tap a winner through the goal posts in the last few moments of the match. The final whistle blows.

Oh my God.

We won. *We won!*

The entire team, including the grooms, pours onto the pitch as the players bring their ponies in to dismount and embrace each other, cheering exuberantly. Even Lady M has lost her demure demeanour and has thrown her arms around a friend, jumping up and down in joy. After giving Jules a hug, I rush in to join the grooms who have to cool down the ponies from the last chukka, weaving my way through the celebrating team to get to Fitz as he jumps down from his pony before throwing his arms around Malcolm and bouncing together screaming, 'We did it! We did it!'

Happily unnoticed by either of them and laughing at their display of camaraderie, I lead the pony off the pitch, my jaw aching from smiling so hard. I wait for my orders from Eduardo, who beams at me while he's giving me instructions, every now and then muttering words of disbelief in Spanish, and then I get started on hosing down the ponies.

I've just set down the hose to brush the water off Violet's coat when I hear footsteps approach.

'Hey,' Mateo says as I spin round.

His hair is damp from sweat and champagne that's been sprayed over his head, his cheeks are flushed from the exercise and the win, and his eyes are glistening with joy. My heart somersaults at his smile that lights up his face.

'Mateo, you did it!' I gush, laughing with excitement and nerves, feeling drunk on the high that comes with a win like this one. 'Congratulations!'

'To you, too.'

He steps forward to kiss me on the cheek. His face lingers near mine a moment too long for either of our willpower to hold. Mine snaps first. Angling my head towards him, I wrap my hand around the back of his neck and smash my mouth against his. He exhales with relief against my lips, his hands grasping at my hips and pulling me closer as he deepens the kiss, pressing himself against me. A low groan emits from his throat that sends my heart into overdrive. Butterflies explode into a frenzied dance in my stomach as he kisses me like he's been starved of me for years and years, his hands roaming up the curve of my waist, round to my back, sliding up and back down again, exploring everywhere all at once.

Violet stomps and whinnies, and we suddenly remember where we are, breaking apart and catching our breath. Mateo leans in to kiss me one more time, a gentle peck that takes me by surprise, before stepping back to pat Violet's neck, his hand slapping against her wet coat.

'We're… we're going to have a team photo on the pitch,' he says, collecting himself as I stand in a daze. 'Come join us for it.'

I nod, my breathing shallow and heavy like I've just played in a polo match myself.

KATHERINE REILLY

'I-I'll be there in a minute.'

Satisfied with my answer, he gives Violet a kiss on the nose and then jogs back to his waiting teammates. I hear a cheer go up as he reappears, Fitz's voice above the others shouting, 'Where have you been, mate? You saw the *prince* coming over to us, didn't you? What could be more important than that, you glorious fucker?'

Eighteen

Gazing out of the window at forty-thousand feet, I pick up my glass of champagne from the glossy walnut table in front of me and nestle back into my big, squashy leather chair. I acknowledge with a sigh that it's going to be difficult to fly economy after this.

Flying to Paris by private jet is definitely one of the more surreal experiences in my life. Grooms don't usually fly with the team in this kind of luxury, but Jules extended the invitation to me, citing her last experience flying with the lads as her reasoning – apparently, Fitz and Eric got so drunk, they started stripping and asking the air stewards to set up karaoke.

'It would be nice to have an ally, should things spiral,' she said drily.

It's the closest she's come to calling me a friend.

She's currently sitting with her mum and Mateo discussing tactics and changes for the Paris Open; Malcolm is fast asleep with his mouth hanging open, while a giddy Fitz has engaged Eric in a hilarious story about his failed attempts to woo a beautiful Iranian heiress last night, the contents of the champagne flute in his hand sloshing around with each animated gesture. Garfunkel the corgi is curled up, dozing on a seat next to Lady M.

When Garfunkel hopped up the steps of the plane, he knew exactly where he was going and was given a warm and familiar greeting from the stewards. Lady M informed me that, while she doesn't bring her other dogs, who are mostly rescues and would be too nervous of the noise and various new places involved in international travel, Garfunkel is a frequent flyer.

'If I could come back as anyone in my next life, I'd come back as that bloody corgi,' Fitz muttered, waiting for Garfunkel to select his seat before any of us were allowed to sit.

As soon as we step onto the tarmac in France, things will go back to the way they should be: the team will be whisked off to their opulent suites at the Ritz Paris, while I'll be making my way to a much smaller, much less luxurious hotel where the grooms are staying, one near Polo de Paris, the prestigious club hosting the tournament so we're close to the ponies. As amazing as I imagine the Ritz Paris to be, I'd prefer to be with the team close to the stables where our ponies are staying.

Putting down my glass, I pick at my thumbnail, distracted.

So distracted, I don't notice Mateo has risen from his seat and made his way down the plane to sit with me until he slides into one of the seats on the opposite side of my table. He sticks to the aisle, though, rather than sitting directly opposite me at the window, retaining enough distance between us that I can keep my legs safely from knocking against his. One touch of his body anywhere near mine and I swear, I would find it hard not to lose myself in that feeling of when he was pressed up against me and consequently launch myself at him.

'Hello,' he says with a knowing smile.

My heart races. 'Hi,' I reply nervously.

We haven't spoken about the kiss we shared after winning the Queen's Cup just two days ago. We haven't actually spoken *at all* since. As bizarre a decision as Sam thought it was when I told her, I opted to go in the lorries taking the ponies home rather than stay for the celebrations of our win. I'd heard that the party after the Queen's Cup was particularly raucous and it was such an exciting day, I was seriously tempted. But it had also been a tiring week, Paris was looming over us and the kiss with Mateo had shaken me up. It had felt too real and instinctive, like there was nothing else I could do. I'd kissed him like an addict, no control and powerless, clambering for my hit of him I knew that if I went to the party, something was going to happen. I knew I couldn't trust myself with him.

I'm starting to realise how much I like him.

And I'm scared.

'What's wrong?' Mateo asks, clasping his hands in his lap. 'I can tell you're worried about something. You have that face.'

'What face?'

'The one you get when you're worried.' He rubs a finger in the gap between his eyebrows. 'The little crinkles you get here.'

My hand instinctively flies up to my face. 'Do I? That sounds sexy.'

He lowers his hand and gives a shrug. 'I think so.'

Fuck. The flutters in my stomach feel more intense than ever. It must be partly down to the altitude and not just the way his eyes seem to be simmering with heat.

'So what's wrong?' he repeats as I shift in my seat. 'Do you not like flying, either?'

'No, it's not that. It's stupid. You'll laugh at me.'

He tilts his head, looking at me expectantly.

'Fine. I'm worried about the ponies. It's a long way to travel and I know that you do this all the time and they've travelled lots, but I... I feel guilty I'm not with them.'

'Why would I laugh at that? Any time we travel anywhere, I'm worrying about the ponies, even if it's just to Guards or Cowdray. In fact,' his lips twitch into an amused smile, 'I worry about the ponies whenever I'm not with them, even when they're in our stables, safe and sound. But Eliza doesn't spare any expense when it comes to their travel and they are monitored the entire time to make sure they're happy and comfortable.'

'Are all polo ponies treated as well as the ones at Maycourt?' I ask with genuine interest, relief easing the tightness in my chest at his reassurance.

'Almost always. Polo ponies tend to be very pampered. Patrons aren't in this sport for the money, because all they do is spend it. There has to be a real love for polo and ponies at the root of it.'

'Or a real love to win.'

'That too.' His eyes twinkle at me. 'But the love for the ponies comes first. I've never personally been on a team or worked in a polo yard where that isn't the case. And if the patrons don't love them intensely, then the grooms do.

Why else would they do what they do? But you know more about that than me.'

I smile down at my lap.

'Don't worry about the ponies, Ash,' he adds gently. 'They are fine. I promise.'

When I bring my eyes back up to his, my stomach backflips at the way he's pinning me with his gaze. For a moment, he looks as helpless as I feel.

'You didn't come to the Queen's Cup party,' he says quietly.

'There was too much to do. I had to help with the ponies.'

'Is that really the reason?'

I swallow, my heart beating faster. My lips part to say something, but no words come out. He already knows the real reason for me avoiding the party; he wants me to say it.

I can't. I can't say out loud that I am trying to protect myself from him and what he does to me. How I instinctively brighten at the sight of him. How I'm always looking for him at the stables, always that bit distracted while I do my job by hoping he's going to appear somewhere. How I feel woozy and unsteady when he comes too close and I breathe in the smell of the cologne on his skin. How when I know that I'm the cause of a certain smile, the one that lights up his eyes and forms deep crinkles around the corners of his mouth, a tingling feeling starts all the way down in my toes and makes its way up through my body at alarming speed, accelerating my heart rate and stealing my breath.

I know all too well how this will end if I let it begin.

Before I can think of a good enough excuse that neither of us will believe, we're interrupted by a steward who has come to let us know that we're starting our descent. Mateo thanks her and rises to his feet, sliding into the aisle. He hesitates.

'I'll see you later,' he says eventually before returning to his seat.

I go back to looking out my window at the city below, my heart aching for something I know I can't have, Basilio's warning ringing in my ears.

He sets his sights on his quarry and he won't be satisfied until he's got it. Then he disregards it once it's served its purpose.

I don't think I'm imagining it. Every time Mateo scores a goal in this tournament, he looks for me. I know that sounds absurd, but he comes cantering towards the pony lines after each one, his eyes darting across the sea of Maycourt shirts and slowing until he finds me. And when I look up, our gaze locks and he grins while I applaud him.

I noticed this pattern in the first match of the tournament but now it's the middle of the semi-finals and I don't think I can get away with brushing it off as coincidence anymore. He's actively seeking me out when he scores a point to see if I, what, approve? To see if I'm *impressed*? I honestly don't know what's going on, but it's strange and adorable and making my determination to stop falling for this guy wobble and crack.

We're up fourteen-thirteen in the final chukka when Mateo is awarded a sixty-yard penalty. You can practically hear the groans from his opponents as he calmly measures it up before swinging his mallet and sending a stinger of a ball zipping through the air and over the middle of the goal posts, the flags going up to an eruption of applause. Moments later, the match ends and we're through to the final.

As the team celebrate by swarming in droves onto the pitch, I look for Mateo amongst the crowd, my cheeks flushed with excitement. Suddenly, I spot him and our eyes meet across the field, his chest heaving with heavy breaths. I beam at him, my heart soaring. He holds my gaze until one of the grooms jumps at him, throwing his arms around Mateo and making him stumble backwards in surprise. Laughing, Mateo claps him on the back and, free from his gaze, my brain clears and I'm able to get back to work.

We have the next day off before the tournament final. Like all the grooms, I've been up bright and early, feeding, exercising and mucking out the ponies, but have been granted the rest of the day to enjoy the city. Back at the hotel, I shower and put on a pretty summer mini dress, excited to explore. When I came here with Ren, we zipped over on the Eurostar and I spent every waking moment scurrying around after him, stressed about whatever appointment or show we had next, barely noticing our surroundings, before we returned home. As far as I'm concerned, I haven't been to Paris, and I cannot wait to spend the day seeing the sights and eating as much delicious food as possible. I don't care that I'm on my own. This is *Paris*.

Grabbing my bag, I leave my room and practically skip down the stairs, before crossing the lobby. With a polite smile to the receptionist, I notice the guy sitting on the bench to the side and then double take, coming to an abrupt halt in front of him.

With a bashful smile, Mateo rises to his feet.

'What are you doing here?' I blurt out, too surprised to remember basic manners.

'You said last night that you were exploring the city today,' he says, sticking his hands in his pockets sheepishly. 'I wondered if I could join you.'

I stare at him. 'I thought… aren't you all invited to that swanky rooftop pool party today? Fitz was talking about it. He said it's the hottest invitation in town.'

'I've heard. But I thought your plan sounded more fun.'

All the breath in my body is knocked out by the way he's searching my gaze, his expression apprehensive but hopeful. God, it's *unbearable* how cute he can be sometimes.

'You thought my plan of going full-on tourist for one day in Paris sounded more fun than spending the day with the rich and famous at a glamorous rooftop pool party with free booze and food?'

'Yes,' he says, deadpan.

'*Really?*'

'Really.'

'Haven't you been to Paris many times before?' I check, folding my arms.

'Yes. But I'd like to explore it with you.'

My heart is hammering too hard for me to speak.

Studying my face, he frowns. 'If you'd rather spend the day on your own, though, I—'

'No, no. I'd like the company,' I admit, unable to fight a smile.

He breaks into a relieved grin. 'Great. One day in Paris. Where do we start?'

Nineteen

I have a strong suspicion Mateo is trying to talk me out of going up the Eiffel Tower.

'It's better from the ground,' he claims, as I lead the way to join the ticket office queue. 'There's not much point in going all the way to the top. Here, you can appreciate it, but spending money to get, what, a good view? It's not worth it.'

'That must be why no one ever does it,' I reply sarcastically, getting out my phone and replying to Jasper, who's messaged to ask how it's going out here.

'It's like all these tourist things in cities, though. The locals don't do it. They know it's a trap. I can take you to a dozen rooftop bars across Paris where we don't have to pay to get just as good a view – better, even, because the view from those has the Eiffel Tower in it.'

'Mateo, I warned you that this is how the day was going to go,' I tell him, busy typing my reply to Jasper. 'If you don't want to come, then you don't have to. But I am not spending a day in Paris and not going up the Eiffel Tower.

I'm sure the views from your rooftop bars are lovely, but,' I glance up from my phone and point to the top of the tower, 'they're not that high, are they?'

Tipping his head back, he squints up at it, before relenting. 'No. No, they're not.'

'Are you getting a ticket with me, then?'

He sighs, his shoulders slumping. 'Fine,' he mutters.

'That's the enthusiasm I'm after!' I cry, giving him a playful jab on the arm.

With a reluctant smile at my quip, he folds his arms across his chest and looks towards the top of the tower again while I shuffle forwards in the queue. When we enter the elevator to go up, I hear him mumble something under his breath, questioning the necessity of the glass windows, but it doesn't make any difference anyway since it's so crowded, I can't see a thing as we ascend. Mateo is gabbling on at about one hundred miles per hour at how the view is good enough from the lower floors, but I'm determined to go to the summit.

'I know you've done this before, but I want the full experience,' I insist as we make our way to the smaller elevator that takes visitors all the way up. 'We don't have to spend long up there, but apparently, the views are spectacular. Don't worry, there's still plenty of time to do everything else.'

It's not until we reach the top and everyone files out that I realise something is wrong.

Expecting him to be next to me, I walk out and realise I've somehow lost him in the few paces from the elevator onto the viewing platform. Turning round in confusion, I see that he hasn't exited the elevator at all. He's pressed up against the side of it in one corner, the colour drained from his face while the elevator attendant attempts to coax him out in French and then, when that's not working, excellent English.

'Mateo?' I come back to him as the operator steps aside to let me closer. 'Are you all right? What's wrong?'

His eyes are wide with fear. I've never seen him like this before.

'I probably should have m-mentioned that I'm not g-good with heights,' he stammers.

'*What?*' I gape at him, guilt hitting me like a gut punch to the stomach. 'Mateo! Are you serious? You're afraid of *heights*. Why wouldn't you say something?'

'You wanted to come here so badly.'

'If you'd said, I never would have—'

'That's why I didn't say.' He gulps audibly. 'I… I want to do this. I just… can't.'

My heart swells as I watch him try to build up the courage to step out the elevator. His bottom lip trembling slightly, his eyes gleaming with panic, he looks consumed by fear, but there's a hint of determination in his expression, the look of someone who's not ready to give in quite yet. I step towards him and reach for his hand, linking my fingers through his, squeezing it tightly. His eyes flicker down at me as I give him a reassuring smile.

'It's okay, I'm here,' I say so gently, it's almost a whisper. 'We'll do it together. This lower level is completely enclosed.'

He gives a sharp nod, his throat bobbing.

'Big, deep breaths,' I encourage as we begin to walk out, his legs wobbling enough for him to put a hand out against the elevator wall to steady himself.

'I… I want you to know, that there are many things I am *not* afraid of,' he stammers, his hand clutching mine so tight,

I'm beginning to lose all feeling in it. 'Sharks, no problem. Snakes or spiders, they don't bother me. You ever have a spider in your room that you need handling? Come to me, I will rescue him and put him outside for you.'

Oh God, he's so cute. The way he's hating being this vulnerable in front of me. How he's specifying that he wouldn't harm a spider. This is disastrous.

How am I going to stop my feelings for him after *this*?!

'I am fine in enclosed spaces,' he continues to ramble, shutting his eyes now that we're officially standing on the viewing platform and I bring him to a stop. 'And I'm good with speed. I can go fast. You've seen me on a horse.'

'I have seen you on a horse,' I confirm quietly, gazing up at him as he talks, completely ignoring the view of the entire city stretching out around us and choosing instead to study his face, so strikingly handsome even when scrunched up in angst.

'So you know that I-I am a strong a-and f-fearless person. Usually.' His eyes still clamped shut, he swallows again, his Adam's apple bobbing. 'Oh God, I hate this, Ash. This is horrible, I can't… I can't do it, I'm sorry. I need to—'

The rest of his sentence dissolves on my lips as I've reached up to cup his face in my hands and draw his mouth to mine. I couldn't fight my need to kiss him a moment longer. Any sensible thought has been squashed by the need to be as close to him as physically possible when he's standing in front of me like this, exposed and worried. In this moment, I can't help my raw and overwhelming urgency for it to be me that comforts him, and only me.

I want him to need me the way I think I might need him. *The way I know I need him.*

He's stunned by the kiss at first, his breath hitching at my lips, but then I feel the warmth of his hands find my waist before sliding slowly round to the small of my back, locking me in place against him. My arms loop around his neck as I arch my body into his, kissing him tenderly and firmly at the same time, my heart thrumming as he responds by deepening the kiss, his arms tightening around me.

I'm not going to let you fall, my lips are telling him.

I'm not going to let you go, his are telling me.

When we break the kiss, he doesn't release me quite yet, his forehead pressed against mine. Digging my front teeth into my bottom lip, I slide my palms down to rest against his warm, solid chest as it heaves up and down with heavy, shaking breaths.

Bollocks. I've never wanted anyone as much as I want him.

'Are you okay?' I ask.

'Better than I was,' he croaks, the corners of his mouth tugging into that small, secretive smile of his, before he draws his head back to glance to his right. His face crumples and he closes his eyes again. 'Oh fuck. *Mierda.*'

'We'll go back down.'

'No, you need to… get your fucking pictures or whatever the fuck you want up here in the sky,' he says, making me laugh. '*Then* we'll go back down.'

'Are you sure? If you're uncomfortable then—'

'Please, *go*,' he insists. 'And enjoy the view. Don't rush it and let this all be a waste.'

'Thank you for coming with me. I wish you'd told me you were scared of heights, but… thank you.'

He shrugs. I run my hands down the curves of his arms,

finding his hands and grasping them in mine. He sighs heavily, dropping his head as his eyelids reluctantly flutter open and he keeps his eyes determinedly locked to mine.

'I won't be long,' I add.

'Sure, sure,' he says, clearing his throat as though wanting to give the impression he's in full control, the unease flickering in his eyes giving him away. 'You go.'

'I'm going to go up onto the upper deck.'

'The upper—' He stares at me, aghast. 'You can go *higher*? Than *this*?'

'The level above is open air.'

A small, strangled sound emits from his throat.

'There's literally a cage around the deck, so it's completely secure,' I add calmly, easing my fingers loose of his grip. 'I'll be back in a bit.'

'Fine. Be careful,' he says gruffly, folding his arms across his chest as he remains frozen to the spot, refusing to go near the window.

'I will,' I say, heading to the elevator to go up a level. 'I just want *one* picture of me hanging over the edge…'

As his jaw drops open with his gasp, I cackle with laughter.

'I'm *joking*!'

'*You*…' He blows the air out of his cheeks, shaking his head. 'I'm going to make you pay for that.'

I'm still smirking as I step onto the open-air deck, gazing out at the breathtaking panoramic views of the entire city. I take a moment to appreciate how beautiful it is, how peaceful and calming it is up here, and how I wish Mateo was looking out at this with me.

'This better be good,' mutters a grumpy voice behind me.

I spin around to find him stepping out of the elevator in a

comically dramatic fashion, clinging to the rail and pressing his foot down very slowly and carefully onto the deck.

'Fuck me. This better be *magical*,' he emphasises in a strangled voice.

Rushing over to him, I throw my arms around him.

'You came up here!' I exclaim in disbelief.

'Yes, I had to come find you,' he says, in between deep inhales and exhales as he tries to steady his breathing.

I take a step back, holding his shoulders.

'Aren't you scared?' I ask in amazement.

He swallows and nods after a long exhale. 'Yes,' he admits, his eyes shining at me. 'I'm terrified. But usually, that means the reward is greater.'

My heart aches for him. Before I can think about what any of this means, I take his hand and lift it to my lips, planting soft kisses across his knuckles. When I look back up at him, he's watching me intently, his mouth parted slightly, his eyebrows knitted together.

'Here,' I prompt, leading him cautiously to the edge. 'Come with me.'

As a born-and-bred Londoner, I find it hard to imagine any other city ever coming close to being as cool as mine, but Paris sure does put up a good fight. There's so much to see and do here, I'm disappointed we only have a day to enjoy it. After coming down from the Eiffel Tower, Mateo had an adrenaline rush so big, he could barely stand still, glancing back over his shoulder constantly as we walked away from it, going, 'What the *fuck*? You see how tall that thing is? You see how *high* it is? We were up there, Ash! Right at the top!'

It is such a gorgeous sunny day, we went for a coffee by the river and I sat there sipping from my tiny espresso cup, looking at the Seine through my sunglasses, feeling like Audrey Hepburn. We went on to the Louvre where both of us tried to out-bullshit the other talking about the exhibition, neither of us knowing anything about art, and sending each other into fits of laughter. My favourite moment was when Mateo gasped suddenly and I turned to see him waving me over eagerly.

'There's a horse in this one!' he exclaimed, pointing at a painting in front of him.

He's never been cuter.

He insisted on taking me for a long lunch at one of his favourite bistros, which thankfully turned out to be a tiny place down a narrow street I never would have come across without him. They greeted him warmly and treated us both like royalty. Mateo explained that there used to be a young French groom at Maycourt from Paris who once brought him here and introduced him to the maître d' of this restaurant. Ever since, whenever he's in the city, he makes a point to come here because the food is unlike anywhere else.

'That groom has moved to Argentina now,' he told me with a proud smile. 'He was a talented player already. After his training, he'll be up there with the best.'

I realise as the lunch is concluding that the conversation has mostly revolved around me. Without it seeming like an interrogation, Mateo has asked me questions about growing up in London, my close relationship with Jasper, and how I came to work for Ren through Mum. The questions continue as we stroll across the bridge towards Notre Dame, but take a pause while we stand in front of the magnificent, imposing cathedral, both of us awed into silence. I made it clear to Mateo this morning that I wanted to finish the day with a cruise down the Seine, emphasising it was non-negotiable as I suspected he was fighting the urge to roll his eyes. But when I walk in the direction of the boat-tour signs, Mateo puts his arm around my shoulders and gently angles me another way.

'Hey!' I protest, ducking away from his arm. 'We're going on a boat tour, Mateo.'

'Yes, we are.'

'Then why are we walking *away* from it?'

'We're not. We're walking away from the large, public boat tours, and walking towards the small, private boat tour that we'll be going on.'

He nods towards a small boat bobbing at the jetty, a skipper standing next to it, waiting for us with a beaming smile. I stare at him in bewilderment before turning to Mateo, who looks very pleased with himself.

'You... you booked a private boat? *When?*'

'This morning, when you said you wanted to go on a boat,' he replies simply.

'But... I was with you this morning!'

'I made a call when we were queueing for security at the Eiffel Tower. You were distracted by those people holding everyone up by filming a dance for TikTok.'

'You really booked a private boat for us?'

'Yes, I did.' He smiles hopefully at me, a thousand butterflies dancing around my stomach. 'Is that okay?'

I laugh lightly. 'Mateo, it's *amazing*!'

'The least I can do after everything you've done for me.' He offers me his arm. 'Shall we?'

Twenty

It feels like I'm in a dream, drifting through Paris on our own private boat. We've turned down the offer of bubbles – Mateo has a rather important match tomorrow and I'm up at the crack of dawn – but honestly, I still feel drunk because of how surreal this is. The city is even more magical from the water. I marvel at the architecture of the buildings we pass, exquisite stone structures and stained-glass windows clashing with the pockets of noise floating from vibrant bars and restaurants right next door.

Mateo is sitting opposite me at the front and his frequent glances my way haven't gone unnoticed, as though he's anxiously checking I'm having a good time.

'I'm not going to want to go home after this,' I joke as we go under the most magnificent and ornate bridge. 'Maybe I'll stay here in Paris. I could work for the polo club and spend all my free time eating amazing food and going on boat trips.'

He smiles. 'Sounds like a good life.'

'We'll have to transfer all the ponies from Maycourt to Paris, though.'

'Ah.'

'I couldn't be without them. Especially Serafina,' I shoot him a look, 'who you've benched yet again.'

'I've been wondering when that was going to come up. We're through to the finals of the Paris Open, Ash. I think I was right with my line-up of ponies.'

'If DQ were playing this tournament, it might be different.'

He quirks a brow, looking mildly insulted.

'I'm not saying you can't beat them, because you can; you've already proved it,' I say quickly. 'But at some point, you might need the biggest weapon we've got, and that's Serafina. I think Eduardo would agree with me.'

'He didn't think she was ready for Paris,' he gives a knowing smile as I sigh with irritation, 'but would it make you happy if I told you I was considering her for the British Open? The biggest tournament of the season. How's that?'

'It would make me happy… but that's not why you should pick her. I want you to believe in her as much as I do.'

He nods silently.

Chewing my lip, I go back to admiring the sights we're passing. I was hoping to see the Eiffel Tower sparkling at night, but it's too light still, the summer evening shading the city in a warm-orange glow.

'It's interesting that when you move to Paris, you'll still work in a polo yard,' Mateo says lightly. 'Do you think polo is it for you, then?'

'You know, I didn't even think when I said that,' I admit, laughing, 'but there it is in my subconscious. It's strange for me to think of doing something else now. God, the younger me would be *dying* of joy knowing I was going to end up working with ponies.'

'I thought you didn't know much about horses when you were a child.'

As I fill him in on my horse-riding experience through the school programme, I watch as he listens with great intrigue and then his face falls with devastation on my behalf when I get to the part about it being shut down.

'They should start it up again!' he declares, as though he's suffered the injustice himself. 'How else can children like you learn to ride? If you hadn't come to Maycourt, you never would have known about your talent. You might have gone your whole life without riding again!'

I smile at his passion. 'Maybe.'

'That's a scary thought. I hate the idea of another kid not having that chance.' He sighs, the weight of the world suddenly pressing down on his shoulders. 'Horses can do so much for children, you know? Without them, I wouldn't have lasted long, I don't think. They see the good in you that everyone else misses. They make you feel like you are… like you are worth something.'

I could listen to you talk like this for hours.

'You say your mother was never interested in horses?' he asks, interested.

I shake my head. 'Nope.'

'And what about your dad?'

'He's completely indifferent to animals and pets.'

He nods sadly. 'Do you speak to your father often? What is your relationship like?'

'Mateo, I feel like I have talked about myself this entire day!' I say, chuckling. 'Sorry for going on about myself so much.'

'No, I asked you too many questions,' he reasons with a shrug. 'I wanted to know about you. I'd like to know more.'

I shyly fiddle with the hem of my dress. 'There's honestly not a lot to know. And surely it's your turn in the hot seat now.'

He leans back in his seat with a bemused expression. 'You know everything about me. In our jobs, we're always talking about my work, what I do and why I do it. It's been a while now that I've been wanting to take you out so I can do what I really want to do when we're together.' He takes a beat, sending heat flushing up my neck and through my face before he says, 'Which is talk with you about you.'

It's impossible not to laugh at the playful smile on his lips.

'May I ask you one more question?' he checks.

I pick up my glass of sparkling water and nod. 'Sure.'

He takes a deep breath, and asks quietly, 'Why do I feel like you're... fighting this?'

My glass pauses midway to my mouth. 'Fighting what?'

'Whatever this is between us. I can't work it out. Sometimes, I think that it's going the way I want it, then it's as though it doesn't exist. I know how it is on my side, but I can't read you. So, I guess I want to check whether I have a chance.'

I lower my glass back down without taking a sip.

'When you say you know how it is on your side,' I begin, the wobble in my voice betraying my nerves, 'what does that mean?'

I'm not going first.

His throat bobbing as he gazes at me, he takes a moment to form his answer then leans forward. 'You're all I think about, Ash,' he says in a low, gravelly voice that sends warm, glowing sparks through my body. 'I can't bear it when you're not with me. And when you are with me, I feel like I can breathe again.'

My heart is pounding so hard, surely he can hear it. Surely the whole *bankside* can hear it. I try to form words, something to say in response, anything, but my brain has gone blank. I'm lost in his dark eyes that continue to blaze at me as though they never want anything else in their sight. As though I'm the only one that matters.

'What about Emma?' I blurt out, my stubborn lines of defence not giving up yet.

He frowns, baffled. '*Emma?*'

'Basilio told me about her. How you pursued her until she fell for you and then you dropped her. And what about that actress you met at Guards? Or the model you met in Florida, the one I saw you with in your car? And all the other women that flock to you and the other players. Look, I know how it goes in polo and I'm not going to get sucked in.'

Flustered, I run a hand through my hair, which has grown wilder in the heat of today. Having been lost for words moments ago, they sure are spilling out of me now. He was right to ask me why I've been pulling away because at least we can get everything out on the table – no more games. I am giving him the chance to back away before it gets messy.

We're too close, we know each other too well; I can't be a fling to him. Maybe if we'd only just met. Sure, I'd love to jump into bed with this guy because *look at him*. But it's too late. I've spent too much time with him and I can't pretend that these feelings don't exist.

The problem is, how do I know he didn't say this exact same shit to Emma?

I know now that it's easy for people to say things they don't mean.

A memory of Chris flits through my mind: we were at his flat in Wimbledon and he saw me admiring a painting hanging on the wall. 'I bought that in Paris from a street artist while I was playing in the French Open,' he told me.

'I'd love to experience Paris properly,' I said, gazing at the picture.

'How about I take you sometime?' he offered, wrapping his arms around my waist from behind. 'It's easy enough. We can pop over, pretend we're there to see the sights and spend all our time in our hotel room.'

I laughed, turning round to kiss him.

He threw that idea out so easily, so convincingly, when he never had any intention of seeing it through. And I was so caught up in the idea myself, I didn't stop to question it.

I sigh, looking at Mateo with pleading eyes that say, *Please don't fuck around with me. I'm too tired, I'm too broken, I'm too decent. Take your games somewhere else.*

'Mateo,' I continue, 'you're right. I have been fighting whatever this is, because I can't take any more risks. Maycourt saved me. You say that horses have the power to make you feel worth something – well, I couldn't agree more and I'm living proof of that. When I arrived at that yard, I may have been functioning, I may have been putting one foot in front of the other, but beneath it all, I was struggling. It felt like the whole world hated me, and I was alone in it because the person I'd trusted had dropped me the moment reality hit.'

His expression is pained as I talk, his jaw clenched, the line between his eyebrows deepening. I pause for breath, my chest feeling lighter somehow.

It's nice to talk about it, I suppose, even if it's with the one person I shouldn't.

'As much as I... want...' I trail off as I gesture at the air between us, unable to say it out loud and hoping he gets the picture. I clear my throat. 'I can't risk what I've managed to find again for a brief, meaningless fling. Something that might not be *real*. And I'm sorry for the mixed messages. It wasn't fair of me to keep giving in to... Look, I'm sorry for kissing you. I should have been stronger.'

He doesn't say anything at my conclusion. There's several moments of unbearable, torturous silence where he doesn't move a muscle or speak a word, his mouth set in a hard, straight line, his hands grasped together. Then, finally he speaks.

'Don't be sorry,' he says quietly.

And that's it. The rest of the boat ride is mostly silence, an occasional bit of side talk, but all the fun and joy of the adventure has been sucked out of it by my hard-hitting summation. I regret the timing of it, after he went to the trouble of organising this trip for me and at the end of such a perfect day, but I can't regret being honest, especially as he doesn't fight back.

As we stop at the door of my hotel, that's what I remind myself. He hasn't tried to persuade me that I'm wrong, that this would be more than it is. He's heard me out and he's drawing away. That's everything I need to know.

'Goodnight, Ash,' he says, leaning forward and kissing me on the cheek. 'Thank you for today. It was...' He doesn't quite finish his sentence, swallowing audibly.

'Yeah.' I smile politely. 'You too.'

I'm not sure that even makes any sense, but it seems like the only way to conclude this awkward exchange. Turning away from him, I walk into my hotel, desperately fighting the urge to cry.

At the overcast Paris Open finals the next day, Mateo seems distracted and more aggressive than ever on the pitch. He barely speaks to anyone in between chukkas, except to give sharp, abrupt orders to his teammates. His dark mood almost goes in our favour and by half-time, we've taken the lead, but it doesn't last. He makes more and more mistakes, fouling an opponent during a ride-off in the fifth chukka and awarding them a penalty. I can see the other three players getting frustrated themselves, only Eric daring to snap at Mateo to get it together. His ponies are as tense as he is, jittery and apprehensive, their boldness wavering as they read his displeasure. The goals slip away from us and by the end of the sixth chukka, no one believes we deserve to win. We accept the loss, disappointment weighing down in the pony lines and making all of us quiet and gloomy.

Mateo barely looks at me all day.

Having missed the after-party at Guards, Jules isn't letting me off so easy this time.

'We may have lost, but we should still celebrate that we made it to the finals,' she reasons. 'You have tomorrow morning off. And it would be insulting to Paris to spend the last night here holed up in your room. Do you want to insult this beautiful city? *Do you?*'

I admit I do not.

At her insistence, I head back to my hotel from the stables to get ready for a huge party in the centre of the city. Our team have stayed at the Polo de Paris bar for initial drinks but will be transported to an exclusive venue, which is where myself and the other grooms getting the ponies to bed will meet them.

When I arrive at the bar as it starts to drizzle, Jules is standing under cover outside vaping with a dark-haired girl wearing striking blue mascara. Gorgeous in a mint-green co-ord, she takes one look at me and her eyebrows fly up, exhaling a plume of smoke before saying, 'Mateo's going to have a heart attack.'

'What?'

She gives me a knowing look. Obviously, Mateo and I haven't been as stealthy as we thought. I'm wearing a short, black fitted dress for tonight with thin spaghetti straps and accessorised with statement gold earrings. My hair is up in a loose do, so there's a lot of skin on show, my collarbones glittering with highlighter, and I'm wearing the highest block heels I own. Come on, this is a night out in *Paris*. I couldn't go casual, could I?

And, when I was choosing what to wear, I knew I had to go with something that would make me feel confident and fierce. I had to show him I was fine.

Jules leads the way across the dark, sophisticated bar to the booth where the team are sitting. Perched at the edge, Malcolm glances over to us and his eyes widen before he says something to the others, prompting Mateo to snap his head up sharply. I pretend not to be intimidated by the group's attention, brushing a tendril of my hair out of my eyes before greeting everyone and gratefully taking the glass of wine Jules thrusts into my hand.

I can feel his eyes on me. Whoever I'm talking to as the evening plays out, I can sense his gaze and it's taking everything in me not to meet it. I laugh with Malcolm as he teases me about wearing a top instead of a dress; I comfort Eric as he gets drunker and sadder over being ghosted by an influencer he was dating back in the UK; and I join Jules for some shots, the whole time fighting the urge to look in Mateo's direction.

Determined to shake off the loss, the team are getting bolder and sillier by the moment, dancing, chanting, drinking, but not Mateo. He remains in the booth with his calm, cool demeanour, attracting friends and admirers, letting them all come to him and barely paying attention to any of them. I'm hopelessly aware of him.

When Jules is pulled into a warm embrace by a French player, I scuttle away to the bathroom but when I come back, I can't find her anywhere. Weaving through what is now a heaving bar, I consider that she may have gone outside to vape. Glancing at the overcrowded booth, I don't see an option more attractive than continuing my search for her. The music is loud and it's a strain to hear anyone in here anyway, so I slowly make my way to the exit, stepping out into the evening air to find it's now pouring with rain and Jules isn't out here.

Ducking into the covered smoking area, I get my phone out to message her.

'Ash.'

I look up from my screen to find Mateo has followed me out.

'Hi,' I say with a nervous smile. 'I-I'm sorry you lost today, Mateo. It was... close.'

'I've been thinking about what you said,' he says with a furrowed brow, ignoring my commiserations and coming to stand opposite me. 'I actually haven't been able to think about anything else. All day, it's been bothering me and... angering me. I've worked out why. I'm ready to respond to you now.'

Stunned by his abrupt statements, I stare at him. 'Respond to what?'

'What you were saying last night. I want to continue the conversation. Is that okay?'

'Uh. Yes. Yes, of course.'

'Ash, I think—'

He's interrupted by someone brushing past him as the smoking area becomes more crowded with people seeking refuge from the rain that's hammering down on the canopy. Mateo looks around us, agitated. I take his hand and lead him beyond the roped-off area into the street, hurrying around the corner and ducking into a doorstop around the side. It's a tight space and not exactly completely covered from the rain, but it's private. He shrugs off his jacket and holds it over our heads as a makeshift cover.

'What is it?' I ask, needing to know whatever it is he wants to say.

'I think if you never take any risks, then you never win,' he states, his eyes bright and wild. 'Ash, I don't know what lies ahead for you, for me – for anyone. But from the moment you came trespassing into that field and into my life, everything changed. I haven't been able to shake you, not for one moment. That scared me. It scares me still. It's made me question everything; *you've* made me question everything. I...' He lifts his eyes to the jacket above us for a second, searching for the right way of putting it. 'I want to be around you all the time. Your stubbornness is very annoying. Your laugh is perfect. I don't feel myself unless I'm with you. You drive me to be better at whatever I'm doing. I want to win every match, every tournament, so that I might have a chance at winning *you*. The way I feel for you... I've never felt anything like this before.'

He pauses, breathing heavily, his expression softening.

The jacket is half-working. Our hair and faces are protected, but our arms are soaked, his shirt see-through and plastered to his toned muscles working hard to keep the jacket held high for our conversation.

'I hated going up the Eiffel Tower, *hated* it,' he continues. 'I've been to Paris so many times and I promised myself I'd never, ever do it. You're the only person I could break that promise for, Ash. I can't persuade you to take this risk, but I can tell you that, if you want to, I will take it with you. I *want* to take it. You won't be alone in it.' His throat bobs. 'Yesterday, you said this might not be real, but I don't know what could be more real than that.'

My heart is thudding at an alarming rate. The rain is roaring in my ears. He's watching me apprehensively, wide-eyed and waiting, as though his sanity depends on whatever it is I'm about to say. But words won't cut it. Because I don't know how to put in words the way he's made me feel on this stoop in the middle of the rain in Paris. He's made me feel a bit stupid, actually. He's right. I wanted to shut this off before it began because I was protecting myself before I knew how he felt. I know now. He's told me.

Time to show him exactly how I feel.

Grabbing fistfuls of his shirt, I pull him towards me and drag his lips to mine, arching my body into his as I kiss him with a hunger and need I've never felt before. He responds instantly, dropping the jacket as one hand cups my face, the other threading through my hair. As his tongue parts my lips, I moan against his mouth and the hand on my jaw drops to press against my back, forcing my hips to press into him. Without our cover, we are open and vulnerable to this unexpected heavy shower of rain.

Locked safely in his arms, I couldn't care less. Let it pour.

Twenty-One

'Shall we make a break for it?' Mateo grins, pressing his forehead against mine.

Biting my lip, I nod and he bends down to pick up his jacket, now too wet to be of any use. He takes my hand in his, interlocking our fingers, and we launch ourselves out into the downpour, hurrying down the road in the direction of his hotel, which I know isn't far. I squeal with laughter through the hammering rain, grateful for Mateo snaking his arm around my waist to make sure I don't slip in my heels.

By the time we burst into the lobby of the Ritz Paris, my hair is dripping wet and my dress sodden. Mateo runs a hand through his hair, droplets beading down his face, his shirt clinging to his solid torso. His grin is making my heart flip. I must look a state, my make-up probably smeared all over my face. Mateo looks hotter than I've ever seen him, his skin glistening with raindrops, his hair damp, messy and tousled, his eyes flashing at me. When he leads me towards the elevator with purpose, I notice everyone glance up and watch us with intrigue, the two of us soaked through and giggling like we've done something that's going to get us in trouble as we cross the marble floor.

The doors ping open and he presses a hand on the small of my back to guide me inside the empty elevator before he steps in behind me, presses the number for his floor, and spins me round to face him, steadying me with one hand gripping my hip, the other cupping the side of my head. Before the doors have closed again and I have time to think, he's dragged my mouth to his. I gasp, his lips devouring me hungrily, my back arching into him as his fingers tangle in my hair and his tongue glides against mine.

This kiss is so urgent, so demanding, it's making me light-headed and reckless. I don't notice when the elevator doors shut; I don't care who's seen us before they do. I'm lost in my hunger for him, all of him, every fucking inch of him, digging my nails into the muscles of his back and dragging them down in slow, torturous motion as he moans into my mouth in response, biting fervently at my bottom lip.

As the elevator shifts into motion, I back against the wall, hauling him with me, needing his body pressed against mine. His hands fall to the back of my thighs and he hoists me up with ease, my dress sliding up around my waist as my legs squeeze his hips, my ankles locking behind his back. As he buries his head in my neck, kissing and licking my wet skin, I inhale sharply at the feel of his hardened erection pressed in between my legs. *Fuck*. He's huge. I can tell he's huge. The idea of him inside me sends jolts of electricity surging through me, dampening the fabric of my underwear. I want him now. I need him now. I grind against him and he groans, jerking his head back to look at me, his eyes flaring with heat.

'Ash,' he says through gritted teeth. 'You don't know what you're doing to me.'

My hand slides to the bulge in his trousers. 'I think I have an idea.'

He punishes my brazenness by lowering me to my feet and stepping back, leaving me cold and gasping for him. The elevator doors slide open. Catching his breath, his eyes drift down my body as I quickly wriggle my skirt back down my thighs.

'Fucking hell,' he mutters, the muscle in his jaw twitching. 'You're so beautiful, Ash.'

For a moment, I'm dumbfounded, struck by the sincerity of the compliment. The doors threaten to close again, but he presses the button to open them and reaches for my hand, guiding me down the corridor towards his room in a daze. Unlocking the door, he ushers me inside and turns on the light.

'Whoa,' I say, taking in the vast, elegant suite with its gold-gilded walls, marble fireplace, private balcony and the biggest bed I've ever seen. 'This is—'

He doesn't let me finish my sentence and, to be honest, I'm okay with it. Stepping in front of me, his hands grab my hips and he captures my gasp of surprise with his mouth, kissing me like this is the first time he's been allowed to, the pent-up frustration feeding into his lips and tongue that are exploring mine hungrily. My lips are going to be bruised tomorrow, but I don't care, I want more, moaning with desire so he's left in no doubt of it. My back against the door, my hands pull at his shirt, yanking it free from his trousers and I start fumbling with his buttons until he pulls back from me, forcing me to stop.

For a moment, he studies me intently, his dark eyes roaming from my face down my neck to my collarbone, from one strap of my dress to the other. He slowly slides a hand round my back to the top of my dress, his fingers finding the zip. A small smile appears on his lips.

'May I?' he asks, pinching it.

'You'd fucking better.'

His smile widening, he pulls the zip down, before easing the straps down my arms with the lightest trail of his fingertips, my skin burning beneath his touch. The dress falls to the ground in a crumpled heap around my heels. His eyes glaze as he looks at me in my sheer black lace strapless bra and matching thong. He swallows and his lips part as my chest rises and falls with each shaky breath, my peaked nipples pushing at the material of the bra, begging for him. His gaze fixed on me, he lifts his chin and inhales deeply.

'What?' I ask, glancing down at my underwear to check there's not something wrong.

'I'm taking a moment,' he says, his voice strained. 'I'm wondering how the hell I'm going to last more than a couple of seconds with you looking like,' he gestures at me, '*this*.'

Tucking my hair behind my ear, I smile bashfully.

'You're perfect,' he adds.

His warm hands come to my waist, soft and gentle now, and he dips his head to kiss me slowly, his lips brushing against mine tentatively like they were dealing with something precious, something that might be easily broken. My heart thrums at this new variety of kiss in Mateo's arsenal, melting into him, resting my palms against the damp material of his shirt plastered to his chest. He breaks the kiss for a moment, looking at me with soft, hopeful eyes.

'I want you so fucking badly. It would never be meaningless,' he says, his voice thick and hoarse. 'Fuck, Ash, how could you not know how badly I want you over and over and *over* again?'

I crack first, drawing his lips to mine and kissing him deeply as his hands roam up and down the skin at my waist, covering me in goosebumps. Sliding my tongue against his, I groan into his mouth and he responds by kissing me harder, flutters erupting in my stomach at the sensation of his hard length pressing against my hip. But when I go to undo his belt, he grabs my wrists with both hands, lifting my arms above my head.

'You first,' he says in a low voice.

Pinning my wrists against the back of the door above me with one hand, the other drops to my stomach. I draw a sharp breath, as his fingers trace teasingly along the waistband of my thong, heat building and aching between my legs. A desperate whimper emits from my throat, my body arching towards him as it hums with need.

'Tell me I can touch you,' he says, his throat working as though somehow nervous about whether he's done enough to earn my permission. 'Let me do to you what I've been thinking about for weeks. What I haven't stopped thinking about.'

'Touch me,' I beg him, a low, tortured sound rumbling in his chest. '*Please.*'

He slips his hand beneath my thong, drawing a gasp from me as his fingers stroke over my clit, my body jolting in response. I whimper with something like relief and ecstasy as they slide lower and push inside me.

'You're so wet for me,' he murmurs, his eyes blazing. 'So fucking *perfect.*'

Dragging his fingers back and sinking them inside me again, he captures my groan with his mouth, his tongue caressing mine as pressure builds and tightens between my legs.

'Do you know how long you've made me suffer?' he says, his jaw tense as he watches me. 'How restrained I've had to be around you every fucking day?'

Holy fuck, I think I'm about to combust.

The way his fingers are making my muscles tighten and ache, how he's taken control by not letting me touch him, how he kisses me like he's worshipping me. I've never felt so fucking powerful, like this man is completely at my mercy even though I'm the one pinned up against the wall. All of it combined is making my head spiral and my orgasm build impossibly fast. He moves his thumb to my clit, rubbing with the perfect amount of pressure.

'*Oh my God,*' I breathe, bucking into his hand.

He lets out a groan at my reaction, the hand holding my wrists releasing them to drop to my waist and hold me firmly in place, while mine rake roughly through his hair, down his neck and cling to his shoulders for dear life. His eyes flare as I bite back a moan, desperately trying not to fall too fast, wanting this fluttering, building, rippling sensation to last forever.

'Come for me, baby; don't you dare hold back,' he growls, increasing the speed and pressure, reading me like a fucking book.

His demanding tone thrills me, bolts of electricity crackling through my body. As his fingers fill me and the heat mounts beneath his swirling thumb, he kisses my mouth hungrily, along my jawline and down my neck like he can't get enough of me, like he needs to taste me everywhere. No one has ever touched me like this before; no one has made me this close to the edge so quick before. I tip my head back, sinking my fingers into his shoulder muscles, rasping, 'I'm coming, I'm coming.' I clench around his fingers and the pleasure erupts, pulsating through my body so intensely, I can't stop the loud moan that escapes from my lips. I ride out the orgasm before slumping against him, catching my breath.

'Oh my God,' I say hoarsely, my body still tingling.

'You have no fucking idea how good you look,' he says, kissing me as I lift my head, tangling a hand through my hair and gripping it. 'You're driving me crazy, Ash.'

My mind still hazy from the world-shattering orgasm I just experienced, I arch my body into him, pressing my breasts against his chest, nipping at his bottom lip to let him know I want more from him. I want *everything* from him. My move has its desired effect. A low, rumbling, almost pained growl comes from his throat and he kisses me harder, his mouth claiming mine. My hands slide to his chest and grab fistfuls of his shirt.

I'm addicted to you, this kiss is telling him.

Pushing myself away from the door, I turn us around without breaking the kiss so I'm walking backwards towards the bed with his shirt locked in my grasp, dragging him with me. He smiles against my mouth, his hands on my hips until we stop as the edge of the bed hits the back of my legs and I draw away to spin us around again. He sits down on the bed, his hands clawing for me, but I step back out of reach. Breathing heavily, he leans back on his hands and watches as I reach behind my back to undo my bra, tossing it to the floor, before I reach down to unfasten and step out of each shoe, kicking them away.

'*Christ*. You are the most beautiful woman I've ever fucking seen,' he says in awe, in a way that sounds like it's true even though it can't possibly be.

Completely naked, I move to straddle him, working at the buttons on the shirt while his warm hands cover my breasts, squeezing them, his fingers toying with my nipples.

'So fucking beautiful,' he murmurs, his voice ragged with desire and eagerness.

I finally get to the last button of his shirt, yanking it open and helping him to pull it down his arms and drop it on the floor. Oh my God, this man.

'You're too much,' I breathe, shamelessly admiring him, letting my hands explore the curve of his muscled shoulders, the hair on his solid chest, down his washboard abs.

'No,' he counters, 'I'm just right for you.'

Cradling his face, I give him a wicked smile, dropping my hands to his shoulders and bringing my lips achingly close to his before I murmur, 'Let's find out, shall we?'

His eyes darken and I feel his cock pulse against my clit, making me gasp and grind against him, while he groans with pleasure. God, I *love* that. I love that I'm the cause of that sound. I want more of it. Driven into a frenzy of need, I rake my fingers through his thick, messy hair and bring my lips to his ear to whisper, 'I want you so badly.'

I'm rewarded with another desperate groan, his hands winding round to my arse and gripping me there as I rock against him once more, shivers of pleasure and anticipation rolling in waves down my spine.

'Please,' I murmur, taking his ear lobe between my teeth and squeezing it gently, 'please fuck me, Mateo.'

He breaks, wrapping an arm around my waist and lifting me to the side, lying me flat on my back across his bed in a movement so swift and fast and sexy, I can barely keep my head straight. Holy *shit*, he's strong. I mean, I knew he was strong, but he made me feel as if I didn't weigh a fucking thing. He presses down on top of me and kisses me, my hands flying to his belt but I only manage to unbuckle it before I'm grabbing onto his hair again because the way his tongue is sliding against mine so urgently and roughly is making me lose my fucking mind and apparently all ability to do two things at once. He moves his kisses from my mouth to my jawline, giving me time to gasp for air, before his lips trail down my neck, collarbone, down my right breast and stopping to suck at my nipple.

'Mateo!' I whimper, my back arching off the bed, and the bastard chuckles.

He finishes what I started, taking his belt off and the rest of his clothes, while I prop myself up on my elbows to watch. When he peels his boxers down, I'm forced to wet my lips, my mouth has gone so dry. I could feel he was big, but even so, I underestimated him. He glances at my expression and a rogue smile appears on his lips.

'Are you sure you want this, Ash?' he says, running a palm softly over my stomach and bending down to kiss me just above my belly button. 'We don't have to. There's plenty more we can do if you're not ready. We have all the time.'

'Not ready?' I practically splutter, sitting up and wrapping my hand around his length, stroking it and earning the groan that makes the ache between my legs throb. 'I thought I'd made myself clear. Mateo, I want you more than *anything.*'

His eyes light with something like fire and his hand cups my face as he draws his mouth to mine, gasping at my lips as I pump his cock and moan into his mouth, imagining him inside of me, how incredible he would feel.

'Fuck, *fuck*, Ash. Stop, it's too good.'

He grabs my wrist to halt it and I let go, before he opens his bedside drawer and finds a condom, ripping the packet and sliding one on. I shuffle backwards and ease myself down as he moves to hover over me, his hand sliding between my legs, my stomach fluttering at his touch. I can feel his heart pounding as I press my palms against his chest, before looping my hands around his neck, closing my eyes giving in to the sensation of swirling heat that begins to build beneath his fingers. He's so good at this. Like he knows exactly how I tick.

I moan his name as he drags his thumb over my clit, a satisfied sound rumbling in his chest as he hits my spot, swirling and increasing the pressure. My eyes flash open to find him gazing down at me, his dark eyes piercing, his jaw tense.

'Fuck me,' I plead helplessly, pleasure rolling through me at an alarming rate. 'I need you inside of me. I want you. Fuck me, please.'

Am I begging? Christ, I'm *begging*. This guy is so good at what he's doing, he's made all inhibitions vanish and the truth spill out of my mouth without any thought whatsoever. I've never felt so needy for anyone before and for a moment, I panic at how pathetic I must seem to him. But any worries are crushed by his lips finding mine, his moan of pleasure filling my mouth as his control snaps, kissing me like he can't get enough of me.

'When you say things like that, you don't know what you do to me,' he tells me, grabbing his cock and brushing the end of it teasingly against my clit. 'I've wanted to fuck you for so long. Only you.'

He edges himself into me and I gasp at the instant sparks of pleasure that ripple in waves through my body. He's watching me closely, watching me take him.

'Oh my God,' I breathe, dragging my nails up and down his biceps, wound up, every part of me aching for him to go deeper. 'More. More.'

His hand angles my leg so I spread wider for him, crying out in ecstasy as he pushes himself fully inside of me, filling me and touching a spot that's never been reached before. He pulls out and pushes back in, groaning loudly into my neck, his breath tickling my skin and driving me wild. I feel feral, clawing at him, begging him for more, lifting my hips up into him, losing myself in this overwhelming sensation.

'Fuck, Ash, you feel so fucking good,' he grits out, moving slowly at first, every thrust sending me to a different plane, the rest of the world vanishing from existence.

He picks up the pace, driving into me quicker and harder, telling me raspily how beautiful I look like this, how he's not going to last, capturing my moans in his mouth. His hand finds my clit and I clench around him. He swears profusely in Spanish.

'More,' I demand again, grinding into him, a woman possessed. '*Harder.*'

'Fuck,' he grits out, pounding into me harder and harder, and I love that he's lost control, that he can't hold back any more. 'Ash—'

He doesn't need to tell me, I can feel him pulsing inside of me and knowing he's close is all it takes to tip me over the edge. The most intense feeling of pleasure I've ever experienced ripples through my entire body, leaving me bucking and writhing beneath him as he groans into my neck at his own release. He shudders, collapsing on top of me.

'You're incredible,' he whispers through heavy breaths, kissing my neck lightly.

You're everything, I want to say, but find myself unable to, fear flickering in my heart. Instead, I cling to him tighter, hoping I never have to let go.

Twenty-Two

Without opening my eyes, I sigh dreamily into my pillow as I feel Mateo's fingers trail over my shoulder, sweeping my hair over one side, so the bare skin of my back is exposed for him to explore with his lips. Beats an alarm clock.

'Good morning,' he murmurs at my neck.

I smile, nestling further into the pillow. When he draws away, my back suddenly feels cold without the trail of kisses he was busy leaving there, and I huff in disappointment as I hear him get out of bed and go to the bathroom. The excitement of last night, of being here with him – *I'm in a suite in the Ritz Paris!* – has fully woken me up and, thanks to the ponies, I'm used to absurdly early mornings now, anyway.

I kick away the sheets from my legs, sit up and stretch and then jump to my feet. Swiping up his shirt from the floor where it was haphazardly dropped last night, I slip it on, only bothering to do up a couple of buttons, and then stroll across the room to the balcony. I step out onto it and lean my arms on the rail, looking out at the view in the early-morning light. It's still and silent, the city barely waking.

I hear his footsteps approach behind me.

'Nice shirt,' he says with approval, his hands slipping under it to hold my waist while he rests his chin on my shoulder. I exhale with contentment. 'Enjoying the view?'

'It's not bad.'

He chuckles. 'You are hard to please.'

One of his hands slides round to my stomach before dropping between my legs. I gasp as his fingers find my clit, caressing it gently.

'Maybe I can improve things for you,' he suggests, moving my hair to kiss my neck, my head rolling back as heat pools between my legs.

He grabs my hips and spins me round to face him, his eyes lit with desire as they roam from my lips to my cleavage, landing on the button of his shirt done up there. My chest heaving under his hungry gaze, I acknowledge how hot he looks first thing in the morning, his hair dishevelled still from my fingers working through it last night, his muscled torso on full display in the early-morning sunshine as he stands in front of me in only his boxers.

Is he real?

Is this real?

Fuck, I hope this is real.

As if he can read my mind, as if to dissipate any intruding doubts that he might well be an impossibly beautiful figment of my imagination, he reaches out to undo the buttons on the shirt I'm wearing and push it open so his hands have access to the bare skin beneath, leaving me shivering at his touch. My heart races as I catch the muscle in his jaw twitch, the way his eyes flare with longing as he explores my body. He runs his hands up over my hips and along the curve of my waist, leaving my skin covered in goosebumps. He brings them to my breasts, playing with my hardened nipples before he runs them back down my body.

'I can't believe you're here with me,' he says so quietly, it's as if he's saying it to himself. 'Standing on my balcony, wearing my shirt…'

He slides his hand between my legs again, watching my lips part with pleasure.

'So wet,' he says, his gaze searing into me and making my heart thrum. 'Say it's for me, Ash. Say it's me who does this to you, who makes you this fucking wet.'

'Only you,' I say hoarsely.

A low, guttural noise emits from his throat and he sinks to his knees.

'Mateo. Oh God,' I whisper, glancing nervously at the rows of windows and empty balconies surrounding his.

But he doesn't give me much time to think about the consequences of being caught because he's kissing along my thigh and between my legs and—

My breath hitches as his tongue finds my clit, my hands flying back to the balcony rail I'm pressed up against and gripping onto it, already spiralling as I feel the vibrations of the soft moan of satisfaction he releases before increasing the pressure of his tongue and sinking his fingers into me. My knees almost buckle, his other hand gripping my hip and holding me in place as I begin to succumb to the mounting pressure beneath his tongue.

'Oh my… *fuck*… Mateo,' I breathe. 'Oh my God!'

Holding onto the rail with one hand, I let the other fall to his head and grip his hair, feeling the cool breeze on my peaked nipples, unable to bite back a moan as I lose myself in this all-consuming pleasure.

'You look so fucking hot like this,' he murmurs, glancing up at me with a look of disbelief, his face flushed, his eyes gleaming with greed, before his tongue sweeps against my clit, groaning with gratification like he's been starved of this and is making up for lost time.

'Fuck,' I say breathlessly, the vibrations of his groan bringing me right to the edge as I grind into the rhythm of his tongue and hand. 'I'm coming. *Mateo!*'

My muscles clench round his fingers and my body spasms as the pleasure unfurls in relentless, pulsing waves, his name reverberating around the buildings around us. My legs trembling as I cling onto the balcony rail, he leaves several kisses on the inside of my thighs, before standing up and lifting me into his arms, carrying me inside in a post-orgasm daze, with my arms looped around his neck, his shirt draped on me still.

'That was... oh my *God*,' is all I can manage to say while he eases me down on the bed.

Moving to lie alongside me, he trails his fingers up and down my stomach, from my bellybutton to just underneath my breasts, watching me attentively as I catch my breath.

'That was the sexiest moment of my life,' he says quietly, pressing his lips to my temple.

I've never had this before. It's never been like this with anyone before. Mateo acts as though getting me off is more fulfilling for him than seeking his own satisfaction. He makes me feel safe and sexy and confident. I've never felt so admired, so wanted. The way he looks at me, the way he touches me – in those moments, he makes me feel like there's nothing else that matters. And that turns me on big time.

I sit up and move to straddle him, the swift change in position taking him by surprise, but he doesn't fight it. He grabs my hips, grunting as he adjusts me onto his hardened erection straining at his boxers. Sliding my hand beneath the waistband, I lift myself off him to wrap one hand around his length and use the other to tug his boxers down. He groans as I release his cock and stroke it, a throbbing ache already building again between my legs.

'Fuck yes,' he grits out, his eyes fluttering closed.

'I need you now,' I breathe, watching his Adam's apple work, his cock pulsing in my hand and sending flutters through my stomach.

Determined to remain the lead on this one, I do the honours of finding a condom in the bedside drawer, before handing it to him to roll on while I shrug his shirt off my shoulders and let it drop to the floor. Moving back to straddle him, he positions his cock at my entrance and I lower myself down onto him, exhaling with a mixture of pleasure and relief to have him inside me again, to feel this full as I slide down to the hilt. His fingers dig into the skin at my hips as he guides me into a rhythm, his groans making me wetter and more ravenous for him.

'Ash, *fuck*,' he says in a throaty voice as I grind harder and faster against him, challenging his slower pace and taking command.

He moves to sit up, leaning back on one hand, his fingers grabbing a fistful of the sheet, and holding me in place with the other. My hands press on his shoulders, using him to control my movement as I rock against him, urged on and on by every ragged exhale, every moan, every gasp that I prise from his lips, driven wild by the feeling of his length throbbing and pulsing inside me.

'Oh my God,' I cry, muscles clenching around him as I realise that this movement at this angle is hitting my spot without any help from his hand.

'Ash, baby, I'm coming,' he grits out.

As I feel him surge deep inside me, my own orgasm hits and I ride it out on him, capturing each other's moans with our mouths, bodies shaking and shuddering together.

Panting and sweating, he brushes my hair from my face and kisses me. I think it's a quick kiss at first, but he comes for more, his fingers threading through my hair as he kisses me tenderly and slowly, savouring it. Meaning it. It's a kiss that sends a shiver down my spine.

I wonder if he knows what he's done to me.

I wonder if he has any idea how easily he could break me.

'You know, your bathroom is as big as my hotel room,' I inform him after a shower, emerging from the bathroom in one of the white fluffy towel robes that was hanging on the back of the door and I've helped myself to the slippers, too.

I stop in surprise when I see the breakfast spread laid out on the table by the balcony doors: coffee, freshly-squeezed orange juice, a huge selection of steaming, buttery-looking pastries, colourful fruit platters and several plates of cooked food.

'I thought you might be hungry,' he says, brightening at my appearance and coming over fully dressed to give me a kiss on the lips, his hands resting on my hips. 'I wasn't sure what you'd like, so I ordered a few different things from the menu.'

'Mateo, you ordered the whole menu,' I laugh before reaching up to the back of his neck and hauling his mouth to mine again. 'Thank you,' I say against his lips, kissing him.

With a gentle kiss on my forehead, he draws back to move to the table and pull out a chair for me, gesturing for me to sit down before taking the other seat and pouring us coffees.

'Flying private jet, sleeping in a bed of custom-made linens, showering in a bathroom made of marble, eating a breakfast fit for a king,' I list breezily, picking up the delicate cup from its saucer. 'Not too shabby being a professional polo player.'

He smirks. 'It's not always like this.'

'I think you can relax, Mateo. You've been playing so brilliantly, every team is going to be begging you to join them next season.'

'I didn't play well yesterday. I let my emotions get the better of me,' he says, troubled.

I feel a stab of guilt. 'I'm so sorry you lost.'

He brings his eyes up to meet mine. 'I'm not sure I did.'

As I blush furiously, he offers me the plate of pastries and I select a croissant.

'If I'm on a team for Argentina, I'll be happy,' he adds.

'Is Argentina the big one?'

He nods slowly. 'It's the big one. It's nerve-racking. Very fast, very aggressive – the best players in the world. There's a lot of pressure.'

'Uh-huh, I know how that feels,' I say, liberally buttering my croissant with a solid silver knife. 'I mean, the grooms' match is on the horizon. Talk about high stakes.'

My sarcasm makes him chuckle. Satisfied, I bite into the pastry. It's so delicious and warm and buttery, I suddenly feel more devoted to this croissant than anything else.

'Oh. My. *God*,' I cry as I chew, holding the rest of the pastry in my hand aloft.

He quirks a brow. 'Good croissant?'

I swallow the mouthful in disbelief. 'Are you fucking *kidding* me? What kind of bullshit croissants have they been feeding us back home?'

He bursts out laughing.

'I'm serious!' I insist, my lips curving into a smug smile at his reaction. He's so calm and serious a lot of the time that I love making him laugh. It's like a shell exterior cracking and revealing the gooey centre beneath. 'This is the most incredible thing I've ever tasted. It's so warm and soft and buttery. Mateo, we're going to need to snaffle a bunch of these. How many do you reckon you can fit in your bag? I don't even have a jacket, so you're going to have to shoulder a lot of the work.'

'You want us to steal pastries from the Ritz Paris?'

'Yes. Have you *tried* one of these? I can't casually eat this croissant now and be expected to simply walk away knowing that they exist in this magical hotel while I'm going about my life across the sea. I'm not asking much. Just sweep that platter into one of your bags and we're golden.'

'I'll tell you what,' he begins, his eyes twinkling at me, 'how about we come back here to Paris together whenever you want and we can stay here and you can eat all the croissants you like? I think that's a better plan than stuffing pastries in my bag.'

I swallow my mouthful. 'We can come back to Paris whenever I want, huh?'

'Whenever you want,' he repeats, gazing at me. 'Although I'd rather avoid the weekends of the big tournaments. Otherwise, you say the word and we're right back here.'

'That's quite the offer. One craving for croissants and you'd whisk me away to Paris.'

'Ash,' he says, inhaling deeply, 'I'd whisk you away anywhere you want to go.'

Wiping my hands with a cloth napkin, I smile bashfully at the sentiment, but the memory of Chris flashes across my brain, and apparently, I don't do a very good job at hiding the stab of worry that accompanies it. Mateo's expression falls and he frowns in concern.

'What's wrong?'

'Nothing. It's nothing.'

He wiggles a finger at my face. 'The line in between your eyebrows. There it is. If something has upset you, I'd like to know if you'd like to tell me.'

'This conversation reminded me of a similar one I had a while ago, that's all.'

His frown deepens. 'Chris Courtney?'

'Sorry. I don't want to ruin this amazing moment talking about him.'

'You wouldn't ruin anything by telling me what you're thinking or how you're feeling,' Mateo urges, reaching over to take my hand in his and bring it to his mouth, his lips grazing across my knuckles, warm flutters erupting in my stomach as I watch him. 'I want to know if you want to talk about it.'

'Not really,' I say with a nervous laugh. 'He promised to take me to Paris, but it was only meaningless words. It was hard to tell.'

Mateo listens and then sighs as I finish. 'If I ever see that boy…'

I snort. 'What? You'll beat him up?'

'If I have the chance, yes,' he growls so darkly, my smirk vanishes. I believe him.

'Well, I wouldn't want you to,' I say, squeezing his fingers and pulling my hand away to pick up my coffee again. 'He's nothing to me now, so none of it matters.'

Mateo's whole face changes at my words. He goes from vengeful warrior to hopeful golden retriever in a split second and it's mind-blowingly cute. It makes me want to jump on him and kiss him until our lips bleed.

'Good,' he says, reaching for his own coffee. 'I'm pleased you feel that way. And if you have any doubts, I understand, but you will soon see that I don't want anyone but you. Give me a chance to prove myself with actions. Not just words.'

'You did a good job at erasing most of my doubts last night. And this morning,' I add, smiling into my cup, trying to hide my furious blushing at his statement.

'I think I see a doubt or two still left in you, though, so we should probably stay here all day working on them.'

'Probably. In fact, now that I think about it, I have quite a few doubts left.'

'That sounds serious. Better make it a couple of days.'

'Maybe a week.'

'Maybe a month. You know what, make it a year. Let's just move in here.'

We smile mischievously at each other until he breaks into a laugh. I sip my coffee triumphantly. He sighs.

'I can't believe how much you went through because of

him. All those things that were written in the press. You are so resilient and strong. I'm in awe of you.'

'Surely not at the beginning. You didn't want me in the stables.'

'I was worried you didn't know what you were doing, but I still thought you were the most extraordinary woman I'd ever met,' he says casually whilst ladling some fruit into a bowl, as though he hasn't just said something so wonderful, it's winded me. 'You didn't care what people thought. It's the sexiest thing I've ever had to suffer. I couldn't take my eyes off you, so I had to force myself to. Otherwise you'd have thought I was creepy, staring at you all day. Christ, when you were half-naked in the tack room on the first day, I didn't know what I was going to do.'

'It was so embarrassing.'

'No,' he counters. 'It was torture.'

I smile down at my lap, admitting quietly, 'I did care what people thought when I started at Maycourt. I do care.'

He doesn't say anything, waiting for me to expand.

'I care what people think of me. I've had to train myself to put up a shield to it. I wouldn't have survived the fashion industry without it. My mum's always been good at that and I admire that about her; I think I've tried to emulate it. But it still hurts, feeling like an outsider. I've felt like that a lot, especially this year. The truth is, I act tough but everyone wants to be liked.'

His eyes are glistening as he watches me, his jaw set.

'I know how it feels to see yourself as an outsider,' he says. 'I'm so sorry, Ash.'

'Actually, it's reassuring to know that you were thinking

nice things about me when I started at Maycourt, when I was feeling so grim,' I admit, ready to lighten the tone.

'"Nice" isn't the word I'd use,' he says, shooting me a dangerous grin. 'Those riding lessons were excrutiating. Being around you all the time, no idea how you felt.'

'I obviously fancied you. Look at you. I'm not a robot.'

He laughs. 'That's something.' He hesitates, a thought suddenly bothering him. 'I've been good at shutting people out before, but what I'm not, Ash, is a person who goes around sneakily stealing someone's girlfriend and breaking her heart for the hell of it.'

'You're talking about Emma.'

'I did date her soon after she and Basilio broke up. Too soon, to be honest. I was young and proud and too focused on living in the moment to think about consequences. And very drunk. But I didn't steal her. They broke up because they cheated on each other.'

'Oh! That's a sign of a healthy relationship,' I remark drily.

'She did not cheat with me either, I would like to say. But Basilio determined I did.' He sighs heavily. 'He hated me, anyway, so why not throw that in? It didn't matter that he'd cheated on her countless times – I was chosen to be the bad guy.'

'Guess you shagging her so soon after they broke up didn't help.'

'No, it did not,' he says, grimacing. 'I didn't break her heart, though. We only had one night together and she graciously told me the next morning it was a huge mistake.'

'Ouch.'

'She didn't hesitate to tell Basilio that she'd had her revenge, though. She was infatuated with him and was doing everything she could to get his attention.' He pauses, his lips curving into a playful smile. 'I know how that feels.'

'What?' I scoff. 'Are you saying you've been sleeping around to get my attention?'

'The opposite!' he exclaims, horrified. 'Do you know how shit I felt when that actress showed up on the polo field? What I knew you must be thinking about me? I felt sick to my stomach. I was about five minutes into that date when I told her nothing was going to happen and this was all a mistake, because there was someone else, someone important to me. I couldn't sleep thinking that you were out there believing I didn't care.'

'Why didn't you tell me?'

'Then I'd have had to admit my feelings to both of us. I wasn't sure they were reciprocated. And the intensity of my feelings for you was scaring me. I'd never had that before. I was trying to get my head around it all myself.'

My heart somersaults at his earnestness.

'I can't believe you thought I was saying that I was sleeping around to get your attention,' he adds with a laugh. 'I meant I was trying to get your attention by scoring goals.'

'You thought I was like the High Fives and would be impressed by a higher handicap?'

'You do know that the handicap isn't based on goals, yes?'

'Yes, Mateo.' I roll my eyes. 'I was making a generalised statement.'

'Just checking.'

'I *was* impressed, you know, not only by the goals but your skills on a horse in general,' I inform him, prompting him to sit up straighter. 'I was impressed by that from the very start. The first time I saw you ride.'

'But not impressed the first time you saw me drive.'

'Good thing neither of us believe in sticking with our first impressions,' I say, tearing off my next bit of croissant.

'Hey, I was right about you,' he claims.

'That I was a naïve city girl who had no idea what she was doing?'

'That you were the most extraordinary woman I've ever met,' he says, casually pouring me some orange juice as though that's the sort of thing I hear every day.

Twenty-Three

Ash

It's not a pair of socks

Sam

Huh?

Ash

It's not a pair of socks down there

It's all real

Sam

Wait

What.

Are you saying what I think you're saying?

DID YOU SLEEP WITH POLO HOTTIE????

Ash

Many, many times

Sam

IN PARIS????

Ash

And back home

Sam

I am disgustingly happy for you

THIS IS SO EXCITING

I need details

All the details

Damn work!!! I'll have to call tonight

So are you guys like a thing now?

Ash

I think so

Yes

We're a thing

Sam

YAY!!

Wow

Fucking Paris

City of lights

Works every time

I adored Chris Courtney. He craved that adoration, not just from me, but from everyone he met and the audiences he played in front of. I was an added boost for his ego, a fan who panted after him, there when he needed someone to make him feel brilliant. I was so dazzled by him, I didn't notice that he wasn't the least bit dazzled by me. He promised me glamorous weekends away. He disguised a deceitful affair with thrilling stolen kisses, stashing me away in his flashy apartment where I was distracted by flashy things. He told me about his ascent to greatness, all of his achievements, the challenges he faced and overcame. He never asked about my life, my family, my friends, my job or even my likes and dislikes. He fucked me like I was lucky to be with him. And that's how I felt. Lucky to have him.

Strange, isn't it, how easy it is to lose yourself in a relationship mirage of your own making, to be so enchanted by the idea of it, you choose to ignore the prickly reality. I only wish I'd smashed and shattered the illusion before the world did it for me.

With Mateo, it's as though my eyes have been opened to what it can be like.

When he sees me, his whole face lights up. He looks at me like there's no one else in the room. He's made no effort to keep our relationship secret, insisting on coming back to my hotel after the Ritz Paris to help me pack up my stuff so we could travel to the plane together, taking my hand the moment I got out the taxi and leading me towards the steps so that no one in the team could be in any doubt about what had happened. A hungover Jules gave me a thumbs up while Lady M peered over the top of her sunglasses at us and then proceeded to follow Garfunkel up onto the plane wearing a knowing smile.

'Took you long enough,' she muttered when we sat down next to each other.

At Maycourt, he acts so proud to be with me, it makes me shy. He's attentive, calm and kind when we're working together. When we spend the night together, it tends to be at his place – it's too weird to bring him back to my brother's – but one night, when everyone was drinking at The Old Greyhound, it made sense to stay there. He knew I wasn't completely at ease in this group of his teammates and friends – although I'd consider myself liked by Malcolm and Eric, the jury's still out on Fitz and I'm definitely not a welcome addition for Clara and the High Fives. But even if he wasn't talking to me, he found a way to let me know he was there, right at my side if I needed him – a hand resting on my thigh, his fingertips brushing along my arm, his knee pressing into mine. It felt like he wasn't just showing everyone else that he belonged to me and I belonged to him, but showing me, too.

'So we have you to blame for Mateo's late arrival to practice the last few times,' Fitz said, tipping his wine glass at me. 'You must be *very* distracting to have turned Mateo's head from the game. I didn't think that was possible.'

'You've never been on time to anything, Fitzy-boy,' Malcolm said, carefully putting him back in his place. 'And until Mateo starts playing badly, I don't think any of us are in position to say anything, do you? He's been a bloody bull, recently. With him on our side, the Gold Cup is ours, I know it.'

'You're so cocky, Malcolm,' Clara teased, flicking her hair behind her shoulder.

'I have reason to be very cocky, Clara, believe me,' he responded, licking his lips suggestively while she giggled with Paige.

'I think we'll win,' Mateo said calmly. 'We have the quickest pony in the tournament.'

I gasped, swivelling to face him. 'You're going to use Serafina in the Gold Cup?'

'Yes,' he said, smiling at my excitement, 'I'm willing to take the risk this time.'

Fitz suddenly announced a rumour about a well-known player being done for fraud and embezzlement and all eyes consequently turned to him. But not mine, and not Mateo's. I was lost in his gaze as he reached to brush a lock of hair back behind my ear before leaning forwards to kiss me slowly and deeply, the kind of kiss that sends a tingling sensation all the way down to your toes so you have to scrunch them up in your shoes. Everything and everyone around us faded away.

Which was actually quite embarrassing because it was a loud throat-clearing that broke us apart and I looked up to see the throat being cleared belonged to none other than grumpy Jasper, who had come to take the empties on our table.

'Sorry,' Mateo said, picking up a couple of glasses and passing them to him.

He narrowed his eyes at Mateo and swiped the glasses away.

'I thought he liked me,' Mateo murmured when Jasper had marched back to the bar. 'He was a bit hostile then.'

'Yes, but how many girls have you brought to his pub before?'

He hesitates. 'I may have brought one or two.'

'Uh-huh. He's my brother. He's going to be protective.'

'I respect that,' he said thoughtfully.

In bed that night, when my hand drifted down the ridges of his abs to the waistband of his boxers, he gently moved it away and insisted on nothing more than cuddles.

'We can't do that,' he said on seeing my puzzled expression, before holding me close so I could nuzzle into his neck. 'We're in your brother's house.'

As frustrating as it felt at the time, it was also kind of sweet.

While wary at first, Jasper came round to the idea of Mateo and I dating and, when I saw Noor and Rhys at the pub, they made a joke about the high life of a polo WAG.

'Hey, I'm not a polo WAG, I'm a polo *groom*,' I corrected haughtily.

Despite their affectionate teasing, I assured them I was much happier mucking out and helping in the pony lines than sitting in the stands.

After the Argentine Open, the British Open is the most coveted title in the polo world. That's what the Cowdray Gold Cup brochure tells me anyway, and on the first morning of the tournament, I can believe it. There's an unspoken tension simmering across the fields as grooms prepare the ponies and players prepare their minds.

It's hard to imagine this level of prestige could be topped anywhere else in the world, especially with the backdrop of Cowdray Ruins, a strikingly grand Tudor mansion once destroyed by a fire, rising behind the manicured lawns and pitches. The Cowdray estate is vast and the Gold Cup is a long-awaited spectacle of a tournament that comes with a funfair, live music performances, and rows and rows of marquees housing sophisticated, upmarket fashion, equestrian, interior, and jewellery shops, as well as a host of bars, cafés and food trucks for visitors to choose from. For the spectators, Cowdray is quite the day out, but for the players, it's serious business.

Mateo finds me in the pony lines brushing Serafina.

'How is she?' he asks.

Serafina recognises his voice with a gleeful whinny. Shaking her head, her ears move back and forth to listen out for him as he makes his way around to her front, reaching up to stroke her nose. She nibbles at his shirt playfully.

'She's ready,' I tell him, patting her on the neck. 'I'm trying not to let my own nerves rub off on her. Lots of deep breaths and mindfulness going on over here.'

He breaks into a smile, scratching her cheeks as she leans into him.

'What's the big deal? If she messes up, all that will happen is I'll never use her again and you'll be fired.'

'Mateo!'

'I'm joking, I'm *joking*.' He laughs as I prepare to throw the brush at him. 'I thought you English love a bit of sarcasm.'

'We also know that timing is *everything*. Now is not the right time.'

I put one hand on my hip and I use the back of the other that's holding the brush to push any hair that's escaped from its ponytail back from my face. Mateo walks round to me, grabbing my hips and pulling me into him, his arms wrapping round my back.

'It is going to be fine,' he assures me.

I peer anxiously up at him. 'What if she doesn't do as you say? What if I've got it wrong and Maycourt loses because of me pressuring you to add her to your string?'

'Ash, these are always the risks of polo. Ponies are living, breathing creatures – it's not like relying on a car or bike;

you can't know how they're going to be on the pitch or how they'll react to things that happen. We train them as best we can and hope they trust us as much as we trust them. I've made the decision to use Serafina for the last chukka because *I* have judged her on recent training and matches. She manoeuvres brilliantly, she's listening to me, she's fierce in ride-offs, and she's quick. I haven't picked her because she's my girlfriend's favourite horse.'

My heart skitters in my chest.

'What?' he asks, confused as he watches my lips part with surprise.

'You… you called me your girlfriend.'

'Aren't you?'

'Am I?'

'I hope so.'

'I hope so, too.'

His smile stretches, crinkles forming around the edge, eyes sparkling. 'That settles it.'

Leaning towards me, he lets his lips graze softly against mine, hesitating as his eyes notice something over my shoulder.

'What is it?' I ask breathlessly, desperate to nip at his bottom lip, which is full and mesmerising and so damn close.

'One of the official Gold Cup photographers is lurking nearby,' he murmurs quietly. 'He's been taking photos of Fitz and Lady M, but he's looking this way and… yep, he's lifting his camera now. The lens is definitely pointed at us.'

'I don't fucking care, Mateo,' I whisper, prompting his eyes to lower back to mine, a heat blazing into them. 'I want my boyfriend to kiss me.'

A low, frustrated, guttural sound emitting from his throat, he dips his head to kiss me. I smile against his lips, wrapping my hands around his neck and letting the brush drop to the grass with a thud. No secrecy, no shame, no scandal. This is real.

Twenty-Four

I'm no use to anyone in the final chukka of the first round match against Ember Crest. The best groom in the business, Eduardo already knew I'd be too nervous to cool down the ponies and so had assigned me the duty of holding a spare mallet so I could be with the other members of the team at our end of the field, watching the action right in front of us. It's nerve-racking enough watching Mateo charge into the thick of it or face an aggressive opponent in a ride-off, but now Serafina is out there, too, and I have to stand here helpless, wishing with all my might that she's going to be okay and make us proud.

She does, more than I could have hoped.

When Eric manoeuvres spectacularly to block a shot from Ember's number one, Malcolm is able to intercept the ball and pass it to Mateo, currently being emphatically pressured by the Ember number four who is taking his role of having to mark the most dangerous member of the opposing team very seriously. But on Serafina, Mateo appears unbeatable. When he swings her around, she does so swiftly before accelerating down the pitch with remarkable speed and stamina as Mateo knocks the ball ahead of them, looking like she's hardly breaking a sweat. Unopposed, Mateo scores the goal with ease.

During the last couple of minutes, Mateo scoops up the ball and Serafina bolts down the side of the field, a blur of chestnut, a thundering of hooves and heavy snorts, breaking away from the two opponents hunting her down. Mateo positions her perfectly, curving towards the centre, and with a stunning offside forehand, he smacks the ball in between the posts. The noise from the Maycourt team is deafening, the cheer from the stand heartwarming. Mateo lifts his mallet in the area triumphantly as the end of the match rings in and Maycourt is safely through to the next round.

The relief engulfs me.

Hearing my name being called out behind me, I spin around to find Lady M striding towards me across the grass in her pastel-lemon dress and wide-brimmed straw hat, tears in her eyes, her arms outstretched. Before I have the chance to speak, she pulls me into her and holds me tight. I'm too stunned to hug her back, my whole body tensing.

'Thank you,' she whispers in my ear, before drawing back and holding my forearms, her nails digging into my skin. 'You have no idea what this means to me, to see Serafina out there. God,' she clasps a hand over her mouth as she attempts to rein in her emotion, 'William would have loved this. He would have really *loved* this.'

Moved by her reaction, I swallow the lump forming in my throat.

'I didn't have much to do with it; it's Mateo who has

trained her to perform like this, and her natural talent,' I remind her with a giddy smile. 'I knew she had it in her.'

'That's what I mean, Ashley. Your belief in her made today happen. You may not have trained her, but you didn't give up on her. That means everything.'

She pulls me into another hug and then, with a parting squeeze on my arm, steps around me to congratulate Fitz as he comes rushing off the pitch. In moments, I find myself in the middle of a group hug as Mateo grabs me from behind swinging me around and then, as my feet are planted back on the ground, Malcolm jumps on top of him, Fitz piles in, too, and anyone else in the vicinity gets involved. In the centre of it all, I laugh until my jaw aches, held firmly in Mateo's arms. I officially feel like I'm part of the team.

It's a good feeling.

Throughout the tournament, the Maycourt team provides a masterclass in teamwork and mental resilience, refusing to let mistakes or bad luck affect their performance. When tensions mount during the semi-finals and Fitz is sent tumbling to the ground in a ferocious ride-off, a chorus of gasps and yelps ripple through the stands. Once we can all breathe a sigh of relief as he stands up and dusts himself off, seemingly unharmed, I expect his temper to flare, but instead, he has a few words with the groom who assists him in getting him back up on his pony. He thanks his teammates, who'd come rushing to check on him, and nods in agreement with the umpire awarding a penalty in his favour. After a shock like that, he'd be forgiven for a wobbly hit, but he lines himself up and hits the ball with measured composure and we cheer as it rolls through the centre of the posts.

Maycourt win the match and will face DQ in the finals.

On the final day of the tournament, the sun is shining and the estate is heaving with spectators. The bars are noisy, there are screams of joy reverberating around the fields from the funfair, and everywhere you look, celebrities and influencers are having their photograph taken as they get into the spirit of the event. I love admiring all the fashion and smirking as I overhear yet another *Pretty Woman* reference. Everyone who has come along today seems impossibly beautiful and elegant, handles of designer bags looped over their elbows, their towering block heels wobbling across the grass, decorative and colourful hats perched on their heads, chosen to catch the eye. And everyone is smiling. That's one of the best things about the polo: people are here to have a good time. The atmosphere is buzzing.

Somewhere amongst the crowd are my mum, Jasper and Sam, all of whom have made the journey to be here today. They're in one of the private enclosures and I'm sure are making the most of the complimentary champagne and gourmet dining.

I can already feel the layer of sweat forming on my forehead as I finish braiding and taping a pony's tail. It's been a busy morning and it's a hot day. Across the pony lines, you can see a trail of ears flicking and shaking to ward off the pestering flies, the string for today impatient and agitated, raring to go. Serafina is at the end being checked over by Eduardo.

Please do well today.

She's been the talk of the polo set, drawing the eye of envious patrons and even prompting Ambrose to reluctantly congratulate Lady M on sticking to her guns on that 'fine chestnut mare'. When a mutual acquaintance asked her whether she'd ever agree a price, Lady M believed they'd been sent by Ambrose to sniff around.

'She's not for sale and never will be,' she said, shutting down the conversation.

There's not much conversation in the pony lines before the final. I think everyone's too nervous, trembling with anticipation. Double checking the tail is neat and securely fastened, I give the pony a pat and a kiss on the nose to wish him luck, and then spot Mateo with the rest of the team in the shade of the Maycourt tent, hashing over tactics as they zip up their boots. He catches my eye and gives me a fleeting smile before pulling back his focus.

Biting my lip, I turn to find Basilio jogging past on a grey speckled mare, slowing as he sees me. I can't pretend I haven't seen him – our eyes have accidentally locked and he's on a horse for Christ's sake, so he's kind of hard to miss.

'Fine day for it!' he calls out in a mocking posh English voice, as he gestures to the blue skies with his mallet.

A laugh escapes me before I can stop it and he gives me a spectacular grin before cantering away. It was funny and completely innocent, but I still glance back at Mateo, feeling awkward that he's witnessed the exchange. I'm almost certain he saw it, but he looks calm and controlled, no hint of irrational anger that his enemy should joke with his girlfriend. Satisfied that I haven't accidentally scuppered Maycourt's start by fuelling the fire between those two, I get ready for the match to start.

*

'Fuck me, what a shot!' Jules cries.

I'm still too shocked to speak, but she's spoken my thoughts exactly as we've just witnessed Mateo accelerating towards the right-hand corner of the pitch only to play an angled neck shot towards the goal, putting such spin on the ball that it curls in between the posts. It has to be the most skilled shot I've seen him, or anyone else for that matter, play all tournament, and the crowd are cheering wildly, their applause reverberating across the field.

I can see Basilio at the other end of the pitch roar something in frustration at his teammates, violently gesticulating as he speaks. His flare of anger is understandable: it's the last chukka and Mateo has nudged Maycourt into the lead from being tied in the fifth chukka at ten-ten.

My heart is pounding so hard as the play continues. I want Mateo to win every match he plays, but this one feels particularly important. Not only is it the final of the British Open, it's a final against DQ, a team that goes out of their way to make Maycourt feel inferior. How *good* would it taste to beat them here today on a ground as prestigious as Cowdray in front of a crowd as VIP as it gets. That sort of thing is important to Ambrose, I bet. It would sting much more for DQ to lose here today than anywhere else. Watching Eric, who currently has the ball, spin his pony round in a lovely bit of false play to shake off Basilio, I clench my fists as he sends it firing upfield to Malcolm.

Come on.

Glancing up for Mateo or Fitz, Malcolm finds his own path ahead clear and makes a go for it, thundering past the halfway line and setting up a perfectly placed pass to Mateo who streaks ahead on Serafina, the goal in his sights. I hear

Basilio shout in fury before the ball has even gone through the posts, but he knows as well as everyone else that it's about to. We hear the resounding, satisfactory *thwack* of the mallet striking the ball.

There's a moment's pause as everyone holds their breath, the flag goes up and the noise from the stand is deafening. Jules is screaming in my ear, her arms flinging around me and squeezing me tight. I don't hear the whistle declaring the match is over, but it must be because everyone around me is hugging and jumping and running onto the field. I'm released by Jules and caught in a tornado of purple shirts as every member of the Maycourt team celebrates this unbelievable win together; players, grooms, trainers, vets, partners and children descend upon the field in elation.

Somehow in the midst of the chaos, Mateo finds me, spinning me round to face him and, before I can say anything, kissing me hungrily, one hand on my hip, the other gripping into my hair. He pulls back, his hair damp from sweat and plastered to his forehead, his eyes blazing, his breath ragged.

'That win was a reminder to Basilio that he doesn't always get what he wants,' he says gruffly, nipping at my lip. 'Promise me later I can get what *I* want?'

I laugh, the adrenaline pumping through my veins. 'You've already got the Gold Cup, Mateo; what more could you possibly want?'

Later that night, when the celebrations are in full swing, I'm tending to the ponies with the other grooms. As tempting as it is to sack in work to hang out with my champion boyfriend,

I'm determined to show everyone that my priorities are in line. I'm a Maycourt groom first, a polo WAG second.

Things are winding down in the stables and there's only a few of us stragglers left. When Eduardo has done the final checks of the ponies, I volunteer with a junior groom called Jay to finish checking the tack is all clean and sorted while the others head off to join the party. I'm hanging a bridle when I hear the creak of the door as someone leans on it.

'Oh hey, Mateo,' Jay says, brightening as I spin round to face him. 'How's the party?'

'Good,' he replies, his eyes locking on me. 'You should go join it, Jay.'

'That's okay, I said I'd help Ash finish up here.'

'I'll help her,' Mateo says. 'Go have fun. I insist.'

'Honestly, it's fine, I don't mind—'

'Jay,' Mateo says, turning to look at him. '*Go*.'

Fuck me. He's so commanding and calmly authoritative. It's fucking sexy. My breath is caught in my throat, my nipples hardening beneath my bra, my heart pounding.

Jay's eyes dart from him to me and back to him again before he nods and says, 'Sure. Got it. See you later. Well done again for today, man; it was awesome.'

Mateo gives him a gracious nod and then waits for his hurried footsteps to fade away.

'What are you doing here?' I ask, fighting a smile.

I know exactly what he's doing here.

'You know exactly what I'm doing here,' he answers, staying put where he is. 'I've come looking for someone who appears to be doing her best not to have fun. Tell me, Ash, what is it about this tack room that is so appealing to you that you'd rather hide away in here than come celebrate with me after we won the Gold Cup?'

'Who says I'm hiding?'

'The person who's been looking for you all night.'

My breathing quickens and my stomach twists with anticipation, a pool of warmth building between my legs. *Fuck*. Just from a hard gaze, Mateo makes me wet. Just from the *thought* of what he can do to me. I scour his dark eyes, down to his full lips, along his stubbled jaw, across his broad, muscled shoulders, thinking of my nails digging into them until they leave bruises. *Marks that he's mine*. I wet my lips and his eyes sharpen.

'I'm glad you've found me,' I say.

'Me too,' he says, pushing himself away from the door frame. 'I seem to remember a promise you made earlier. I've come for collection.'

'That's funny because *I* remember you asking me to promise you something, but I never actually agreed to it.'

'That's a shame,' he says in a low voice, stepping across the room towards me. 'Maybe I can do a little bit of persuading.'

'That could work in your favour. Although,' I smile up at him as he stops in front of me, 'you did win the Gold Cup today. So maybe you do deserve whatever it is you want.'

Placing my palms on his chest, feeling it rise up and down with each heavy, ragged breath, I slide them down in a torturously slow motion until I reach his belt. With a thrill of satisfaction, I watch his throat work as I unclasp the buckle and pull the belt loose, dropping it on the floor with a clank.

'Ash,' he says, his voice strained, 'I don't have a condom on me.'

'We don't need one. I'm on the pill.'

His breathing's ragged, his dark eyes piercing as he cups my face in his hands. 'I'm clean. But if you have any hesitation, any worries, we—'

'No hesitation. I'm sure. Now tell me, Mateo,' I say, undoing the button of his trousers and pinching the zipper before dragging it down, 'what is it that you want?'

'You know it's only you I want,' he rasps, his fingers raking through my hair and gripping it tight. 'All day, you've been torturing me in these tight fitted jeans,' his other hand drops to my arse, squeezing it, 'and I've had to watch the other players look at you like they might be in with a chance.'

'Ah, so that's what this is about,' I say, my finger tracing his skin just above his waistband. 'You *were* jealous that Basilio made me laugh.'

'Wildly,' he admits. 'I don't like that feeling.'

His eyes linger on my mouth as I dig my teeth into my bottom lip. 'Poor baby.'

Exhaling through his nose, his eyes flare with heat and his Adam's apple bobs, and I savour every single moment of causing these physical reactions, desperate to be the only one who ever does. My hand drifts to the huge, hardened bulge in his boxers and a shudder rolls down my spine with anticipation. Hooking my fingers into his boxers, I pull them down with his trousers, releasing his cock and bending to my knees.

'Fuck, Ash,' he croaks before I've even touched him.

Wetting my lips, I lick the tip of his cock before taking him in my mouth, bringing him as far as I can to the back of my throat, sucking and tasting him as he groans in tortured pleasure. Oh my God, seeing him like this, doing this to him, is making my underwear wet. When I draw back, licking and sucking the tip before taking his length again and moaning as my hand strokes at his base, he lets out a rough, guttural noise and leans a hand against the wall behind me for balance.

'Yes, *fuck*, that's good, that's amazing,' he rasps as I begin to speed up, feeling him pulse in my mouth, his low moans making my body ache.

His hand falls to my head, his fingers threading through my hair as I moan with approval around him, my tongue dragging up and down the underside of his thick length.

'Stop,' he pleads, and with one last suck, I come off him, gazing up in curiosity. 'I need to feel you.'

Rising to my feet, I kiss him, his mouth devouring mine, his hand not hesitating to unbutton my jeans and slide beneath my pants, a growl of satisfaction rumbling from his chest. 'I knew it. I knew you'd be so fucking wet for me.'

'Fuck me, Mateo, before anyone finds us in here,' I demand bossily, my hand stroking his length until he grabs my wrist to stop me.

He turns me around, bending me over slightly and placing my hands against the wall. Crouching down, he undoes the zippers on my boots and takes them off, before undressing me from the waist down. Shit, this is hot. I swallow audibly as Mateo grips my hip with one hand and guides his length into me from behind, a thrill rippling through my chest. I bite back a moan as he pulls back and thrusts into me again, harder and deeper this time, hitting a spot at this angle that makes my muscles flutter and clench around him, an aching pressure swelling inside me.

'God, you feel good,' I say, my palms pushing against the wall, being driven closer and closer to the edge as he rocks into me over and over.

'Say it again,' he grunts, thrusting deeper and making me cry out with pleasure.

'You feel so fucking good.' I moan louder, desperate to give him whatever he needs. 'Like I was made for you.'

He groans, his hand reaching around me to delve between my legs. *Oh fuck.*

'Mateo!' I gasp as his fingers swirl around my clit while his hips find a faster pace, tremors of electricity zipping through my body and making my legs shake.

'You're so fucking tight. It's too good,' he grits out, winding me higher. '*Ash—*'

A blazing, frenzied orgasm hits and shatters me into a million pieces, and as our moans echo around the stables, his release filling me as my muscles clench and flutter around him, I know that no one has ever made me feel like this and no one else ever will.

It's amazing. It's perfect.

It's terrifying.

Twenty-Five

The high from the Gold Cup begins to ebb in the lead-up to the charity grooms' match, which takes its toll on the yard's confidence. Maycourt lose three consecutive matches in two weeks. After winning the Gold Cup, an online polo magazine dubbed us, 'The Mighty Maycourt', but a fortnight later and the headline reads, 'Maycourt Malfunctioning?'

I think the losses are easy to explain away. The boys were so driven to win the Gold Cup, especially after the near-win in Paris, they put their all into their focus and training prior to Cowdray, but once they lifted the trophy, the pressure eased and they relaxed. The UK polo season is coming to an end. It has been such an intense time, it's natural for their minds and bodies to want a break.

'Something has to change before Soto,' Mateo grumbles, driving back to his house after the third loss, his sunglasses doing little to hide his furious expression. 'I don't know what happened out there today, but we weren't at our best.'

'You played well,' I say vaguely, knowing he can play better, whilst tying my hair.

I've made the mistake a couple of times now of forgetting a hairband when driving with Mateo in his convertible, emerging from the car with my hair even more wild than usual. Mateo claims he likes it that way, untamed and dishevelled, but I can't agree.

'I couldn't focus.' He exhales through his nose, irritated. 'When we get home, I need to run through the match. I'll ask Malcolm over to work on our tactics. Three losses in a row is not good.'

'Fitz was hungover for two of them and Eric is broken-hearted,' I remind him.

The girl who ghosted Eric had picked up where they left off after his win at the Gold Cup, only to drop him again for one of the DQ players whose father recently hit headlines for overseeing a major financial merger.

'Go easy on yourself and the others,' I add gently. 'You'll be ready for Sotogrande.'

Glancing at Mateo as he stares silently at the road ahead, I frown. I hate seeing him like this, taking the weight of responsibility on his shoulders, disappointed in himself when, even if he hasn't played his best, he's still the most exquisite polo player I've ever seen.

We pull into his drive and he shuts off the engine, slumping back in his seat. I undo my seatbelt and lift my hips so I can pull my denim shorts down my legs, leaving them in the footwell. He glances over at me and then does a double take, his eyebrows lifting above his sunglasses.

'What are you doing?' he asks, intrigued.

I move to straddle him before hoisting my top up over my head and chucking it down on my empty seat. His lips part with a groan, his hands flying to the curve of my waist, greedily moving up to slide under my bra and over my breasts.

'I have an idea of how I can ease your frustration,' I say, taking off his sunglasses and dropping them on the passenger seat I've vacated, driven wild by his hardened length pressing between my legs.

I grind against him, my breath growing shallow as my thong grows damp, and he grabs the back of my head, dragging my hairband down until my hair falls free of it. Gripping my hair in his fingers, he hauls my mouth to his, moaning against my lips, lowering his other hand to push aside the flimsy fabric of my underwear. I gasp as he slides his fingers into me.

'Fuck, you're so wet already,' he growls, thrusting his tongue into my mouth as his fingers work back and forth.

The sensation causes me to whimper helplessly and I remind myself that this was meant to be about him, not about me. Batting his hand out of the way, I undo his trousers and slip my hand beneath his boxers to grasp his full cock, my body aching for him to be inside me. He grits out my name in a low, strained voice that almost fries my senses and I clumsily free him from his underwear before lifting myself up and then sinking on top of him.

'Oh fuck, *fuck*,' he grunts, his head tipping back at the sensation as I begin to ride him harder, his hand sliding to the back of my bra and unclasping it in one quick, easy motion.

My eyes fluttering shut, I let the straps of the bra fall down my arms before I toss it out the car, leaving it lying on his driveway. His mouth finds my left nipple, sucking and licking as I grind against him, before he tips his head back to watch me, his hands gripping at my hips and he begins to guide me up and down harder, his full length filling me deliciously. His hand moves between my legs, his thumb finding my spot instantly and the pressure almost makes me come straight away.

'Mateo,' I gasp, my nails digging into the back of his neck as his fingers relentlessly increase the pace. 'I'm close.'

'Fuck, me too. You look so fucking good,' he grunts. '*Fuck*, Ash, I can't hold out.'

As he thrusts up one more time, driving himself fully into me, I let my head fall back and moan in ecstasy, bucking and clenching around him as he cries out with me. We unravel together, the pleasure shattering and pulsing through my body. Breathing heavily, his gaze softens as I smile at him, biting my lip. He reaches up to push my hair away from my face before gently guiding my mouth to his, kissing me softly.

'Feel better about polo?' I murmur.

'What the fuck is polo?' he replies in a daze, catching my laugh with his lips.

My fingers are trembling as I do up the zip of my boots. The grooms' match has come around a lot faster than I thought and suddenly, the day is here. Under a grey, cloudy sky threatening to drizzle, Maycourt is bustling with people, hosting a much bigger turnout of spectators than we'd expected. All the locals have come out to support us and DQ's fans have responded in kind, a line of Range Rovers and convertibles parked up along the pitch with family members and friends lounging against bonnets in animated conversation. My mum has made the journey and Jasper is here with her, while Sam asked to take the day off from *Studio* only to be sent here on assignment.

'My editor Toni thinks it will be a great piece for the blog, so I'm getting a day at the polo whilst being paid. What a win!' she cried down the phone.

I did have to manage her expectations, reminding her that this was a local weekday charity match with the teams made up of stablehands.

'It's not going to be a big spectacle like Cowdray. It's all very casual. There's no stalls or shops or anything like that. It's just a polo match without any frills. It's a low-goal match, so there will only be four chukkas. I don't want you coming all this way to be disappointed.'

'Will there be hot men riding horses?' she asked bluntly.

'Yes,' I said, acknowledging the wildly handsome looks of the largely Argentine Maycourt grooms and having no doubt that DQ followed suit.

'Sounds like a hell of fun to me then,' she stated.

Supporters of Ambrose and Lady M have also come along, two of whom arrived in their helicopters at roughly the same time, leaving one hovering in the air, waiting its turn to land. My heart pounded in rhythm with the beating rotators that echoed across the estate.

'Ready?' Eduardo asks me, holding out his hand to help me up from the bench.

'I guess so.'

He pats me on my shoulder. 'We will win.'

I wish I had his confidence. We haven't had the chance to practise much as a team, although the few sessions we have managed to squeeze in in the evenings have been fairly positive. As expected, Eduardo is brilliant and the natural leader. When we've played together, I've focused on doing everything I can to support him and I'm counting on him today to guide me on what I should be doing and when.

I follow Eduardo out of the stables, my heart beating so loud, it's roaring in my ears and drowning out my surroundings into a haze of white noise. My breathing is coming fast and shallow as I see the amount of people lining the field and the other grooms leading the ponies for the first chukka towards us. It takes me two goes to mount Pip, a wobbly start that doesn't go unnoticed.

'She can't even get on the damn horse,' a DQ player jeers, his arms folded as his entourage sniggers. 'Don't worry, lads,' he calls out to his team, 'I think we might have this in the bag.'

Steering Pip away, I jog to the opposite side of the field where I see Mateo and the Maycourt team deep in conversation, eyeing up the DQ grooms and their ponies before muttering remarks to one another. Clara and the High Fives are here, sharing out a bottle of champagne between them, while just along the way from them, I spot Jasper introducing Mum and Sam to Noor and Rhys who are here with their families. If I wasn't so scared, I'd be moved by the amount of support from the local community. People around here really care about this yard and this sport, and it brings them together.

Instead, I wish they weren't here.

I wish the field were empty and I was practising stick and ball on Pip on my own. Why did I put myself in this situation? I didn't want the glare of the spotlight. There are a couple of photographers here and I already know how it works. They'll be looking for a photograph that sells.

If I humiliate myself, all the better for them. I can see the headline now if I take a tumble or get knocked off my pony in a ride-off: 'Chris Courtney's Ex-Lover Falls From Grace... Again!'

The neutral umpires, agreed upon by both Lady M and Ambrose, prepare for the match to start and I adjust my glasses, my exhale shaky. I glance at the DQ supporters huddled together, leaning on their car bonnets, arms folded, sharing thoughts and laughing. *I bet they're talking about me.*

I'm so distracted, I almost miss the throw-in, finding myself rendered useless almost straight away as a DQ player takes off with the ball before I've even located where it's emerged from. I encourage Pip into a canter to keep up with the action, my brain muddled as I try to remember what Eduardo and Federico told me about which position to take and when, but all their instructions have become jumbled in my head like a tangled ball of yarn and I can't pull out a single strain that makes sense. DQ score and I wheel Pip round to find the High Fives shaking their heads and sharing unimpressed looks before glancing my way. My cheeks burn with embarrassment. I can't bring myself to look at Mateo.

'It's only the beginning,' I mutter to myself, my mouth so dry, it's hard to swallow. 'You're finding your feet. It's just one goal.'

The DQ grooms have had a boost to their confidence, while mine has deflated with a gut punch. Play has started again while I'm still giving myself a pep talk, and I'm left flustered and guilty as Federico takes control of the ball and looks for me, only to find me at a standstill behind my opponent. He thunders upfield past me but his shot is blocked, and the DQ defence gets it out of the danger zone, whacking it up the other end.

By the end of the first chukka, which seems to stretch on for years, we're down two-one, our goal scored in the final minute by Eduardo, who was awarded a thirty-yard penalty. I'm brutally aware of how much I'm flailing out there, bringing absolutely nothing to the team and even letting down Pip, who's desperate to do more and no doubt furious that she's been stuck with the dud of the group riding her.

'I'm so sorry,' I mutter to Eduardo as he passes me a bottle of water.

'Don't be sorry; you can do this,' he insists as I take some sips. 'Don't be afraid to make a mistake. It's better to try.'

He's meaning to be encouraging, I know that – but all I hear from his statement is that the other members of my team think I'm not trying. I'm failing them, too.

Determined to at least make contact with the ball in the second chukka so all that practice I've been putting in hasn't been for nothing, I receive a lovely pass from Federico but as I take the swing, I find my stick hooked by the DQ player marking me. I hadn't even noticed he was there.

'Hey!' I cry, while he roars with laughter at my indignation.

The ball has gone the other way now and my heart sinks as I catch a glimpse of the grimace on Eduardo's face and watch Federico having to leg it back with our fourth player, Harry, to try to block DQ's follow-up attempt to score. I almost redeem myself minutes later when I'm cantering to keep up with Eduardo, who is dribbling the ball towards our goal. I assume he's going to have a go, but spotting me, he knocks it my way. My breath catches as I clumsily swing at the ball in surprise, sending it wide. The groans from the spectators swamp my brain and fill my eyes with tears.

Dismounting Pip after the second chukka to switch ponies at half-time, I whip off my goggles, feeling wracked with guilt that she's barely done enough work to warrant a substitute. Eduardo has planned for me to ride Gimli until half-time, a slightly bigger, faster and more experienced pony who might be able to take the lead on this one and not suffer Pip's fate of waiting for me to make a move. I'm so angry at myself, I'm grinding my teeth, my jaw aching as I blink back tears.

'Are you okay?' Mateo asks, having volunteered to bring Gimli over to me.

'I'm so sorry,' I say, sniffing. 'I'm a mess out there. I'm sorry for embarrassing you. Is everyone angry? Are they—'

'Whoa, whoa,' he says gently, handing the reins of Gimli to Harry so he can place his hands on my shoulders. 'Ash, look at me. Please.'

Reluctantly, I force my eyes up to his, a tear rolling down my cheek.

'Deep breaths. You are not embarrassing anyone out there. A few months ago, you'd never watched a polo match, let alone played one. We're all so proud that you've got the guts to take part in this competition. My God, Ash, do you know how many people would have stepped away from this the moment it was suggested?' He lifts a hand to waggle a finger at me. 'Not you. No, you were *in*.'

'It was blind arrogance,' I murmur.

'It was courageous,' he contests sternly. 'Look, I can see what's happening out there. You're nervous, which is expected. And you're getting in your own head. Let me tell you something: if you lose today, nothing happens. So Ambrose gets to boast a bit more; he finds a reason to do that all the time anyway.' He shrugs. 'We can always challenge them to another grooms' match next year. The point is, this is fun.'

'It doesn't feel fun.'

'But it should,' he insists as he wipes another stray tear from my cheek. 'Forget the noise around you and focus on all those reasons you've told me you love polo. How it feels to have a connection to your pony, how good it is to ride so fast, the joy of hitting a really good shot. You're here for the love of the sport, nothing and no one else.' He flicks a hand in the direction of the spectators. 'They will continue with their spats and rivalries no matter what happens today, so don't let that pressure weigh on you. Play the rest of this match because you love it and because you're good at it. You deserve a spot on this team. I've seen you play so well, with so much passion and joy, it took my breath away – that's the Ash I want to witness out there in the next chukka, yes?'

Gazing up at him, I sigh. 'God. You're good at speeches.'

'I know.'

I break into a smile as Harry passes Gimli to me, telling me it's time. I mount Gimli with a grateful nod to Mateo, who gives me such a carefree, *you've-got-this* kind of grin, it lifts the heavy cloud in my chest casting shadows over my heart. He's right. I've been acting as though I have something to prove today, but I've forgotten how far I've come to even get here in the first place. The Ash from the day I arrived at the Maycourt yard in that tight, white shirt and those gorgeous, immaculate boots would never have believed that

I'd be playing in a polo match by the end of the summer with the ability to ride a horse in the way I can now.

'We've got this,' I tell Gimli, patting him on the neck, trotting into position for the throw-in, already feeling like I'm sitting better in the saddle: calmer, more balanced.

The advantage to such a bad start is that it lures your opponent into a certain impression of you. The DQ player meant to be marking me has lost interest and is far more focused on his own movements than keeping an eye on mine. Having kept control of the ball since the throw-in, Eduardo is being chased by two DQ players and looks up to find me open and heading towards the centre of the goal. He hasn't lost faith in me yet. He passes the ball my way and I knock it between the posts with a nearside forehand, closing the gap in the score to three-two.

'Yes!' I cry, leaning forward to pat Gimli's neck as we circle back.

The DQ grooms look stunned, the Maycourt spectators are cheering and clapping with all their might, and my teammates are beaming at me. I seek out Mateo and find him watching with his arms folded across his chest, a knowing smile on his lips.

My confidence swells, my mind clears, and a wave of determination lifts me up off my saddle as I canter, my stick held high in the air in celebration. *I will spend the rest of the match chasing this feeling.*

The goal seems to have lit a fire of inspiration in the Maycourt team, as though my decision to believe in myself has rubbed off on the others, too. Within the next minute, Harry blocks a shot from DQ and Federico taps the ball on to Eduardo, who streaks up the side of the field with it, passing it to me as I charge up alongside him towards the centre. As the ball loses momentum, I hit it ahead, unfazed by the sound of galloping hooves approaching behind me, and with a quick glance to the goal, I swing back my stick and wallop it hard in the direction of the posts, cantering after it to make sure it stays on track, cheering as Gimli and I follow the ball straight through the posts.

'Go Ash!' Sam cries from the sidelines.

We enter the fourth and final chukka with a tied score at three-three, but I care more about the pride on my mum's face as I trot past her into position and the way Mateo is looking at me as though I've surpassed even his expectations today. I want to win, but at least now I feel like I deserve to, whichever way this match goes. At least now I feel like I've earned a place on this team as much as anyone else has.

The DQ number three marking me is looking a lot more tense and alarmed than he did in the first half of this match. It's hard not to feel a tad smug that I've baffled him. With the pressure mounting in the final chukka, the aggression rises and DQ start off with a devastatingly good goal as their number one weaves through our defence, but his cockiness gets the better of him and he crosses Federico moments later, awarding us a penalty.

We're back to a tie at four-four when a mishit sends the ball dribbling in my direction to the surprise of the others, who are still looking for it as I scoop it up and take it upfield. My opponent charges behind me for a ride-off, but I won't be intimidated, staying the course and managing to pass it across to Eduardo, who knocks it between our posts.

'*Fuck!*' bellows the DQ number three, shooting me glares as he mutters something else under his breath.

But I don't care what he's saying about me. My heart soars, adrenaline pumping hard through my body from the intensity of the ride-off, my hands trembling a little as I lift one of them to pat Gimli's neck, checking in with him as he breathes heavily, excited to go again.

'Oh my God,' I say in amazement. 'We can win this.'

Pumped with resentment, my DQ opponent is all over me for the last few minutes of the game and when I have the line, he comes thundering alongside me and crosses right in front, the whistle blowing for a foul as I have to pull up my pony before we collide.

'What the fuck do you think you're doing?' I yell furiously at him.

His jaw set, he ignores me, which angers me even more.

'Ignore him, he's a sore loser,' Eduardo says, coming up next to me. 'He's cost his team the match. You've got a penalty now and we're down to under a minute left. If you score this, they'll be two goals behind.'

Oh shit. I gulp, anger giving way to fear.

'Ash,' Eduardo begins, studying my expression, 'you know you can do this.'

I look at him as he holds my gaze and nods slowly, like someone trying to persuade you of something that's so obvious. *God, the pressure.* I move Gimli into position while the field falls silent, the spectators watching on in tense anticipation. I inhale a deep breath and try to shut out the noise in my head, the panicked thoughts knocking around in there like an uncontrollable, deflating balloon. I exhale shakily. And without another moment's hesitation, I swing my mallet and I strike the ball with a loud *thwack* that vibrates through my bones.

Twenty-Six

A cheer erupts in The Old Greyhound as Mum announces a round for everyone on her in honour of her daughter scoring 'England's best ever penalty'. Jasper and I share a look, both of us shaking with laughter as she tells a flustered Lucas to 'bloody well crack open that champagne', before placing a hand on the shoulder of Malcolm, leaning on the bar next to her, and asking him how he came to play polo.

'I think your mum has taken a shine to my teammate,' Mateo remarks, raising an eyebrow at them.

Everyone has come back here to celebrate, even the DQ team who played today and their supporters. It was the Maycourt lot who persuaded them to join us. While Ambrose may have looked as though he was suppressing a ball of fury ready to explode in his chest at any moment as he marched away to his helicopter, everyone else appreciated that today was ultimately a bit of friendly rivalry between stables equally passionate about ponies and the sport. DQ has already requested a re-match and Lady M has announced that if Ambrose is game, she'd happily make it an annual event. Jules is working up ideas for a trophy.

One of the best things about today has been Mateo getting on with Sam and Mum so well. It made my heart swell when I watched them chatting away on the sidelines earlier and Mum has already taken me aside to tell me she heartily approves. She's also hit it off with Lady M. When I think about it, they have a lot in common, even though they've had wildly different lives. Both underestimated in professions where they've been made to feel as if they have to earn their position there every day, while their male counterparts never question themselves and certainly never wonder if anyone else is. It makes sense that while my mum might be brash and Lady M is reserved, they'd be fans of one another.

What I wasn't expecting is how many *other* fans Mum would acquire today. When I emerged from the stables earlier, I noticed she was surrounded by Malcolm, Fitz and a couple of the DQ lads, and they were howling with laughter at one of her anecdotes.

My mum's funny. She's not *that* funny.

'If Molly lands a polo player tonight and I don't, I'll be fuming,' Sam says in response to Mateo's comment about Malcolm, surveying her options in the crowded bar.

I wrinkle my nose. 'Please don't talk about my mum "landing" anyone. If anything, it would be a... flirtation. Right? *Right?*'

'Have you seen your mum? She's brilliant, successful, authoritative and *hot*,' Sam points out. 'Malcolm would be punching big time. He knows that.'

'Ugh! Can we please change the subject?' I grumble. 'This is weird.'

She brightens, throwing an arm around me and squeezing me tight. 'Yes! How about we talk about how amazing you were out there today? Ash, you are a fucking pro!'

'She is.' Mateo grins, beaming at me, his eyes sparkling with pride.

I smile bashfully down at my shoes. 'Hardly. But it was fun.'

'And you proved to everyone that you were born to play!' Sam gushes, releasing me. 'If you'd never left London to escape to here, you might never have tried polo in your life. Isn't it funny how life has a way of working out?'

'It is funny,' I say, gazing up at Mateo, who winks at me.

'Ren made a huge mistake letting you go, Ash, but he knows that by now. I'm surprised he hasn't been calling you day and night begging for you back!' Sam exclaims, momentarily distracted by a handsome DQ groom who brushes past her, flashing her a winning smile.

'Why would he do that? I accidentally sabotaged the biggest launch of his career, remember,' I remind her drily.

She frowns at me as though I've lost the plot. 'Sabotaged? Honey, you made him. He should be thanking you! His sales are through the roof. Your… um… *involvement* made sure his brand became a household name. The publicity was more than he could have dreamt.'

'But it was bad publicity.'

'What, that a guy wearing his clothes can attract beautiful girls like you?' she says, eyebrows raised. 'That jacket that Chris wore to the launch, the one in the photographs? Sold out faster than any other piece. Trust me, Ash, I know you went through a shitshow, and I'll forever hate that disgusting pig of a tennis player – but Ren? That moron is laughing all the way to the bank.'

I blink at her, astonished. 'Wow. I did not see that coming.'

'Like I say, sometimes, things have a way of working out. You have to keep the faith.' Sam shrugs, accepting the three glasses of champagne that are passed to us from the chain of people surrounding the bar. She holds her glass aloft. 'To our polo champion, Ash. Cheers!'

'Cheers!' Mateo echoes, clinking his glass against hers.

'Thank you for coming today, Sam,' I say, taking a sip.

'Oh, the pleasure is *all* mine,' she murmurs suggestively, her shoulders rolling back and her wicked smile broadening as we're joined by Fitz and Eric.

'Here she is!' Eric cries, nudging me with his elbow. 'Feels good to win, doesn't it? That penalty was spectacular. Are you sure you've never played polo before you came here to Maycourt? It's a shame you didn't come to it sooner. A bit of training in Argentina, Chile, maybe Florida, and you could have made pro.'

I laugh. 'Thanks, but I'm happy to stay behind the scenes in the polo yard. There are a thousand grooms more skilled than me when it comes to polo, so if anyone should be backed to play, it's them. I was by far the weakest on the field today.'

'It's great that you feel so at home at Maycourt.' Eric smiles at me. 'I hope we'll see you back here next summer. Have you thought about what you're going to do in the meantime?'

I hesitate. 'Uh…'

'A lot of the grooms work for my aunt on a seasonal basis. Not as much to do around here during the winter months,' Fitz reminds me. 'They go where the high-goal polo is.'

'Singapore, Australia, and Argentina coming up,' Eric says.

'Eliza also hires grooms all year round,' Mateo notes.

'The all-year round positions are filled with grooms who have been here a long time,' Fitz says. 'Did she say this was a permanent position when she hired you?'

'We didn't go into specifics,' I say, biting my lip. 'She spoke about Serafina and the summer season...'

As I trail off, Eric clears his throat. 'Well, during today's performance, you made the whole Maycourt yard proud.'

'I think you played well,' Fitz decides, taking a sip of his drink. 'Room for improvement, but I'm sure Mateo will dedicate *more* than enough of his time to that.'

His comment is noticeably pointed. There's an edge to his tone. A dash of irritation, maybe? He's miffed about something and he's choosing not to hide it. Mateo picks up on it. I feel him tense up next to me.

'It wasn't just Mateo's teaching that got me out on the pitch today, but also his calming effect,' I say chirpily, refusing to rise to it. 'I was terrified, playing in front of all those people. I don't know how you lot do it!'

'The lead-up to the match is always worse than playing it,' Eric says, nodding in understanding. 'You've got to have the right mindset.'

'Composure under pressure,' Sam says.

He smiles at her. 'Exactly.'

'I work for *Studio* magazine and one of our writers, Iris Gray, profiles athletes. She often writes about their mental resilience and its importance to their success,' she explains.

'Interesting. Has she ever written a polo article?' Eric checks.

'I'm not sure; I don't think so. It would have to be a good story to get her attention,' Sam warns. 'A player having a big comeback or facing an unexpected new challenge. Something along those lines.'

'How about an inexperienced stable groom who blazes to the top at a polo yard and ends up replacing Fitz on the Maycourt team?' Eric says, grinning at me.

'I like it!' Sam cries, while I laugh it off.

Fitz balks. 'Oh, very funny. If anyone should be replaced, it's not me, is it? I'm not the one who's been bringing us down recently.'

'Whoa, it was only a joke,' Eric says hurriedly, slapping Fitz on the back and glancing nervously in Mateo's direction.

Mateo isn't laughing.

'What does that mean?' he asks sharply.

'It means that we're all aware that priorities have been changed,' Fitz answers, boldly refusing to wither under Mateo's glare and instead meeting it head-on. 'Come on, Mateo, you're not going to admit it to yourself? It's blindingly obvious to everyone else.'

'All right, Fitz,' Eric says, noticing Mateo's eyes flare with anger. 'Come on, you've had a drink or two today. Let's not bring down the—'

'I'm only saying what everyone is thinking,' Fitz claims with a shrug.

'And what is everyone thinking?' Mateo demands to know.

'That since you took up with your pretty groom, leading our polo team to victory is no longer your main concern,' he responds loftily, the alcohol giving him an air of confidence to say what he's obviously wanted to say for a while.

Sam looks at me, wide-eyed. I swallow, hit with a wave of guilt and embarrassment that I've been earmarked as a major distraction by the rest of the team.

Mateo looks to Eric. 'Is that what everyone thinks?'

Shifting uncomfortably, Eric opens his mouth to speak but Fitz intervenes: 'You're late to practices. You're distracted. We've been losing but you don't seem to mind. Revised tactics promised never come to fruition because you're busy doing... *other* things. I suppose it is the end of the season, but I thought every match mattered to you pros.'

'Every match does matter,' Mateo contends.

'Could have fooled me.' Fitz holds up his hands, the liquid sloshing over the top of his glass at the jerked movement and splashing on Eric's arm. 'Look, I'm no saint. It's not like I'm one to talk, and I'll admit it. I've had my fair share of delightful distractions, shall we say.' He winks at me and I shudder. 'But I'm also not the one being paid to do a job here. I'm not the one trying to get an all-expenses paid trip to Argentina. After we won the Gold Cup, I thought you'd be a shoo-in for every patron on the lookout, but I guess things change.'

A muscle in Mateo's jaw flicks.

'All right, let's drop it there, Fitz,' Eric says desperately. 'This is meant to be a celebration! We don't need this kind of talk.'

'Do you agree with him?' Mateo asks Eric directly, not letting it go. 'You think I've been bringing down the side?'

'Hey, we're a *team*,' Eric says kindly, prompting Sam to give him a wistful look. 'This isn't about individual play. We all have bad days. Maybe your focus has been a little bit off recently, but you want to know what I think? It's a good thing! It's healthy. I mean, let's face it,' he forces a chuckle, 'you were way too intense about polo before, mate.'

Mateo doesn't say anything. Eric realises his take hasn't been as welcomed as he'd hoped, his face falling.

For the rest of the night, Mateo is lost in deep, brooding thought.

'Hey, are you all right?' I check cautiously when I get him on his own.

'I'm fine,' he says with an almost-convincing smile.

But I've seen his real one and that's not it.

'Don't take what Fitz says to heart, Mateo,' I beg him, reaching for his hand. 'He's always been jealous of you and he's only saying things to take the heat off of him. He's late to everything! And never focused.'

'Eric didn't deny that things have changed.'

'Yes, but—'

'It's fine, Ash, I'm okay,' he assures me, squeezing my fingers. 'Maybe I have been a little too invested in training you for the grooms' match, but it's over now. Polo can go back to being my main priority.'

Knowing he's thrown tonight by this revelation from his teammates, I try not to read into that statement too much. Malcolm appears next to us to ask if we're up for another round. Mateo drops my hand, my fingers cold without his grasp.

'No, thank you. Early morning tomorrow,' he says, looking around for his jacket. 'Apparently, I have a lot of catching up to do.'

Twenty-Seven

In the final match before we fly to play for the Sotogrande Gold Cup mid-August, Maycourt lose to the Titans at their club with a humbling score of eleven goals to six. My heart sinks as Mateo hands Serafina over to Eduardo and comes storming off the pitch, undoing his helmet and yanking it from his head as he mutters a string of expletives in Spanish. I make the mistake of accosting him – I should wait until he's cooled down, but the pull in me to speak to him is too strong.

My desperation to engage with him is heightened by how he's been gradually distancing himself from me ever since the night of the grooms' match.

He didn't try to pretend that things hadn't changed; he told me it might be best if we don't spend every evening together so he could get early nights and be on better form first thing in the morning. He's become a little less affectionate with me in the yard, but he said that was because he needed to boost morale for the rest of the team, and he needed them to know that he wasn't distracted at work. He's gradually pulling away more and more to the point where I think it's actually making his performance worse. He won't let me comfort him when he loses; he's harder on himself, which only adds to his frustration; he's actively avoiding me during half-times or even after stick and ball. It's like he doesn't want anyone thinking I'm in his ear.

But every athlete needs their support team.

'I'm sorry about today,' I say, falling into step with him as he barely acknowledges me. 'You played so well in the first chukka. We were leading and—'

'I wasn't focused.'

'You were focused; it was a bit of bad luck. That foul in the third chukka wasn't completely your fault in my opinion and I thought it was great that you were playing with a bit more aggression.'

He shakes his head.

'Mateo, it was one match.'

He stops abruptly, turning to me. 'It wasn't one match, Ash. It's been the last few. Soto is right round the corner. If I keep playing like this, no patron with a brain is going to sign me to their team. I'm not showing any consistency. I'm... distracted.'

I bristle. 'You're acting as though you were the only person who lost today. Like the responsibility is all on you.'

'Those guys were right,' he says, running his fingers through his hair. 'I've lost my way. I should have ended the UK season on a high. It's finishing on a disaster.'

'That's not true. Fitz said a stupid comment when he was drunk and you've let him get to you! He's inside your head; that's why you're not playing at the top of your game. You need to be kinder to yourself.'

'This is my career!' he cries, emphasising his point by pointing his helmet at me. 'You know how this goes. I'm signed for a season, Ash. I can't just do whatever I want and take some days off to be *kind* to myself.'

'That's not what I'm saying and you know it.'

'Everything is at stake. We won the Gold Cup. We should be seen as a serious threat. Instead,' he gestures to the opposing team high-fiving their supporters, 'we've become a joke.'

I try to reach for his hand but he pulls away. My cheeks flush at the rejection.

'Ash, if I want to go to Argentina, I need to prove I'm not a fuck-up,' he mumbles.

'Oh my God, you are not a fuck-up!' I say in exasperation. 'It is *one match*, Mateo.'

'As a polo player, you're only as good as your last match. Or your last two or three. All of those, I've lost.'

'You're a great player. You have an amazing handicap.'

'Not for long. Fuck's sake. How did this happen? How did I let this happen?'

'You need to fight the demons in your head telling you you're not good enough.'

He sighs heavily. 'What I need is some time to think about my mistakes during that play. I'm sorry, we'll talk later, okay?'

My stomach twisted into a knot, I nod, letting him walk away from me. I wait a moment to collect myself and then turn around to almost stride straight into Basilio, who has sauntered over to me without me realising. He's here to watch the youngest player on the Titans team, a Brit named Tom, who quit school at sixteen to complete several stints in polo yards abroad before returning a top-league player by the age of twenty. This is his first season with the Titans, but everyone knows Ambrose has been sniffing around him.

'Ash,' Basilio says with a dashing smile, placing a warm hand on my arm as he gives me a kiss on each cheek accompanied by a waft of expensive cologne. 'I'm sorry I couldn't stick around after the grooms' match. You played beautifully.'

'Thanks,' I mumble, eyes downcast.

He sticks his hands in his pockets. 'Forgive me. I heard your argument with Mateo.'

'It wasn't an argument. He's upset from the match.'

'I wanted to make sure you're all right.'

'I'm fine. It was nothing.'

Sympathy flashes across his expression. 'You can't blame yourself, you know that, right? Mateo is who he is. No one can change him. Not even someone like you. Others can achieve balance, but Mateo has always felt like he had something to prove and there was never any time for anything else in his life. I tried to warn you...'

'He's dedicated,' I state, immediately defensive. 'Unlike other people in this sport, he wasn't handed the opportunity on a plate. He had to work hard to get where he is. I admire that and I understand that that means losses hit harder. He doesn't take it for granted.'

'Believe me, Ash, I of all people admire his work ethic,' Basilio says in a serious voice. 'But don't you see? That only serves to prove my point. For Mateo, polo is life. It always has been; it always will be. Sure, he might have got caught up in something that made him forget it, but in the end, he will always come back to putting polo first. No one can compete with that.'

Chilled to the bone at the hard-hitting truth, I blink back tears.

'You want my honest opinion? I swear, no agenda here,' he claims, raising his hands up. 'Mateo is an idiot. There have been times this season that I've never seen him play better. I think that's because of you. If he pushes you away, he'll lose the momentum you've inspired. It's like he found his lucky charm in you.'

I hang my head. 'I don't think so.'

'Ash, look at me.' He waits until I've forced myself to bring my gaze to meet his. 'Just because Mateo can't see what he has, it doesn't mean no one else can.'

He leans in to give me a kiss on the cheek, lingering a moment too long, as though considering something before thinking better of it and pulling away. He emits a small sigh.

'I hope I'll see you in Spain,' he says, before strolling towards his car, looking back over his shoulder at me as he goes.

I return to the ponies, hurt, rattled and confused, and with the sense of foreboding that's been niggling at me for days thumping at my heart, demanding my full attention.

The Ayala Polo Club is a beautiful setting with long stretches of trees around the polo fields providing shade for the pony lines and immaculate stables and pitches. Spectators are dedicated to cooling their faces with fans, or play schedules if they're less organised, the stands a sea of flushed cheeks, dark sunglasses and Panama hats.

In the sweltering heat of Sotogrande in August, the ponies are changed during chukkas at a constant rate, led from the pitch with their coats glistening with sweat, their nostrils flaring, exhausted from just a few minutes of thundering across the ground at speed. Cooling them down is, like always, a military operation, but there's absolutely no room for mistakes and the Maycourt grooms and vets work with sharp focus throughout the first match to make sure the ponies are well looked after. I barely catch a glimpse of Mateo playing and am too busy to speak to him in between. There's a loud cheer at the end of the match and I have no clue who might have won, having forgotten to check the scoreboard the last time I passed it. When I look up to see our team congratulating one another, I give a nod of satisfaction before wiping the sheen of sweat from my forehead with the back of my hand and returning to scraping the water from Violet's steaming coat. My only moment of pause is when I hear Fitz's bellowing voice floating across the pony lines:

'He's back! Now, *that's* more like the Mateo we know.'

Everything seems calm early the next morning when I'm exercising the ponies. I feel better after getting an early night last night – by the time we'd finished with the ponies, it was late and all the grooms were exhausted. I'd had to message Mateo to let him know I'd be staying at my hotel which is much closer to the stables. I was tired, sweaty, dirty, desperate for a shower and fantasising about climbing into bed and passing out, which is essentially what I did as soon as I got back. I knew he wouldn't mind. He's got an important networking event tomorrow with patrons he thinks might be considering him for Argentina, so I knew he'd be happy to be well-rested for that – he's talked more about that party than the actual tournament.

I'd slept solidly the moment my head hit the pillow and feel refreshed and in a brighter mood. Walking the ponies under glorious sunshine and clear, blue skies also helps.

When I've finished the sets, I grab some water and check my phone, laughing with Jules over Violet playing up with her this morning.

But as I notice my screen, my blood runs cold.

While I've been out this morning, I've received a *lot* of messages. Too many. An absurdly unusual amount. And I know what that means. I've been here before. No one is this popular. You don't get this many people messaging you unless you're in the news. At a glance, I can tell that a lot of the messages are people asking me if I'm all right. Others are calling Chris Courtney a host of insulting names. My chest feels tight as I open my web browser and google his name. A list of fresh news stories appears. My fingers trembling, I click on the top one.

'She pursued me and I was weak enough to give in.'

Exclusive extracts from Chris Courtney's new memoir to be released in time for Christmas.

In the tennis star's new memoirs, he details the challenges he's faced and overcome in his extraordinary career. In this candid and soul-baring book, Courtney takes us on the journey of his life, from the local tennis courts that offered him an escape from his parents' embittered divorce as a child, to rising up the ranks and winning international championships, to meeting the woman who would save him from the empty clutches of fame and who he'd go on to marry, to one scandalous photograph of a misguided affair that threatened to destroy it all. A raw and commendably honest account, Courtney leaves no stone unturned.

In this exclusive book excerpt, we're treated to a glimpse into the mind of a broken man whose world explodes when his drunken kiss with fashion assistant Ashley Slater is exposed: 'Ashley Slater is the kind of girl who, if you haven't noticed her, she'll make sure you do. She'd made no secret of her desires from the moment we met and one night in the blurry haze of alcohol, I let my guard down. That's when she made her move. Let me take you back to my first meeting with Ren, a talented designer who

I feel too sick to read on, my hand trembling as I lower my phone.

'Jules, I… I have to go back to the hotel. I don't feel well,' I say, my voice wavering as I gather up my things. 'Is that okay?'

'Sure, everything here is sorted.' She frowns at me and I can understand her confusion seeing as moments ago, I was completely normal. 'You all right? Maybe it's too much sun.'

'I need to lie down for a bit. I'll see you later.'

My head in a whirl, I manage to get back to the hotel where I sit down on the edge of the bed and close my eyes to focus on deep breaths. *Oh my God*. How could he do this? I know why he's doing it: money. A book like that coming out so quickly after the scandal is bound to sell well. But to write such horrible, blatant and *unnecessary* lies about me. To make out as though I was the predator and he the innocent prey. Does he dislike me so much? Does he really think I deserve this? Does he care what kind of impact this is going to have on my life? A life I'd managed to piece back together after it fell apart just months ago?

As I begin to spiral, a voice in the back of my head speaks up: *I won't let him win.*

I grip the edge of the bed in determination, like I'm clinging to a cliff edge I refuse to fall from. The people that matter will see through this. I won't let a coward like him knock me down, I just won't, not when I've come so far.

My phone vibrates relentlessly until I reach for it and see Mateo has tried calling.

He's messaged, too:

Are you OK? Jules says you've gone back to hotel xx

My fingers hover over my screen. He tries calling again, but I can't pick up. If I speak to him, I'll crack, I know I will. And I don't want to. Not quite yet. He rings off. He's been practising with the team this morning before the big event. He hasn't seen the story yet, but he will soon and then he'll know why I had to get out of there.

He messages again:

Going into a meeting now with a team sponsor, then we've got the party. Will try calling later xx

As I try to think of what to reply to him, my phone continues to buzz in my hand as more people look at the news and gossip columns today. I feel overwhelmed and quickly reply to Mateo:

I'm fine, speak later xx

before turning off my phone.

Silence rings through the room. I go back to focusing on my breathing.

Collecting myself and needing something to do, I stand up and go run myself a bath. It's when I immerse myself in the comforting hot water that my strength buckles. The tears spill down my cheeks and I let my face crumple as I tip my head back to rest it on the tub. *I wish Mateo were here.* He's who I need right now. I need him to come here and tell me that everything is going to be okay.

When I'm out the bath, my head pounding from the heat and all the crying, I will myself to turn my phone back on. I'm hoping that he's seen the story by now so I don't have to tell him about it. But he must still be in his meeting as there's no more messages from him.

My heart sinks. I turn on the TV to some rubbish and climb under my covers.

When Mateo finally messages, I read it twice to make sure I'm reading it right:

Just heard about the memoirs. Can't believe it. I'm at the networking event and then I'll come to you straight after xxx

I thought he'd come straight away. Why wouldn't he come straight away? Surely he knows how serious this is.

How hurtful it is. After everything, _surely_ he knows. As more tears escape the corners of my eyes, I realise that he must know but he's choosing to stay because this event is important to his career. And polo always comes first.

I tell him not to come over. I tell him I'd rather be on my own.

And later that afternoon, when someone posts a photo on our Maycourt Grooms WhatsApp group of the team on what looks like a massive yacht, I look at Mateo in the middle holding a drink in the sunshine, surrounded by players and a host of rich, important-looking people I don't recognise, and I cry some more.

Twenty-Eight

The next morning, I'm crouched down, bandaging Byron's legs for the match, when I feel the presence of someone behind me. I assume it's Mateo and tense, pretending I don't know he's there, waiting for him to speak first.

'Ash, hi.'

It's not Mateo's voice. It's Basilio. I glance over my shoulder to make sure and then straighten, masking my disappointment with a polite smile.

'Hi, Basilio.'

He looks extremely concerned, studying my face intently. 'I hope you don't mind me disturbing you. I only wanted to check that you were okay. I saw the news yesterday and I was… shocked. For someone to do such a thing. He is scum.'

I pat Byron's neck as he snorts.

'I'm fine, thank you,' I say briskly.

'If you need someone to talk to,' he gestures to himself, 'I'm here. I know it's not the same, but I once had a horrible column written about me in a polo publication and I was devastated. I can't even imagine how it feels.'

My eyes fall to my shoes as I shift my weight from one leg to the other.

'But I don't want you to think that no one here cares about you. So, if you want to talk about it, please don't think that because I'm in DQ and you're in Maycourt, we can't.'

I look up at him, fixing a smile. 'Thanks. How are you feeling about the match today?'

After the slog of getting through yesterday in one piece, I'm desperate to talk about anything other than this. Jules messaged to say that if I needed today off, I could have it, but I wanted to keep busy. I needed to. So I came to the stables this morning with my game face on and thankfully, aside from Jules checking in, no one else has mentioned it. I'm hoping from the way I've thrown myself into things this morning, they know I'd rather pretend like nothing had happened. A few pointed looks and whispers from the grooms on other teams this morning have been unavoidable and unsurprising – every article announcing Chris's memoirs has mentioned me, reiterating that after losing my job from the fallout of the scandal, I now work at the Maycourt Polo yard.

As Mum told me on the phone yesterday, this is just another wave for me to ride out and I've already proven I can do it once. I can do it again.

'I'm feeling confident,' Basilio answers, reaching up to pat Byron. 'What about Maycourt? I hope you're planning on giving us a bit of a challenge out there today.'

'No doubt about it.'

The corners of his lips twitch. 'Should be an entertaining match, then.'

'Certainly for our side.'

His smile breaks and he chuckles. 'Don't count on it, Ash.'

We're interrupted by Mateo, who's marching past on the hunt for something when he stops dead in his tracks on seeing us. His expression darkens as he comes over.

'I've been looking for you,' he says to me before glowering at Basilio. 'Shouldn't you be warming up with your own team?'

Basilio sighs tiredly. 'Good morning to you, too, Mateo. How did you enjoy the party the other night? You seemed to be having a great time. I was sorry not to see you there, Ash.'

I frown at him. 'What party?'

'The night before last. It was organised by one of the sponsors of the tournament at a bar on the marina,' Basilio explains, his eyebrows knitting together in confusion. 'You didn't know about it? The Maycourt team were all there.'

'It was the night you went to bed early,' Mateo tells me. 'You messaged to let me know you'd be going straight back to the hotel and the others persuaded me to go last minute.'

I don't say anything, irrationally bothered that I didn't know anything about it.

'And we missed you yesterday on the yacht, Ash,' Basilio adds, 'but I appreciate you had other things on your mind.' His eyes flicker across to Mateo. 'I hope you didn't have to go through it all alone.'

'I think it's time you go,' Mateo says bluntly. 'I would like to speak to Ash.'

Basilio nods. 'Of course. See you on the field.'

Smiling gently at me, he strolls off. My jaw tensing, I avoid looking at Mateo, instead returning my attention to Byron and crouching down to finish bandaging his legs.

Mateo's voice, soft and worried, comes floating above me. 'How are you?'

'I'm fine,' I respond coldly.

'I haven't seen you all morning.'

'I've been working.'

'I wanted to talk to you about yesterday.'

I finish securing the bandage and straighten, moving across to the other leg. 'I don't want to talk about it today.'

There's a moment's pause. 'You should have let me come over,' he says dismally.

'You were busy.'

'Ash,' he says, coming round to join me on the other side of Byron, 'would you stop doing that for a second so we can talk?'

'There's a lot to do, Mateo.'

'You can take a moment,' he presses.

With a reluctant sigh, I stand up to face him. His eyes search mine, his brow furrowed in concentration. I can tell he's puzzled by the way I'm acting and that bothers me.

'Talk to me,' he says gently.

'I've told you,' I say, avoiding his eye contact by glancing around at the goings-on of the other grooms, 'I'd rather not talk about it now. It happened, I've dealt with it, I'm moving on. No point in dwelling on it. And now definitely isn't the time.'

'I want to make sure you're okay,' he says, concern deepening the creases on his forehead. 'You have no idea how worried I was yesterday. You wouldn't let me see you, you turned off your phone—'

'I was being inundated by messages from reporters asking me for comment, as well as friends and family who had read nasty things about me in the press. Of course I turned off my phone,' I say bluntly.

'You shouldn't have been alone. You should have let me come over.'

Trying to keep my temper, I press my lips together and inhale deeply. 'Stop saying it like that,' I mutter.

'What?'

I bring my eyes up to meet his, speaking in a low, sharp voice. 'You keep saying that I wouldn't let you come over. As though *I* was the one making the choices yesterday.'

He stares at me, baffled. 'Ash, I said I'd come and you told me not to.'

'You had a choice to leave the party and you chose not to.'

'What? What do you mean?'

'I think I'm being clear, Mateo,' I say sternly, my thoughts clear and concise having dwelled on them for the whole of yesterday and this morning. 'You found out what had happened. You knew what the consequences would be. And instead of coming to me, you chose to stay at the party.'

'I said I would come!'

'*After* the party.'

'I was already at the event; I couldn't walk out straight away.'

'Why not?' I ask, lifting my chin.

He puts his hands on his hips. 'I'm sorry?'

'Why not? Why couldn't you walk out straight away? As soon as you heard, why weren't you running off that yacht and coming to my hotel? Were there barriers stopping you? Guards?'

'*Guards?*' he splutters, bewildered. 'Don't be... Of course not! But it would have been… rude to the hosts. And the team. We were there together, you know it was an important event for everyone.'

'It was important for your career, you mean.'

He looks me straight in the eye, swallowing. 'Yes. It was important for my career. You know that. But that doesn't mean—'

'I know what it means, Mateo,' I say wearily, walking away, wanting out of this conversation. Suddenly, I feel completely drained.

'Ash, wait,' he says, falling into step with me, keeping his voice low as we pass by others on the way to the stables. 'If I'd known you'd feel upset by this, I would have left. I was so worried about you. I wanted to see you, but from your messages, you made it clear you didn't want to see me or anyone else. I called you so many times. I wanted to come to the hotel to be with you.'

'Once you'd done enough schmoozing to secure a place on a team for Argentina.'

'That's not what I—'

'You know what I find funny, Mateo?' I say without looking at him, still marching onwards, the frustration and anger that's been building recently starting to spill out of my mouth before I can decide whether or not it's a good idea. 'I find it funny that spending time with me is distracting for your work, but yachts and parties aren't.'

'What are you *talking* about?' he asks earnestly, looking completely thrown by my comment, which is equally confusing to me.

'You know what, you need to go prepare for the match and so do I,' I decide, as we reach the stables where Eduardo is directing other grooms and I stop to face Mateo head-on, my volume dipping. 'Now isn't the time for this.'

'I'm still trying to understand what *this* is,' he confesses. 'I'm sorry if you think I wasn't there for you yesterday, believe me, I tried to be. But you also have to understand that polo isn't just about how you play on the field. I've told you before how important it is to attend these events to meet the right people.'

'Yes.' I sigh crossly, tucking a loose tendril of hair behind my ear. 'I *know*.'

'So how can you be so angry at me?' he asks, irritated now.

His obvious impatience and peevishness at the situation makes things worse. A fiery rush of resentment swells in my chest.

'Because, Mateo,' I begin in a low, sharp tone, 'if things had been switched and it was you in the news and me on that yacht, *guards* wouldn't have stopped me running to you.'

His lips parted, he finds himself unable to respond. Without waiting for him to gather his thoughts, I turn on my heel and march to Eduardo, asking him where he needs me next. Mateo doesn't follow me and I don't speak to him again before the match.

'What the fuck is going on out there?' Jules mutters as we walk the ponies round during their cool-down period in the sixth and final chukka.

It's a good question and one I've been asking myself ever since the start of the Maycourt versus DQ match. The team are all over the place; no one seems to be listening to each other and rather than being supportive, they're snapping irritably at one another. Even Eric has lost his cool today, and DQ has taken advantage of our mess, leading the game since it began. We're twelve-six down and it seems impossible that we'll catch up now.

At the heart of this turbulent wreckage of teamplay is Mateo, who seems to be pissed off with absolutely everybody, whether they're on his side or not. He's given away two penalties to DQ this match and the umpires are getting shirty at his combative attitude, and he's gone wide on three attempts at goal by hitting the ball way too hard.

In the final moments of the match, as though in a last-ditch attempt not to let DQ streak any further ahead than they are, Mateo lumps himself in with our defence and goes to ride-off Basilio with ferocious energy and rage, like he's been waiting for this all match. My breath catches as I watch their ponies thunder down the field together, neither of them giving in. Basilio goes for the pass, knocking the ball across to his teammate and almost coming out of his saddle thanks to the pressure from Mateo and only just managing to keep his balance, crying out for a foul. Mateo yells something over his shoulder as he follows the ball, only to witness the DQ number two knock it through the goal.

We lose thirteen-six.

Twenty-Nine

After that match, none of the Maycourt team are in a mood to party, except maybe for Fitz, who is always in the mood to party. But Lady M insists that we make an appearance at the event tonight hosted by the team's major sponsor at the exclusive beach club, La Reserva Club de Sotogrande. It's a breathtaking space, the decking around the turquoise-blue man-made lagoon bathed in a warm-orange glow of lanterns, candles and festoon lights draped from the palm trees. Smartly dressed waiters serve drinks in crystal glasses, and the crooning singer of the live jazz band providing background music to the guests' conversation is setting a classy tone for the evening – although I spot a DJ checking his decks at a booth on the other side of the space, so I'm guessing things get livelier later.

After a dismal couple of days, it was calming to put the time in to doing my make-up and hair, and getting into a dress that makes me feel good about myself. I knew that the Sotogrande post-polo social scene was high glamour, so I'd packed appropriately: tonight, I'm wearing a plunged neckline, black, figure-hugging dress with towering heels, statement drop earrings and my hair swept over one shoulder styled in gentle waves.

Arriving on my own, I accept a cocktail and walk out onto the decking, hoping to see someone I know. I'm in luck: Malcolm and Eric, both looking good in their tuxedos, are standing nearby with Jules in a stunning gold satin number. Eric spots me and brightens, mouthing, 'Wow,' at me, before waving me over to join them.

'Tough day today, team,' Eric says, sticking a hand in his pocket.

'It happens,' Jules says with a shrug.

'Shame it happened on our final match all together,' Malcolm muses. 'Mateo and I are off to France to play with another team; Eric is headed for Santa Barbara; and God knows how Fitzy will be spending his time but I imagine the London bars are about to see their revenue shoot up. It would have been good to part ways on a high.'

'We can still do that,' Jules counters, holding her glass aloft.

'Jules is right,' Eric says, slapping Malcolm on the back. 'We've still got tonight. And it's been one hell of a season. A few trophies under our belt.'

We echo Jules and lift our glasses, lightly clinking them together. Before we can even take a sip, Fitz appears at my side out of nowhere, espresso martini in hand.

'What are we toasting to?' he asks eagerly.

'Are your ears finely attuned to the sound of glasses clinking?' I ask, amazed. 'Where did you even come from?'

'It's my superpower, Ashley. If there's a chance someone might be enjoying a tipple, I'm there at their side in a flash to make sure they're doing it right – and getting in a fresh round for yours truly,' he says, adjusting his bow tie.

'We should toast to one hell of a summer.' Eric smiles. 'There have been ups and downs, but it's been an honour to play with you lot this year. Heaps of fun.'

'Hear, hear!' Malcolm cries. 'We won the Queen's Cup and Cowdray Gold Cup, for Christ's sake!'

'And here's to the grooms who keep everything running,' Jules says, smirking at me.

We lift our glasses and carefully – these are full of expertly crafted, out-of-this-world delicious cocktails, not one drop wanting to be wasted – tap them against one another's.

'We're down one,' Eric notes after sipping his drink, craning his neck to scan the party. 'Where's Mateo? I thought I saw him earlier.'

'He's with Mum, being introduced to what's-his-name,' Jules says, jerking her head to the side where a group of people are standing, their backs to us. 'The shipping company director who's taking a team to Argentina.'

'Go interrupt them and drag him over here, would you, Ash?' Malcolm says jovially.

'I think we both know I wouldn't succeed at that,' I say with a light laugh.

If any of them catch my bitterness, they don't comment on it.

The toast has done a good job of lifting spirits and we steam into the evening with more enthusiasm than expected, consuming the cocktails at a faster rate than we should. Putting aside the emotional hazards of the last couple of days, I'm able to finally enjoy the glamour of Sotogrande, talking and laughing with friends I might find myself missing.

I've grown quite fond of these idiots. Will I miss Fitz? Doubtful. But he is such a ridiculous character that he brings a lot of laughs, whether he means to or not. Malcolm is a bit of a lovable buffoon and Eric is soft as anything. I hope I'll see them in the yard again, soon. That is, if I'll even be there. I haven't been brave enough to broach the subject with Lady M or Jules, yet. This was never meant to be long-term. Sussex was never meant to be long-term. I can't stay with Jasper forever, no matter how much he insists I can. The season is ending and everyone is looking to the future. At some point, I need to make a decision, too.

But not tonight.

While Malcolm and Fitz pounce on the DJ, attempting to persuade him to give them the microphone so they can sing along, I slip away to the bathroom, happy to miss any efforts they make to embarrass themselves amongst this high-society crowd. Mateo has been so caught up in his conversation, he hasn't even noticed I've arrived yet, and I'm determined not to be the one to seek him out. I want him to know I'm still annoyed at him.

Emerging from the bathroom, my heels clack along the decking by the water as I head for one of the bars, but I spy a familiar face on my way there. Basilio glances my way and double takes, his eyes widening. He excuses himself from the group of people he's standing with and comes over to greet me.

'Wow,' he says, placing a hand over his heart as he gazes at me. 'You are stunning.'

'Congratulations on reaching the final.'

'Thank you. Will you be there?'

'I don't think so. We'll probably be heading home now we're out of the tournament.'

'You should stay. The party after the final is always a good one,' he says, his hand brushing against my arm.

From his bloodshot eyes and the way he's standing a little too close, I can guess that our team isn't the only one that's been enjoying the cocktails tonight. I take a small step back.

'I bet. But there will be lots to do at the yard, so hopefully, I'll be needed there,' I say regretfully, even though I'm not regretful at all.

He quirks a brow. 'Hopefully? You're worried you won't have a job there after the season? That might be a good thing. You know, Ambrose has been wanting you on the DQ yard ever since the grooms' match.'

I shift uncomfortably. 'Basilio—'

'I'm serious! He was impressed with the way the ponies responded to you, and your instinct around them.' He takes a step closer, leaning in conspiratorially. 'The best polo yards are the ones with the best grooms.'

'That I agree with.'

'So, you should consider it.' The corner of his mouth hitches up. 'Why not?'

The way he's looking at me prompts me to hug my waist self-consciously, suddenly feeling very exposed. I hear heavy footsteps march up behind me and Mateo appears at my side, his expression thunderous. The tension between them feels sharper than ever after their tussle on the polo field today.

'Mateo!' Basilio cries, like greeting an old friend, before a smirk appears on his lips. 'I hope you're not too sore after your loss today.'

'You've got a lot of nerve,' he snarls.

'Oh, oh, oh, I see, so this is how it's going to go.' Basilio gestures at Mateo. 'Most players are able to leave rivalry on the pitch. Only those who are weak bring it away with them. You should chill, Mateo. This is a nice party.'

'Why is it that whenever my back is turned for a moment, I find you hovering around Ash like a hungry little mosquito?' he says through gritted teeth, his eyes flaring with fury.

Basilio snorts at the analogy.

'Mateo, it's okay, we were just talking,' I say quietly, glancing nervously around the party. 'Let's go.'

'What's wrong, Mateo?' Basilio jabs, relishing the confrontation. 'Worried that Ash is going to come to her senses and realise that she should be with a man who genuinely cares about her? One that can provide for her?'

'Okay, stop it,' I cut in sharply, holding up my hands, 'I don't—'

'You know *nothing* about her,' Mateo seethes.

'I know that she deserves better than you. No wonder she's thinking about moving to the DQ yard, somewhere she'd be valued.'

'*What?*' My jaw drops open. 'I'm not thinking that! Basilio, that's completely—'

'How long are you going to drag this on for, Mateo? How long are you going to lead her on until you break her heart?' he says, taking a step closer to Mateo, whose chin is lifted and fists clenched, the two of them facing off and drawing attention from the other guests now. 'We both know the relationship is past the point of saving. It's always the same with you, isn't it.'

I watch Mateo's jaw tick. Eric and Malcolm have caught

whiff of something going on and come casually strolling over, ready to intervene. Lady M glances over mid-conversation and a flicker of concern crosses her expression.

'Guys, *please*,' I plead, cheeks flushing at being the focal point of a scene.

'Don't talk about me and Ash again,' Mateo growls, low and threatening, ignoring me.

'Or what?' Basilio scoffs, bringing his face closer. '*Or what, Mateo?*'

'Come on, mate,' Eric says quietly at Mateo's shoulder, taking his arm in an attempt to pull him back but Mateo shakes him off, his eyes locked on Basilio.

'You're pathetic,' Basilio sneers, looking him up and down. 'As pathetic now as you were when you first arrived at Rossi's. Never quite making the mark. I proved it to you yet again today. No matter how good you get, you'll never be the player you want to be. The player *she* wanted you to be.'

Mateo flinches, pain and horror flashing in his eyes. He grabs the lapels of Basilio's jacket in his fists, dragging him towards him. A ripple of gasps floods through the party.

'Mateo, no!' I cry, grabbing one of his arms as Eric places his hand on the other. 'Stop. *Please*. Stop it.'

'He's not worth it,' Eric hisses through gritted teeth. 'Come on, man, there are patrons here. Let him go.'

After a moment of roaring silence, during which everyone holds their breath, Mateo relaxes his grip on Basilio's jacket, releasing him. Malcolm pats Mateo on the back and Eric nods, while I feel dizzy with relief. I try to take his hand but he bats all of us away. Basilio laughs, straightening his jacket and running a hand through his hair.

His jaw tense and his chest rising with a long, deep breath, Mateo slowly turns around and starts to walk away, making it clear he doesn't want anyone with him.

'Yes, off you go, Mateo,' Basilio taunts, unable to leave well enough alone, 'and don't worry. I'll take care of Ash.'

Mateo stops in his tracks. *Oh no.*

Basilio sneers triumphantly.

'I'll show her what it's like to be a real man, not a lost little fuck-up of a boy still trying to make his mummy proud.'

Spinning round, Mateo strides back over to him, swings his arm back and, before anyone can intervene, punches Basilio square in the jaw so hard, he stumbles backwards and, with a yelp, tumbles into the lagoon with a loud splash. I clasp my hands over my mouth in shock, gasps and cries come up from our captivated audience, and Eric groans as Basilio splutters and coughs, wiping his face with his hands as he finds his footing beneath the water.

'You fucking—' Basilio begins, but Mateo cuts him off, standing by the edge and pointing a finger down at him.

'Don't ever talk about my mother again. *Ever,*' he says, before he shakes his hand out and storms away, the crowd of guests parting to make way for him as he leaves.

Thirty

'Mateo, wait,' I call out, trying to keep up with his strides as I follow him in my heels out of the club and onto the road.

He finally stops, burying his face in his hands and letting out a cry of frustration. He runs his hands through his hair before dropping them despondently to his sides. The pause gives me time to catch up and step round to face him, my breath coming thick and fast as my heart pounds hard against my chest, shock and adrenaline pumping through my veins.

'I shouldn't have punched him,' he says, looking pained and glancing down at his knuckles, flushed pink from the contact with Basilio's jaw. 'There were important people in that party. I should have walked away.'

'Just... take a moment to calm down,' I advise as he shakes his head, pacing back and forth.

'I'm fine.'

'Clearly, you're not.'

'I'm *fine*.'

Unable to keep still, he walks about, agitated, shaking out his hand and muttering in Spanish under his breath. I watch him, wondering what to say.

'Basilio was out of line,' I reason. 'He was trying to—'

'Why didn't you tell me that you were thinking of moving to DQ? Why didn't you tell me they'd offered you a position there?' he asks gruffly, barely looking at me.

'They haven't! He's screwing with you, Mateo. He's drunk.'

'But you *had* talked about it.'

'No!'

'But he offered you a job,' he seethes, shaking his head in disbelief. 'Again.'

'Nothing formal. Mateo, trust me, you're blowing this out of proportion. Basilio said that to hurt you. He'd literally just mentioned that if I was worried about my future at Maycourt, then maybe I could consider other stables like DQ which might have all-round positions. It was barely a conversation.'

'You're thinking of leaving Maycourt.'

'I... I don't know. I don't want to, but I might have to. This was only meant to be temporary and Lady M never discussed anything further.' I put a hand on my hip. 'But this isn't about me.'

'Of course it's about you,' he contends, coming to a halt in front of me, his eyes flaring with anger and pain. 'He won't leave you alone! He knows how to hurt me and he doesn't fucking hold back, does he? What was he saying to you?'

'Nothing important.'

'I saw him touching you. He was all over you.'

'He was drunk,' I repeat, exasperated.

'Any chance to fuck with me, he'll take it.' He shakes his head dismally. 'If it weren't for him, we wouldn't have argued this morning and I wouldn't have lost my temper during our match today. I played right into his plan.'

I frown at him. 'What?'

'He knew what he was doing,' he tells me eagerly, as though Basilio is some great evil mastermind and we've foiled his plotting together. 'He knows that there are two ways he can fuck with my head.' He counts them out on his fingers. 'My mother and you. My only weaknesses.' He throws his hands in the air. 'And I let him. I fucking *let* him.'

He picks up his pacing and muttering in Spanish again. I watch him in silence for a few moments as he does so, my brain trying to get my thoughts into a sensible order, a task not helped by those delicious summer-in-a-glass cocktails I helped myself to earlier.

'You think Basilio is the reason we argued?' I say eventually.

'Yes! It's always him.'

'We didn't argue because of Basilio,' I state, my brow creasing in confusion that he would have been labouring under this impression. 'We argued because of us.'

He stops, lifting his head to look at me.

'Is that how you really see me, Mateo?' I ask calmly. 'As a weakness?'

He sighs heavily.

'Am I a problem for you?' I continue, narrowing my eyes at him. 'A threat that your enemies can prey on to hurt your career?'

'That's not what I…'

My stomach twists as he trails off.

'I think it is what you meant,' I say quietly, before taking a deep breath. 'We didn't argue because of anything Basilio said. We argued because you're oblivious to me being angry at you for not coming to see me yesterday.'

'I tried! How was I supposed to know that you wanted the opposite of what you said? I'm not a mind-reader! You told me you wanted to be alone!'

'Because by then, I felt too upset to talk to you,' I erupt. 'I *needed* you, Mateo. My ex had just announced to the world that he was releasing a book that details our relationship and, unsurprisingly, apparently, I'm the villain in his story. Do you think anyone is fine when that happens? I needed you to take a moment out of your job to come find me and tell me that everything was going to be all right. I know that your career is incredibly important, but I also *know* that you could have made the time to do that if you wanted to.'

'Ash—'

'For Christ's sake, Mateo, you didn't even come to say hello to me at the party tonight until you thought someone else was hitting on me. Do you know how that makes me feel? *Small*,' I answer before he can try. 'And it's not the first time you've made me feel that way recently. When this thing between us first started, you put on a good show of making me feel like I was important to you—'

'You are important to me!' he croaks, pained.

'No, Basilio was right. *Polo* is the most important thing to you and no one will ever compare. Ever since your team told you I was a distraction, you've been distancing yourself.'

'We've talked about this. It was only while—'

'The season was going, yeah, except the season is over and I feel more distanced from you than ever. That's the British season done, right? But then there's always the next one you need to be signed for. Europe, Australia, the US, Dubai, and, of course, let's not forget the big one: Argentina. What's your plan, Mateo? Keep me at arm's length until you retire? Then we're all good! Then you can have as many distractions as you like!'

'No! You don't understand. Please.' He takes a step towards me, but I recoil. 'I had to focus on polo; I had to try to get back on form the last few matches.'

'And how's that gone for you, Mateo?' I snap.

His jaw tenses. It was a bit of a low blow and probably a sore point right now, but I don't care. The frustration from the last few weeks is violently bubbling in my stomach and ready to boil over. The hurt I've been trying to suppress at being made to feel second best, cast aside until he's fucking ready, is spilling out in resentful, bitter arguments. I don't want him to give up his dreams for me. I'd never want that. But I want to share in them. I want to feel like I'm on the ride with him to get there. I can't pretend that I'm okay being benched.

'I wanted to prove I was good enough to play in Argentina,' he begins through gritted teeth, 'and then I—'

'Oh my God, please *stop* with Argentina,' I beg, lifting my eyes to the night sky glittering with stars overhead, a fanciful romantic canopy at jarring odds with the scene taking place below it. 'It's *one* tournament, Mateo; it's not all there is.'

'It is for me!' he cries, confusion flitting across his expression as though he can't comprehend why I'm not getting this. 'You want me to tell you why I'm this way, Ash? Why Basilio takes pleasure in telling you that polo comes first for me? Why I *have* to play in Argentina?'

'Please!'

'My mother sacrificed *everything* so I could play polo,' he tells me, his eyes brimming with tears, and the sudden overwhelming emotion in his voice making my heart lurch and body ache to hold him. 'She left my father and took me to the Rossi estate. Her family never forgave her for that. They were strict Catholics and disapproved of her actions so much, they cut off all ties. She didn't just lose her husband that day, she lost *everyone*.'

I stare at him, too stunned at this outburst of unchecked feeling to speak.

'She gave up her career for me and got a shitty job on the Rossi estate so I could be around horses every day, so I could work at the yard and get the chance to learn with a pro. That was the deal. She'd work for Rossi, I'd help out at the yard and in return, he would train me to play polo like Basilio and all those other boys.' He pauses to take a breath, hands on hips, his eyes misted with painful memories. 'She sacrificed everything for me because she knew I'd repay her by being a great polo player. She believed in me that much.'

I swallow.

'I'd catch her crying sometimes,' he continues, his voice hoarse. 'She would brush it off if I asked. Make up some bullshit excuse. I asked once if she was sad about her family and she told me she was, but that they would be the ones to regret it. They would see me win the Argentine Open and they would finally know that she was right. That she'd made all the right decisions. I think that's what drove her every day. Knowing that was in her future.'

'But… but surely you've proven you're good enough,' I say, confused. 'You've already played in the Argentine Open.'

'My worst performance in a tournament. It was humiliating. The pressure… it was too much. I was too young. Basilio and his friends made sure I never forgot where I came from, that I wasn't one of them. If any of her family saw or heard of my appearance that year, it only would have served to confirm their feelings: that my mother had turned her back on everyone and everything she knew for a… *failure* of a son.'

It's taking everything in him not to crack. I can see it in his face, how he's fighting the urge to break and crumble. I wonder if he's ever spoken this out loud to anyone before.

'You are not a failure. You're a great polo player,' I tell him truthfully, blinking back the hot tears pricking my eyes.

'You know, she died a year after we moved to the Rossi estate,' he says, tipping his head back and looking up at the sky. 'She didn't even get to see me turn pro.'

'She didn't have to. She knew you would.'

'I promised her I would dedicate my life to this sport. I had the opportunity to honour her memory in Argentina, where it matters most, and I let her down. Now, I have grown as a person, as a player; I am more focused, calmer, braver, more experienced. It has taken time, but I have built up my reputation and I promised myself I would go back to Argentina and make her proud.' He looks at me earnestly, his eyes glistening with regret. 'This was supposed to be my year. Our Maycourt team was good enough to get everyone's attention. I knew I was finally ready.'

'You're talking as though all hope is lost. You can still get to Argentina. It's not over just because of a few local matches and a bust-up at a cocktail party.'

He shakes his head. 'It's going to be harder to persuade a patron I'm worth the trouble. But I *know* I can do this.' He clenches his sore fist. 'I will do whatever it takes to win in Argentina for her. Nothing will get in my way. All I need is someone to recognise that and give me one chance. Just one more chance.'

Fighting back tears, I mutter under my breath, 'You mean no one.'

'What?'

I clear my throat and force myself to look at him. 'You said, "nothing" will get in your way, but I think you mean no one. That's why you've always kept everyone at a distance. You never let them down; no one lets you down. You don't have to walk on the pitch worrying about an argument you had the day before or how you're going to make time for anyone else. All you had to do was focus on scoring the next goal. Easier that way.'

His gaze locks with mine, his chest rising and falling with heavy breaths. 'But then you came along,' he says quietly.

'But then I came along.' I nod slowly. 'So what happens next?'

I watch his throat bob as he swallows audibly.

'I don't know,' he whispers.

It's strange. I didn't know it could hurt like this. Like the sadness is so heavy, you feel you can't stand upright. Like your heart is being squeezed so tightly in your chest, all the blood has stopped running through your limbs so your body becomes numb. And you feel so fucking stupid.

'I guess that's our answer, then,' I manage to say, the brain cells left functioning doing a much better job than I expected them to.

'Ash,' Mateo croaks, panic in his eyes, 'I don't want to lose you.'

'I'm not going to beg you to love me, Mateo. I'm done feeling like a burden. And I don't want to continue like this only to face more disappointment down the line.'

Desperately trying to retain composure, I turn to look for a taxi, spotting one waiting and flagging it over.

'Wait, Ash, let's… let's talk about this,' he says, his eyes darting at the car in panic.

'I think it's best for me to go,' I say earnestly, opening the door to the taxi and hovering there a moment. 'You have more networking to do.'

'I don't want you to go.'

'You need to give your all to polo. That's the only way you'll be happy. And I can't stay with you, Mateo, knowing that I'll never be enough and you'll only grow to resent me if you don't achieve the sporting greatness you crave. I deserve more than that.'

He stares at me, speechless.

'Please don't follow me. I don't want to talk more tonight. Go back to the party. It's important for the team,' I conclude sternly.

Then, sliding into the back seat of the car and slamming the door shut behind me, I ask the driver to go, refusing to look back at Mateo as we pull away.

Thirty-One

When Lady M suggests I have some time off after Sotogrande, I take her up on the offer. The season has come to a close, people are going their separate ways, and they can spare me. It's good for me to get away from Maycourt for a bit – any time I hear footsteps around the yard, I'm terrified and hopeful it might be him, even though he flew straight from Spain to France. Everything here reminds me of him.

He's called. I didn't answer the first couple of times and then when I did pick up, the relief in his voice made me want to cry, so I kept it as short as possible so I could stay composed, telling him we needed time and space. I felt like I'd said all I needed to say in Soto. I want Mateo to win in Argentina and achieve true happiness. But not at the cost of mine. What hurts the most is that I believe we could have had both. If only he'd been able to remove his blinkers to see that, too.

I haven't been neglecting my duties at the yard – whether you're having a good day or a bad day, the ponies need their breakfast and exercise, no way around that – but it's been hard to put my heart into the job. I've been on autopilot, struggling through every motion, every task with a debilitating ache. As the season has come to an end, it's a good time to have a break and I feel like I may need it.

'Ash, I know you have a lot to think about,' Lady M says, leaning on the fence with me as we watch Serafina and Byron graze in the field on a cloudy afternoon, her dogs clustered around her feet. 'We never discussed further than the polo season. I asked you to help us get the best out of Serafina and you did just that.'

'Mateo did most of it,' I mumble earnestly.

'You gave us the first steps with her that we needed to earn her trust. Please don't brush that away as nothing. It's not and I'm grateful to you.'

'Likewise.' I turn to offer her a small smile.

'If you do decide that you'd like to work in a polo yard for the long-term, perhaps you and I could have a serious conversation. I know Jules would like to have you as a permanent fixture around here, as would I, but I'm also aware that you had a life in London before us and you never planned for this to be forever. Take some time to think about it. Let me know.'

She pushes herself off the fence, her dogs scrabbling to their feet and whining with excitement, wondering where they're off to next.

'Thank you,' I say.

'And if I may be so bold as to offer some personal advice,' she places a hand on my arm, 'it sounds obvious, but sometimes, it's not: make that decision based on what *you* want from life. Don't let the actions of anyone else have sway over it.' She pats her fingers on my sleeve, lowering her voice to a hushed tone as she leans in conspiratorially. 'He won't be around here much the next few weeks, so you don't need to worry about seeing him.'

I don't say anything, but I nod appreciatively.

She sighs, dropping her hand from my arm. 'Some people don't know the best thing to happen to them until they let it slip away.'

'Oh, don't worry, I know how much Maycourt means to me.'

Her lips twitch into a smile, her eyes gleaming at me. 'I wasn't talking about you.' She tightens her grip on her dogs leads. 'Right, come on you lot, let's get home.'

I watch her stroll away, the lurchers trotting to heel nicely at her feet, while Garfunkel pulls on the lead to get back to his plush sofa as fast as possible. He had a groom recently and seems to have extra swagger with his impossibly fluffy corgi butt. I can't help but smile as I watch them go, a pack of misfits who fit together perfectly, and then I go back to watching the ponies, wondering if I should accept I fit in here, too.

Staying at Mum's house in North London is a bit like staying at a really cool modern hotel. Everything is clean, sleek and minimalist, with pops of bright colour every now and then. The sofas are white with bright-orange and turquoise cushions. The walls of the kitchen are white except for one bright statement wall that's been painted with bold, vibrant abstract art by an artist friend of hers. The house is lit mostly by long hanging clusters of pendant bulbs ensconced in glass domes, and in each room, there are few but big colourful ornaments or sculptures that bring the room to life, like the graffiti elephant in the corner of the sitting room. It's not so easy to slob in a house this orderly, which seems impressively clean until you realise that that's largely down to Mum rarely being in it.

I didn't let her take time off work, not that I think she could have anyway. But she did make the offer and I was adamant that she only assign one block of time a year to looking after her heartbroken daughter and I've already collected my allotted chunk. That was meant to make her laugh, but instead, she gave me a wry look and said, 'We both know that last time wasn't heartbreak. This time, I think it is.'

She was right, but I still wouldn't let her take time off work.

The first couple of days I was here, I made the most of the opportunity of being alone to wallow in being pathetic. *I miss him.* I don't want to be without him. I can't bear the idea of him ever being with anyone else. I hate the world. Life is so unfair. Why is this so fucking painful? Why does losing him make everything seem worthless and pointless? I never should have let myself fall for him. I'll never trust another man ever again. Every couple I see out there in the world is a lie. Love is a lie. *I miss him.*

Then, one day, I make myself presentable by washing my hair, putting on nice clothes and make-up and I leave the house to meet Sam for a coffee.

'I don't understand how this happened,' she says as I twist my coffee mug round on its saucer absent-mindedly.

'Me neither.'

'He's an idiot.'

'I'm an idiot, too. I fought it at the beginning because I think I knew this was always going to happen. There were so many warnings.'

'But he fell for you, Ash,' she says gently, placing her hand over mine either as a gesture of comfort or to stop me turning the coffee mug round and round because it's getting annoying. 'Anyone could see that. The way he was around you, so in awe, so adoring. He was so proud of you, and proud that you had chosen him. It was like he couldn't believe his luck that you'd landed in his life.'

'We both know how convincing guys can be at this sort of thing.'

She shakes her head solemnly. 'No, that wasn't fake charm or some kind of game he was caught up in. It was real, I know it.' Her brow furrows. 'I hope he comes to his senses before he loses you for good.'

'*I* made the decision to walk away,' I remind her.

She looks at me pensively for a moment. 'What does Jasper think of all this?'

'He says that Mateo is no longer welcome at The Old Greyhound. I told him that was unnecessary and also would be a stupid business move if Mateo is signed to the team again next summer. The team like to be together. They'd just find an alternative local.'

'I think it's nice of him to take a stand. Let Mateo reap the consequences of his stupidity!' She picks up her large coffee and takes a sip. 'What are you thinking about the job offer from Lady M? Are you going to take it?'

'I'm not sure.'

She nods before offering me a warm smile. 'I know you

feel shitty right now, but I'm glad you're back in the city. I've missed you. It hasn't been the same without you.'

'Bet you've got more work done.'

'I have been absurdly productive since you left.'

I grin before asking her to please distract me with some ludicrous fashion stories that might challenge the ludicrous polo stories I've got used to and she does not disappoint.

After the boost of seeing her, I start to venture out the house more over the next couple of days, forcing myself to enjoy London while I'm here and go to art galleries and beautiful parks and important landmarks and basically do all the stuff that I never actually did when I lived here. So far, I've been able to get on with things without strangers confronting me over being the woman who tried to lure Chris Courtney away from his wife, and I'm no longer on social media so I've been able to avoid any trolls online, too.

At least Chris's attempt for garnering sympathy has generally backfired. That excerpt didn't quite have the reaction he or his team expected. He got a lot of heat from the general public and the media for twisting the narrative to play the victim when he's a grown man with his own agency. There was a huge backlash over his attempts to paint me, a junior assistant, as evil, while he, the famous, influential athlete, was, by his reckoning, an innocent bystander who got caught up in my scheming.

'It has sparked a lot of debates about abuse of power,' Mum told me one evening as she pored over notes for her breakfast show the next day.

The cherry on the cake was a Melbourne-based barista named Hazel leaking intimate voice notes he allegedly sent her during the Australian Open last year. She's claiming they had an affair and he asked her to keep it secret while he and his wife were 'in a rocky patch'.

Turns out I wasn't the only one, or even the first.

For now, the release of his memoirs is still going ahead and I'm sure it will sell. People will believe the story they want to. Either way, I'm letting it go and focusing on what's ahead for me.

I've been researching polo jobs, seeing what else is out there and working out what might make sense for my next steps. Being a groom isn't the only option in polo if you're not a player – there's the marketing side to it, the events organisation, sponsorship and hospitality. I don't have to pigeonhole myself if I don't want to.

But I like being around the ponies and riding them. Those other roles would be office jobs, albeit with glamorous perks and the joy of still being in the polo world, plus normal working hours, but I wouldn't be greeted by ponies every morning. I wouldn't have that comforting smell of the stables. I wouldn't get to ride every day or practise stick and ball. My heart lurches whenever I think about Serafina or Byron or Violet or Lyra or Wickham or any of the other ponies expecting to see me every morning and being greeted by someone else.

I think I'm meant to be a groom. Yes, I've decided I want to be the kind of polo groom that players consult. The thought of it gives me a fresh boost of motivation, a sense of purpose that lifts my spirits. I'm going to work in a polo yard and learn as much as possible about the sport, about the ponies, about the players. I'm going to become the Yoda of polo, an all-knowing expert who can advise top professionals on which ponies to choose for which chukkas. I'm basically aiming to be Eduardo.

That dream doesn't have to become reality through Maycourt. There are some lovely polo yards in the country, some of which are closer to London and have great reputations. I note down the ones I like the look of and decide to talk it through with Mum to see what she thinks about applying to them. It might be a good idea to gain experience in a different yard. A new place, new people, new challenges. I might learn something different being somewhere else. I wouldn't have to say goodbye to Maycourt forever. Grooms move around yards all the time. I feel content with this new drive in my life. For the first time, I know *exactly* what I want to do and I'm going to bust my gut to get there.

One evening, Mum calls when I'm in the middle of prepping my dinner.

'Hey,' I say, my eyes scanning the spice rack, 'I was about to call you. Do you have any paprika? I thought I'd try making a tagine.'

'*What?* Ash, don't be ridiculous. You're not a tagine-level chef.'

'You know that most parents tell their kids that they can be whatever they want to be, right?' I mumble, continuing my quest for paprika amongst the jars.

'Sure. Reach for the stars. But listen, before you start your tagine – I was calling to ask you for a favour. We are about to film a segment for the show tomorrow and you'll never guess what it is.'

'A chef showing your audience how to cook tagine?'

'We're talking to an equestrian! Some of my camera crew and a reporter are about to set off to interview him at his stables on the outskirts of London – somewhere in Kent – and get some lovely sunset shots of the horses galivanting about.'

I pick out and examine a pot of red spice that turns out to be cayenne. 'That's nice.'

'The thing is, this segment has all been set up very last minute to fill in for an interview on an actor who's pulled out without any warning whatsoever and none of my team know a thing about horses. Guess what I'm thinking?'

I straighten slowly. 'What are you thinking, Mum?'

'I'm thinking I know someone who is *extremely* knowledgeable about horses. And having someone like that join them for this little excursion and be on hand to make sure they don't make fools of themselves would be very useful.'

'Uh-huh.'

'Ash, do you think instead of cooking up what I'm sure will be a delightful tagine, or something perhaps resembling a tagine, you could get ready to be picked up in twenty minutes to accompany my lovely team on this exciting equestrian excursion?'

I smile into the phone. 'Despite you insulting my culinary prowess, I am tempted. I have missed being around horses.'

'And you'd love to do your brilliant mother a favour.'

'And I'd love to do my brilliant mother a favour,' I repeat dutifully.

'Great! One of them will be with you in twenty, so get out of your sweatpants and into something presentable,' she says chirpily, and I can hear her heels clacking in the background as she marches around the studio.

'I'm not wearing sweatpants,' I lie, still insulted at the assumption.

'Good luck, Ash, and let me know how it goes.'

We say our goodbyes and hang up, before I trudge upstairs and change into jeans and a loose-fitting jumper, brushing my hair and everything. As I lock up the house, I feel excited about spending an evening with horses, proud that I might prove useful in some way. The car pulls up as I'm coming down the steps, a blue Mini Countryman driven by a fair-haired man who I'd guess to be in his forties and most of the back seat taken up with camera equipment. He introduces himself as Hal, the assigned cameraman for this segment.

'The others are meeting us there,' he explains cheerfully, turning down the radio. 'It's a pleasure to meet you. I've heard quite a bit about you from your mum. She tells me you work at the polo? That's interesting. I'm not mad on horses myself. They're quite big.'

'They are,' I say, smiling at his naturally warm, friendly demeanour.

'I'm glad you're coming with us. You can go in first and tell me which ones are safe to film and which ones will kick me in the face with their trotters.'

'Hooves.'

'You know, I've filmed segments in the Houses of Parliament. I've filmed politicians, members of royalty, world leaders. What am I spending tonight doing? Filming a horse. Honestly, this job makes no sense whatsoever.'

'Sounds fun to me, getting that variety in a job.'

'It is, actually.' He grins, putting on his indicator. 'Tell me about yours.'

The journey isn't too long and it goes fast thanks to my companion's ease of conversation. We chat the entire way and by the time the built-up suburbs of London melt away into the leafy countryside roads of Kent, I feel like Hal and I are firm friends.

'We're close now,' he announces as we pass the first of a string of fenced-off fields, slowing as the road grows narrower and Hal starts looking for the turning.

He spots the sign for the stables and we make a right onto the top of the long, dusty, uneven drive. Bumping against my seatbelt, I break into a smile as I see several horses grazing right next to the fence, one of whom lifts her head and walks slowly to stop at the fence curiously as we make our way up it.

'Can you stop a moment?' I ask, undoing my seatbelt as he slows to a standstill.

'What are you doing?' Hal asks when I open the door.

'I'm saying hello.'

Her dark tail swishing in approval, the chestnut horse whinnies and snorts as I calmly stroll over to her, pleased to have human company. I reach up to stroke her nose, admiring her glossy coat and affectionate nature.

'You're a sweetheart, aren't you?' I tell her, giving her cheeks a scratch.

Glancing at the other horses, all of whom are now waiting for the same treatment, I grin, climbing up the fence and hopping over it to introduce myself one by one. Hal waits patiently, not bothering to get out the car or call me back to it, so I'm assuming we have a few minutes before we need to be at the stables – and the action looks like it's here anyway.

'You should get some shots of the horses like this. They're very calm,' I call back to Hal, but he's not concentrating, leaning back in his seat with the engine off, typing into his phone.

Shrugging, I return my focus to the horses, laughing as a magnificent, speckled grey pony with a dark nose nuzzles me a little too enthusiastically in the hunt for treats in my pockets and almost knocks me off balance.

Suddenly, a man's voice carries across the field.

'I should have known it was you who was trespassing.'

I freeze. *I know that voice.*

Thirty-Two

The world around me blurs as I see Mateo striding across the grass. My breath catches, my heart lurches, time slows, and he's there walking through a field bathed in a dim evening glow, his eyes locked on me like nothing else exists. He's more handsome than I remember – his hair thicker, his jaw more defined, his tall frame more imposing and confident – sending all the air whooshing from my lungs. *I've missed him.* I want to run to him. Only when the speckled grey horse pushes me back a step as she nibbles gently at my pocket does everything snap back into action. My brain kicks in, I inhale a deep breath, the horses lift their heads, alert to his presence.

'W-what are you doing here?' I stammer in shock as he nears, his hand reaching to pat the hindquarters of the grey.

'I'm here to see a man about a horse.' His lips twitch into a small, secretive smile like he knows something I don't. 'Lady M sent me.' He comes to a stop in front of me, reaching up to run a hand down the neck of the grey who moves her head round to greet him eagerly. 'What do you think of her?'

'Who?'

He gestures to our curious friend now checking his pockets for treats. 'She's a former racehorse. A very successful one. Lady M knows the owner – he got in touch to say he was selling her. She'd need to be trained up, but Lady M is convinced she'd make an excellent polo pony. What do you think?'

I stare at him, my mouth running dry. 'Uh.' I glance up at the pony, who snorts in frustration that neither of us have provided any snacks. She doesn't move off, though, keen to stay in our company. 'I don't know. You're the one who knows about this stuff.'

'I'd like to know what you think,' he insists.

'I don't know,' I repeat, flustered and confused.

'What does your gut tell you?'

I breathe out all the air in my cheeks, looking up at the pony again, her eyes bright, intelligent and shining beneath long eyelashes, her breathing calm and steady as she waits for my verdict. I reach up to stroke down her nose and she exhales in contentment.

'I like her,' I say eventually, rubbing the soft bit at the end of her nose, her whiskers tickling my cheek as she lifts her head in gratitude. 'She seems to have a calm temperament and she is obviously comfortable around people, not showing any signs of being nervous, which hopefully combine to mean she's responsive. If she's a successful racehorse then we know she's quick.' I shrug. 'I don't know, Mateo. Serafina was hot-headed and independent and she's now the best polo pony in the yard, so I don't know what I'm talking about. I'd have to see someone ride her, I guess.'

'Or you could ride her yourself.' He looks pleased with my answer, gazing up at her happily.

I stare at him, mystified by everything. By my presence, by his presence, by this casual conversation... *What is going on?*

Glancing back at Hal, who must be getting bored and impatient by now, I find he's sitting at the steering wheel beaming at me, not gesturing for me to hurry along, nor looking confused in the least by this stranger's appearance.

'Mateo, what's happening?' I ask, turning back to him. 'Why are you here?'

'I told you, I came to see this pony. Her name is Spud, by the way.' He makes a face. 'We may have to change that.'

Spud snorts indignantly.

'No offence,' he mutters to her.

'Okay, if that's why you're here, why am *I* here?' I say slowly, determined to get answers from him. 'This doesn't feel like coincidence.'

'It's not. I spoke to your mum and I asked her to get you here somehow so we could talk. I didn't want to show up at your house unannounced and I thought you might be more willing to hear me out if you were in the company of horses.'

'Wait, you spoke to my *mum*?'

'Yes.'

'So there's no interview?'

'There's an interview,' he says, wincing slightly, 'but it's with me. I promised her I'd do a piece for her show about polo – we filmed that earlier today. I think it went well.

In exchange, she said she'd bring you here so we could talk. I didn't get away without a lecture. She's scary, your mum. I am pretty sure that if I don't get this right, she might kill me.'

'Get what right?'

'My apology to you,' he answers, his forehead creasing. 'I owe you one, Ash. In fact, I owe you more than that. I owe you... everything.'

He clears his throat, building the courage to say whatever's coming next.

'All my life, I've been convinced that only polo can make me happy,' he begins, his voice wavering with nerves. 'I thought that winning was all that mattered. But since you walked away from me in Spain, I've won matches and lost matches, and... none of it seemed to matter anymore. During every match, I was looking for you in the pony lines, hoping you'd miraculously appear so that my heart might start up again.' He shakes his head. 'I've been so *stupid*. I thought that giving my all to you meant losing what I've worked so hard for – but all you did was make me stronger. It's like...' He pauses, searching for the right way to put it. 'Like, a long time ago, I decided I had to cage off my heart so I could keep my career in check, but by doing that, I dismissed the most important thing in life. The thing that gives everything meaning, makes it all worth it.'

He looks at me helplessly. Spud whinnies in encouragement.

'My mother told me once about the importance of spirit in polo,' he continues, his eyes misting over as he pats Spud's neck, his voice softer, more thoughtful. 'It's not just about skill. It's your heart that tips the game in your favour. "Your heart and your spirit. That is what it takes to win".'

He takes a moment, smiling at the memory, before his eyes flash at me.

'You give me spirit, Ash. You are my heart. Without you, I could win every tournament in the world and I'd be winning nothing at all. Without you, it's empty.' He takes a step towards me, closing the gap between us. 'If you let me, I will do whatever it takes to spend the rest of my life proving to you how much I love you, Ashley Slater.' I inhale sharply and he smiles in relief and fear, like he's been needing to say those words this entire time but he's been scared to. 'Because I do. I love you so much. I don't care if I never win a polo match ever again, but *tell me* I might have hope to win you again.'

He reaches up to brush my hair back from my face as I gaze up at him, speechless.

'I should have run from that yacht the moment I knew you'd be upset. I should have begged you to stay when you left the party in Soto. I should have made you know how much you mean to me every day that we had together.' He frowns deeply as though pained, his throat bobbing. 'I deserved to lose you. I was so frightened of how you made me feel, how you made me question everything. I felt so torn and confused. All these principles I had, the way I'd lived my entire life up until you. The beliefs I'd rigorously stuck to in the hope of being someone worthwhile. But now I know that it's loving you that makes me worth something, Ash.'

I blink back tears.

'I'm so sorry that I didn't see that before,' he says softly, his eyes searching mine. 'I'm sorry that I hurt you. If you let me, I promise to spend every day from now on doing everything I can to protect you from any hurt from anyone ever again. More than anything, I want to be with you, Ash. I'm here to ask you to please consider giving me another chance.'

As he concludes, his chest is heaving with every breath, his eyes soft with hope and fear, his lips slightly parted. He's always so sure of himself, Mateo, but not in this moment. No, right now, he's uncertain and afraid, more vulnerable than I've ever seen him. It's a strange, daunting feeling handing your heart over to someone else. I would know.

I handed mine to him a while ago, even if he didn't know it.

'Ash,' he says so quietly, it's almost a whisper, 'please say something.'

I've been so astounded by this sudden avalanche of information and emotion that I've been stood in total silence while I process it. There's a tingling sensation in my toes spreading up through my body, sending the butterflies in my stomach into a frenzy and causing my heart to thrum and my breath to come out all shaky.

Finally, I manage to think of something to say.

'Is... is Spud part of the deal?' I ask quietly.

Mateo blinks at me, thrown. 'What?'

'If I agree to give us another chance – do I get Spud thrown in as part of the offer?'

His eyes glistening, the corners of his lips twitch into a small, hopeful smile.

'No,' he says regretfully. 'Spud will belong to Maycourt.'

'So I don't get a polo pony.'

'Just a polo player.'

I sigh heavily. 'I suppose that's something. Worth considering, anyway.'

'I'm pleased to hear it.'

I bite my lip. 'Mateo, I'm not very good at this.'

'Good at what?'

'Talking about how I feel. In Paris, you said so many wonderful things. You put it so beautifully how you felt, what you wanted, why we should take that risk together. And now you're here, striding across the field like a fucking… Jane Austen hero, saying things that make me—'

I pause, wishing my thoughts would slot into order. I give up, my eyes falling to the ground as I run a hand through my hair. He waits patiently while I collect myself.

'In Paris, you took me on a boat on the Seine and you told me that when I was with you, you felt like you could breathe again. Later, you stood in the rain and you told me that you'd never felt this way about someone before. I didn't tell you how I felt. You opened up to me and didn't get anything in return.'

He quirks a brow. 'That's not *entirely* how I remember it. I remember getting plenty.'

'I hope I at least showed you how I felt.'

'Oh, *yes.*'

'The truth is, it was easier for me to protect myself that way. I didn't want to say anything out loud because once it's out there, you can't take it back. I guess I never had the guts to tell you how I felt. Until now. Mateo,' I exhale shakily, 'I love you, too.'

He breaks into a smile so big, it reaches his eyes.

I grin back at him, the two of us smiling dopily and silently at each other.

When I don't say anything else, he hesitates, giving me a look.

'Wait,' he says, his eyes twinkling with amusement, 'is that it?'

'Is what it?'

'That is all you wanted to say?'

'That's a big thing to say.'

'Yes,' he says, his shoulders shaking with laughter and relief, 'and it is more than enough, more than I could hope for. But the way you set it up, I thought there was going to be a big speech about us and your feelings! I said quite a lot of things before I said, "I love you".'

'I told you, I'm not very good at this.'

Still chuckling, he cradles my face in his hands. 'You are perfect at it. It was perfect.'

'My point is, I think I loved you then. In Paris, I mean. Before Paris.' I sigh, resting my cheek against his warm palm. 'I couldn't bear it.'

His eyes bore into mine. 'It's terrifying,' he mutters.

'More frightening than going up the Eiffel Tower.'

'Let's not get carried away, Ash. That was *extremely* terrifying.' He shudders involuntarily at the memory.

'Yes, but you did it.'

'Mm. Because I wasn't alone,' he says, his thumb lightly brushing my cheekbone as though I'm the most precious thing in the world. 'And neither are you.'

When he whispers he loves me again before he dips his head to kiss me, it's lucky he drops his hands to hold my waist and pull me close because otherwise, I might float away with the joy that's spreading through every inch of me like wildfire. Somewhere behind me, I hear someone cheer and I realise it must be Hal in the car still. A nudge at my side accompanied by an impatient snort tells me Spud continues her hunt for snacks. But I don't break away for either, looping my arms around Mateo's neck and kissing him deeper, losing myself in this perfect, breathtaking moment that says everything either of us need to know.

For every moment from now, we're in this together.

Epilogue

The stands of the Campo Argentino de Polo of Palermo have been filled with noise from the crowds since the start of the thrilling final of the Argentine Open. Cheers, groans, gasps and screams of encouragement have been drowning out the thundering hooves of the ponies as they tear past in pursuit of the ball, the spectators more passionate and invested than I've ever known in a polo match. But in this moment, mere seconds away from the end of the final chukka, the stand falls silent, as every single person holds their breath.

Mateo, in a light-blue shirt with a navy number one printed on the back, has come charging up our side of the pitch after the ball, his opponent too slow to catch him. He glances across the way towards the goal from the sideline. It's a difficult, wide angle. To us in the stands, it looks an impossible shot. He could try to hold the ball until one of his teammates has made it into position for a pass, or he could take the opportunity of the open ground and try for the goal. *Will he take the risk?*

The crowd falls silent in anticipation.

Jules, sitting next to me, grabs my arm nervously, her nails digging into my skin.

Swinging his mallet, Mateo sweeps the ball under the pony's neck towards the goal.

All eyes are on the small, white dot zipping across the pitch and clipping the post as it sails through it. The flag goes up, the crowd roars with approval and amazement, and the bell rings for the end of the sixth and final chukka. Mateo scored the winning goal. *He's won the Argentine Open.* Tears filling my eyes, Jules and I hug while we cheer at the top of our lungs, jumping up and down in each other's arms. Mateo performs a victory lap, cantering past the stands with his stick in the air, the spectators going wild with appreciation for such a nail-biting and exquisite finish. He won't be able to spot me amongst the sea of people jumping up and down for him, but he will know I'm here.

As his team dismount to celebrate with their grooms and the field is set up for the trophy presentation, we gradually make our way down the steps through the heaving crowds onto the grass, finding a spot at the front of the steel barriers they've set up to separate the podium area from the spectators.

'You should go find him!' Jules is saying to me whilst looking out for Lady M, who is here somewhere but got stuck talking to a former friend of her father's at half-time and couldn't seem to come up with a polite excuse to get away.

'He should share this moment with his team,' I insist, leaning on the barrier, enjoying the goings-on around us, unable to stop smiling. 'I'll be here waiting when he's ready.'

Someone is giving the trophy some last-minute polishing while the winning team line up one side of the sponsor-branded podium, their hair dishevelled from their helmets and sweat, their cheeks flushed with joy. Mateo looks so relaxed, his eyes sparkling as he waits to be called up to lift the trophy. All that hard work over the last few weeks, all that training and dedication and focus, the pressure he endured as he rode and practised for hours every day to feel like he'd earned a place on this team – it's all come to this perfect conclusion. He doesn't need to prove anything to anyone. He's proven it to himself now and that's what matters. When he plays with his heart, he is unstoppable.

Since we reunited that day next to Spud – who has kept her name at my insistence – I have witnessed a notable shift in Mateo's thinking towards polo. He doesn't train any less and his focus is still as intense as it needs to be, but he takes losses and mistakes as necessary challenges through which to persevere rather than stumbling blocks on his way to glory. His ease in attitude has made him even more dangerous, in my opinion. He still gets frustrated, like any athlete, but he's concentrating more on the joy he takes in the sport now and that translates into intelligent and passionate play on the pitch. He's beautiful to watch and now, thanks to his performance today, the best polo players in the world know it.

God, I'm so proud of him.

And I'm proud of myself, too. I've formally taken a permanent position at Maycourt Polo and I've been working my arse off to learn everything there is to learn from Eduardo and Jules and everyone else still working there so that by the time the British polo season returns in a few months, I'm going to be as integral to the show as they are.

If Mateo doesn't ask me which ponies I think he should ride for each chukka then I'm going to be pissed, because I'm starting to know those horses better than I know myself. I still have the closest bond with Serafina, but I have dedicated fans in Byron and some of the others too, who greet me with excited whinnies and snorts when I arrive each morning, their heads poking over their stall doors, waiting for me to come to them. There isn't a better greeting. Eduardo has also been letting me help him get Spud into shape and she is already proving herself to be a great polo pony, if a greedy one. And Lady M, Mateo and I have discussed plans to set up a programme welcoming kids from urban areas to spend time at the stables. It was Mateo's idea.

I'm still staying with Jasper at The Old Greyhound but now that I'm on a proper salary, I'm paying him rent and saving up to find my own place to rent in the area. Jasper is as happy about that decision as I am. We've always been close, but I love that we'll be living in the same area from now on, always on hand for each other if we need. And as much as I miss being in the same city as Mum and Sam, I think they probably knew before I did that Maycourt was where I belonged.

'You've provided me with the perfect country escape from London,' Sam claimed when she last came to visit, warming herself by the roaring log fire in the pub and smiling gratefully at Jasper as he brought her a glass of red wine. 'It's very idyllic here, isn't it?'

It is, and I'll always be weirdly grateful to Chris Courtney for screwing me over and driving me here to this idyllic escape in the first place. In the end, it turned out it wasn't an escape at all. I was coming home.

Thanks to the lull in polo seasons, Mateo and I were able to spend a lot of time together after I came back from my hiatus in London. It got busier for him in the lead-up to Argentina this December and he's had to travel a lot, but our relationship has only got stronger. Whenever he arrives at the stables, he seeks me out to lift me into his arms and kiss me until one of the ponies whinnies and kicks at their stall impatiently or Jules tells us to get a room. He's still giving me polo lessons when we get the chance. We spend evenings cooking and eating together, telling stories, disagreeing over music, and watching films until I fall asleep in front of them and he has to carry me to bed. I've learnt Argentine recipes and Spanish swear words, and asked for and listened to anecdotes about his mother.

'I wish I'd met her,' I said once.

'Me too,' he said wistfully, moving my hair so he could softly kiss my shoulder. 'But she knows I'm happy now, and she knows that's because of you.'

It was such a lovely thing to say. I buried my head against his chest, closed my eyes to listen to his heartbeat and made a promise to his mum without saying it out loud that I would love and look after her son forever.

He's had to make a similar promise to my mum. She was happy to help him with that set-up at the stables in Kent, but gave Mateo the impression that if he fucked things up with me again, it might be the last thing he did.

'It was simple, really,' Mum said breezily when I asked her what it was that had persuaded her to play along with Mateo's ploy to talk to me. 'He told me how he felt about you, the mistakes he'd made and why he'd made them, and I believed him. It takes a mum to know when someone is genuine about their daughter and when someone is full of shit.'

It seemed a reasonable explanation to me.

By the time the players are called up on the podium in Argentina, a lot of the crowd have descended from the stands to swarm around the barriers and I'm grateful to have a front-row spot. The band plays, the smoke cannons go off either side, and the team lift the huge, silver cup in the air, grinning for the cameras and their elated fans. I'm too busy clapping to notice Mateo has been peering at the crowd, his eyes scanning over the faces carefully until they land on me.

A satisfied smile settles on his lips. He's finally found what he's looking for.

Before the others have lowered the trophy, he's jumped off the front of the podium and is walking my way. While the other members of his team are handed magnums of champagne to shake up and open, Mateo ignores the person carrying the bottle meant for him and instead gestures for me to come join him.

'Here,' Jules says, pushing the barrier forward to create a gap between it and the next one along. 'Go through. Go to him!'

I do as she says and slip through the gap. He stops in front of me, wraps his arms around me and lifts me into the air, spinning me around and making me shriek with surprise.

'Where have you been?' he asks, lowering me to the ground.

'I wanted you to have your moment!'

'I want you to be a part of every moment.'

'Mateo, you did it,' I gush, holding his face in my hands as he grins down at me. 'You won the Argentine Open! *You did it.*'

'I can't believe it,' he whispers, his eyes glistening with tears.

'I can. You deserve all of this.' I slide my hands down to lay them flat against his chest, his heartbeat thudding hard and fast beneath my palm. 'So, what's next in your sights? The Triple Crown of Argentine polo? Make history at the US Open somehow? Now that you've achieved your dream, what are you going to do?'

He shakes his head.

'Things have changed. For a while now, I've had a new dream,' he says gently, gazing down at me. 'And I'm looking at her.'

The noise, the people, the music, the cheer at the spraying bottles – everything fades away as Mateo presses his lips to mine. My hands loop around his neck while his arms wrap around my waist. We break away briefly to smile against each other's mouths as his teammates aim the spray of their bottles at us, our hair soaked, bubbles running down our cheeks. He laughs and kisses me again, lifting me up on my tiptoes, the two of us in the middle of a polo pitch helplessly caught in a shower of champagne and the wonder of everything yet to come.

Acknowledgements

A giant thank you to the fabulous Aubrie, my genius editor. Working on these books with you is so much fun, from the brainstorming to the plotting to the editing, and I'm so excited about all our projects still to come – thank you for your excellent guidance and enthusiasm. And a huge thank you to Holly, Yasmeen, Sophie, and the entire Head of Zeus team who work so hard to get my books into the hands of readers, and to the unbelievably talented Sofia and Jessie who have brought these characters to life through such exquisite illustrations and cover design. I feel so lucky to work with you all, thank you.

I am ever grateful to my superstar agent, Lauren. Thank you for all the work you do behind the scenes to make me look good, and for always being in my corner. A huge thanks also to Callen, Paul and the Bell Lomax Moreton team for continuing to cheer me on and keeping me busy. I wouldn't have it any other way – here's to all the exciting projects still ahead!

Special thanks must go to Aggie Stamp at *Country Life* and to Josh Clover of Clover Polo for the expert guidance and advice when it came to researching this book. I so appreciate you taking the time to answer my pestering questions – your love of the sport and the horses is infectious and inspiring.

To my family and friends, thank you for being the best support team an author could wish for, and a giant thank you to my amazing readers – I love writing these stories in the hope of making you smile. From the bottom of my heart, thank you for picking up this book.

It's impossible to write a novel set in the world of polo and not be inspired by the late, great Jilly Cooper, the wittiest and most brilliant of authors. The effortless writing style of her books seems to have been a reflection of her own character: charming, honest, mischievous, heartening, and oh so much fun. She brought so much joy. Thank you, Jilly, for everything.

About the Author

KATHERINE REILLY is the pseudonym for an author of several young adult and adult novels, published globally. Under Katy Birchall, she is the author of *The Secret Bridesmaid* and also writes YA novels as Ivy Bailey. Katherine lives in the Suffolk countryside with her family and rescue dog.

Ride the Wave

He's back for the perfect score

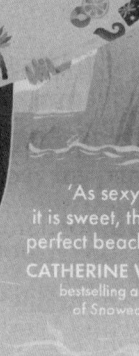

'As sexy as
it is sweet, this is the
perfect beach read!'
CATHERINE WALSH,
bestselling author
of *Snowed In*

KATHERINE REILLY
AUTHOR OF *MATCH POINT*

Discover more sizzling sports romance from Katherine Reilly

In surfing, everyone's chasing the perfect ride...

Twelve years ago, Leo Silva was a world champion surfer – until a tabloid scandal wiped out his career. Holed up in a sleepy Portuguese village, he's dragged back into the spotlight with a wildcard invite to Australia's legendary Rip Curl Pro contest.

Enter Iris Gray, a whip-smart London sports journalist sent to profile Leo's comeback. The catch? The magazine's owner is Leo's famous mother. Now the pressure's on, and the rules are clear: no messing around with the boss's son.

When Iris flies to Portugal, she expects to uncover the truth behind Leo's infamous past, but Leo isn't exactly cooperative. He's brooding, stubborn, and way too easy to fall for.

With a fierce rival threatening to derail Leo's comeback and the competition fast approaching, can they stick to the story, or will love pull them under?

Available to buy now.

Stories to fall in love with

Aria

Thanks for reading!

Want to receive exclusive author content, news on the latest Aria books and updates on offers and giveaways?

Follow us on X @AriaFiction and on Facebook and Instagram @HeadofZeus, and join our mailing list.